力得文化
Leader Culture

Lead your way. Be your own leader!

力得文化
Leader Culture

Lead your way. Be your own leader!

力得文化
Leader Culture

Let Me Teach You
Filthy English

學校沒有教的

髒英文

C D A B

跟著MP3罵到爽！

MP3

欒復倪 Fu-Ni Luan◎ 著

Hello Bitch! Fuck You!

老師不會教！課本不會寫！考試不會考！
但如果不懂，就不知道別人其實在評論你什麼！

跟讀「髒」英文會話大全，就能說出簡潔有力的個人意見！
搭配**字彙Glossary大解**，外國朋友罵什麼都聽得懂！
原來，適當地發洩情緒是件很美好的事！

135篇
經典髒話應用情境

教你如何漂亮地用髒話
**發表己見、處理糾紛、
溝通問題和抒發情緒！**

Author's Preface
作者序

　　大學時期來到美國一晃眼已經過了十多個年頭。當初來到美國之前自以為英文學的還不錯，結果到了這邊才發現，以前在學校學的 proper English 幾乎沒有用武之地。英文的文法固然重要，但是一般人說話並不會老是文謅謅的咬文嚼字，口語化的英文更是重要，罵人呢，更是一門學問，如果被罵還聽不懂跟人家傻笑，那就真的是丟臉了。

　　希望藉著這本書，能夠給大家對英文的日常口語對話能有更深的了解。我盡量取用跟美國最近的時事相關的內容，讓大家有機會感受到這邊目前的文化，以及各式各樣的人對事情的看法以及反應的大不相同。

　　在此我要特別感謝我的先生 Grant Cometa，這是我第一次寫書，在這過程當中，他給了我很多建議跟幫助。當我在為了白天的工作加上寫書的壓力喘不過氣鬧情緒的時候，是他在一旁耐心的安慰與支持，我才能夠完成這本髒英文。也要感謝倍斯特出版社的編輯于婷，在她耐心的指導跟幫助之下，髒英文終於能夠順利地完成。

欒復倪（Fu-Ni Luan Cometa）

Shelton, Connecticut, USA

March, 2016

相信大部分的讀者都有過類似的情況，從課本上吸收了一堆英文知識後，碰到外國友人，卻發現不太懂得怎麼與他們溝通，甚至聽不懂他們的口語，雞同鴨講一番後，有時可能還會鬧了笑話，或是其實自己已經被嘲笑了還不自知。

另一方面，許多人學習一個新的語言通常最快上手的都是髒話。有感於此現象，本書特別選取了一些生活化的英語口語髒話用詞，搭配美國時事與文化，藉由情境對話與 Glossary 髒話大解，幫助讀者能更有效率地吸收日常口語英語，且能於溝通中避開一些容易引發誤會、或是帶有貶義的詞彙，以免影響人際關係。另附光碟，除了閱讀，還能聽聽這類的語彙該如何發音。

非常謝謝復倪老師的用心與耐心！有她的協助，這本書才得以順利出版。

編輯部

Chapter 01 死小孩

 情境對話 Track 01

星期五學校因為暴風雪停課。鄰居的小孩，Elliot 最要好的朋友，Ben 到家裡來玩了一天，而且決定要留下來過夜。

遺看遺聽，學怎麼罵髒話！

...ear yelling?	你聽到他們在叫嗎？
... done yelling for the day.	是啊，但我今天已經罵夠了。
Grant: Yeah... I'm sure they're fine.	嗯…我想他們應該沒事。
Me: Yeah.	是啊。
(Two minutes later)	（兩分鐘後）
Grant: You hear crying?	你聽到哭聲嗎？
Me: They'll come down if they see blood.	誰受傷流血了會自己跑下來。

情境對話中英對照，方便閱讀！

...mping, and screaming from upstairs)	也是。 （碰撞，踩腳，尖叫聲從樓上傳來）

單字標註清晰，容易查找解釋！

Met: [1]**Goddamn** banging? Really?!

Grant: [2]**Assholes.** I'll go check on those two [3]**brats** before they tear down the house.

該死的在撞什麼？有沒有搞錯？！

那兩個混蛋。我去看看那兩個死小孩在搞什麼，在他們把房子給拆了之前。

Glossary 髒話大解

Glossary髒話大解，解析英語口語髒話用詞！

❶ Goddamn，副詞，在此有該死的意思；用來修飾撞擊聲 banging，強調那些碰撞聲很惹人厭。

❷ asshole(s)，名詞，混蛋的意思，本身是指屁眼的意思，常常被用來罵人，在這裡是指在樓上吵鬧的兩個小屁孩。

❸ brat，名詞，死小孩的意思，指那兩個吵鬧的小鬼，這個字通常是用在被寵壞的小孩身上，很讓人反感、老是搞蛋的小孩。

CONTENTS
目次

Faggots

#!@#!*!^%

bitch plaese

Faggots

#!@#!*!^%

bitch plaese

Faggots

#!@#!*!^%

bitch plaese

Faggots

#!@#!*!^%

bitch plaese

死小孩

 情境對話  **Track 01**

星期五學校因為暴風雪停課。鄰居的小孩，Elliot 最要好的朋友，Ben 到家裡來玩了一天，而且決定要留下來過夜。

Grant: You hear yelling?	你聽到他們在叫嗎？
Me: Yeah, I'm done yelling for the day.	是啊，但我今天已經罵夠了。
Grant: Yeah... I'm sure they're fine.	嗯…我想他們應該沒事。
Me: Yeah.	是啊。
(Two minutes later)	（兩分鐘後）
Grant: You hear crying?	你聽到哭聲嗎？
Me: They'll come down if they see blood.	誰受傷流血了會自己跑下來。
Grant: Yeah.	也是。
(Banging, stomping, and screaming from upstairs)	（碰撞，跺腳，尖叫聲從樓上傳來）

Me: [1]**Goddamn** banging? Really?!

該死的在撞什麼？有沒有搞錯？！

Grant: [2]**Assholes**. I'll go check on those two [3]**brats** before they tear down the house.

那兩個混蛋。我去看看那兩個死小孩在搞什麼，在他們把房子給拆了之前。

Glossary 髒話大解

❶ Goddamn，副詞，在此有該死的意思；用來修飾撞擊聲 banging，強調那些碰撞聲很惹人厭。

❷ asshole(s)，名詞，混蛋的意思，本身是指屁眼的意思，常常被用來罵人，在這裡是指在樓上吵鬧的兩個小屁孩。

❸ brat，名詞，死小孩的意思，指那兩個吵鬧的小鬼，這個字通常是用在被寵壞的小孩身上，很讓人反感、老是搗蛋的小孩。

 情境對話  *Track 02*

Grant 在醫院忙了一整天，現在終於得閒手持一瓶 Stella 啤酒坐在客廳沙發上休息，小鬼們則在樓上玩。而我整天下來應付兩個七歲小孩已經筋疲力盡，但還是進了廚房準備晚餐。

Grant: Hey, by the way, have you heard about the new community project in our complex? Guess how much the HOA is asking the residents to pay.

對了，你有沒有聽說我們公寓新的社區工程計畫？猜猜看社區協會要我們住戶付多少錢。

Me: No idea, how much?

沒概念，多少？

Grant: $125,000.

美金十二萬五。

Me: What?! That's a [1]**shit** load of money! Why [2]**the fuck** do they need so much?! What's that for again?

什麼？！那麼多錢！他們幹啥需要那麼多？！你說是要做甚麼？

Grant: Something about the new roof and sidings for the whole complex. The HOA fee is going to be raised by one hundred something dollars per month for the next 5 years.

好像是說整個社區要換新的屋頂還有外牆，接下來五年社區協會費用每個月將要調漲一百多塊。

Me: [3]**Jesus Christ**, we need to move, SOON!

老天，我們得盡快搬家！

Glossary 髒話大解

❶ shit 是用來修飾錢的數量 load 的形容詞，形容那筆錢的數目是該「屎」的多。

❷ the fuck 在這為問句的語助詞，表示認為那數目真「他媽的」多，正常口吻的問句應該是 "Why do they need so much?!"，而在此說的人為了強調她的憤慨而添入「the fuck」。

❸ Jesus Christ，名詞，是大眾非常熟悉的耶穌基督的名字，因為西方人普遍是信奉基督或天主教，通常遇到壞事感嘆的時候，常常會用耶穌的名字來強調震驚度。一般來説是只有信耶穌基督為主的人才會用，其他宗教或是無神論者不會用到這個字眼，因為跟他們的信仰沒關係。

點錯餐（一）

 情境對話  *Track 03*

在一間燒烤酒吧裡……

Lauren: Yeah! About time! I am starving!

耶！終於來了！我快餓死了！

Cindy: Hmm... yah... me too, but this is not what I ordered.

嗯…是啊，我也是，但這不是我點的食物。

Lauren: Oh yah! What [1]**the hell**? Let me wave our server back.

對耶！搞什麼鬼？我來把我們的服務生叫回來。

(Lauren waved at the waiter, but he was too busy greeting other tables to notice her. Finally, he turned around and saw Lauren signaling, and came over to the table.)

（Lauren 對服務生招手，但是他忙著招呼其他桌客人沒有注意到。終於他看到了 Lauren 招手的訊號，走到她們的桌子。）

Waiter: What can I get for you?

你們有需要什麼嗎？

Cindy: Yes, this is not what I ordered. I ordered a beef taco with sweet potato fries, not this burger and fries.

是的，這不是我點的食物，我點的是牛肉 taco 還有地瓜薯條，而不是這個漢堡跟薯條。

Waiter: Let me check. (He pulled out his

我看看。（他拿出筆記本

notes and checked the orders he wrote down for them.) Nope, that's what you ordered.

檢查他寫下的點餐紀錄。）不對，那的確是你點的。

Cindy: I don't care what you wrote on your note pad. This isn't what I ordered!

我才不管你本子上面寫什麼，這不是我點的食物！

Waiter: But it is! What do you want me to do?

可明明就是啊！那你想我怎麼辦？

Cindy: I want the food I ordered!

我要我點的食物！

Waiter: That's what you ordered!

那就是你點的啊！

Cindy: Really! You're telling me what exactly I ordered for myself? Ask your manager to come over, this is ridiculous!

你現在是在告訴我我給自己點了什麼嗎？請你們經理過來，這簡直太可笑了！

Waiter: Yah yah... [2]stupid [3]Chink. (Speaking in a low volume)

嘿啦嘿啦…愚蠢的中國人。（小聲的説）

Glossary 髒話大解

❶ the hell 在這邊是名詞，同時也是語助詞，用來表示 Lauren 對該情形的驚訝以及不耐，在此解釋為搞什麼的意思。

❷ stupid，形容詞，有很笨、很蠢的意思，用來形容接下來的字 chink。

❸ chink，名詞，是用來蔑稱中國人的用詞，是非常沒有禮貌的用詞，就像用在黑人身上的 nigger 一樣極度有攻擊性。

點錯餐（二）

Lauren 跟好朋友 Cindy 先前發現餐點出錯，希望服務生更改，但是對方反而口出惡言。

Lauren: What [1]**the fuck** did you just say?

你他媽的説什麼？

(The manager came over after hearing about all the fuss. Lauren started screaming at him too.)

（餐廳經理聽到吵鬧聲走了過來，Lauren 也開始對著他吼叫。）

Lauren: Your waiter here had insulted my friend with a severely racist term! Either you fire his [2]**sorry ass** or we will sue you until you shut down!

你們的服務生用很強烈的種族歧視字眼羞辱了我的朋友，如果你不開除他的話，我們就告到你關門！

Manager: There must have been a misunderstanding.

這之中一定有什麼誤會。

Lauren: Misunderstanding?! We all hear it loud and clear! Get this [3]**prick** out of our sight. His mere existence disgusts me!

誤會？！我們都聽得很清楚！叫這渾球滾出我們的視線，他的存在讓我覺得很噁心！

(Manager signaled the waiter to go away.)

（經理給服務生打手勢要他走開。）

Manager: I'm really sorry about what happened here. Dinner is on the house, please let us talk it over later.

我很抱歉發生這種事，這份晚餐免費，請等會再好好跟我們談談。

(Cindy has finally recovered from her shock and said.)

（Cindy 終於從震驚中回神說。）

Cindy: No thanks. I've lost my appetite.

不謝了，我沒胃口了。

(Then she stood up, grabbed Lauren, and stormed out of the restaurant.)

（然後站起身來，抓了 Lauren 就急急的跑出餐廳。）

Glossary 髒話大解

❶ the fuck 在這為問句的語助詞，在此說的人為了強調她的憤慨而添入 "the fuck"，正常口吻的問句應該是 "What did you just say?"。

❷ sorry ass 在這是名詞，ass 是屁股的意思，是 Lauren 為了強調那位服務生低劣的品格而用來稱呼他的名詞，在這個情況之下，Lauren 認為那位服務生應該感到抱歉，所以加了 sorry。

❸ prick，名詞，混球的意思，可以用來稱男人陰莖，但是普遍是用來罵人，指那個人沒有存活的價值，是人人喊打的過街老鼠。

Chapter 05

難民政策（一）

Wendy 剛剛在報紙上讀到最新的敘利亞難民資訊，還有政府目前的應對政策。

Wendy: Oh my [1]gosh. I cannot believe these people!

我的老天，這些人真讓我感到不可置信！

Chris: Why? What's wrong?

為什麼？怎麼了？

Wendy: Some [2]idiot named McCaul, the senator of Texas apparently, wrote a letter to president Obama, saying that it would be highly irresponsible to bring in 10,000 Syrian refugees at this point in time because ISIS in their own words have said "we want to exploit this program to infiltrate the West", and that's exactly what they did to Paris.

有個姓 McCaul 的白癡，很顯然的是德州的參議員，寫了封信給 Obama 總統，說現在讓一萬名敘利亞的難民進來的話是很不負責任的一個動作，因為 ISIS 恐怖份子說過：「我們將會利用這個方案來滲入西方。」，而他們也確實對巴黎實行了。

Chris: Wow, that's messed up!

哇，好糟糕！

Wendy: I know! And guess what? He's not the only one! Governors from a total of 17 States have moved to suspend or

就是！你猜猜還有哩？他不是唯一一個！總共已經有 17 個州的州長動員暫

restrict the refugee resettlement, including Alabama, Arizona, Arkansas, Florida, Georgia, Illinois, Indiana, Iowa, Kansas, Louisiana, Massachusetts, Michigan, Mississippi, North Carolina, Ohio, Texas and Wisconsin. Can you believe these cold blooded [3]bastards?

停或是限制難民的安置。包括阿拉巴馬、亞利桑那、阿肯薩、弗羅里達、喬治亞、依利諾、印第安納、愛荷華、肯薩斯、路易西安納、麻薩諸塞、密西根、密西西比、北卡羅萊納、俄亥俄、德克薩斯還有威斯康辛州。你能相信這些冷血混蛋嗎？

Chris: Yah, no sympathy, what a shame...

是啊，一點同情心都沒有，好丟臉⋯

Glossary 髒話大解

❶ gosh 在這邊是名詞，同時也是語助詞，據說是 God 還有 shit 的合體，god shit 上帝的屎，一聽就知道狀況不妙了。通常因為不好的事情而用 Oh my God 來表示驚嘆，其實是對上帝很不禮貌的行為，比較虔誠的基督或天主教徒可能會因此而感到不高興，所以後來延伸出 gosh 這個字。

❷ idiot，名詞，白癡的意思，是指 Wendy 準備罵的參議員。通常就是指那些説出或做出讓人覺得他們智商有問題的人。

❸ bastard，名詞，混蛋的意思，在此是指那些不願接收難民的政客，原本是用來指未婚生的孩子，或是父母不詳的孩子，但是常常被用來罵討厭的人。

Chapter 06

難民政策（二）

情境對話 Track 06

Wendy 繼續表達她對難民們感到不平的憤慨。

Wendy: Leaving innocent refugees suffering out there doesn't sound right to me at all. They have children that need the roof over their head and proper education too, which by the way, could possibly preventing them from becoming future ISIS members! All we need is a stricter screening system, not a death sentence. Besides, cops here need to learn how to do things other than eating donuts, and the news reporters need to learn how not to spread unnecessary fear into the crowd. And look which States are so quick on announcing their refusal of taking in refugees? The ones with the highest number of gun holders! Those [1]**mother fucking** [2]**rednecks** spent all those efforts, fighting for keeping their guns at home or carrying them around, wouldn't they want to at least make some use of them? I mean isn't that what they've always claimed as the reason to keep guns? Self-defense! There you go!

讓無辜的難名在那邊受苦受難聽起來就很不對，他們也有小孩，需要可以安身的房子，也需要上學受教育，而且說不定可以因此預防他們成為未來的 ISIS 恐怖份子成員！我們需要的只是嚴格一些的篩查系統，而不是判他們死刑。況且，這邊的警察也該學著做些除了吃甜甜圈的正事，還有這些新聞記者也該學著如何不要散播無謂的恐懼給大眾。而且你看看哪些州率先公布他們不願意接收難民？居民擁有最多槍枝的那些！那些幹他媽的鄉下人花了那麼多精力，為了可以在家擁有槍械或是隨身攜帶，難道不想在某種程度上使用它們嗎？我是說難道這不就是他們老是說的需要擁有槍械的原因？自我防衛啊！這就是啦！

Chris: Hahaha... You are too funny!

Wendy: 200 people in Paris died and everyone in the world is crying for them. Millions of Syrian refugees who dreadfully need help at this very moment and people chose to close their doors. Look at all the French flag profile pics people are having on Facebook, such double standards truly disgust me. Those [3]**egocentric** [4]**pathetic** individuals better pray that they would never become one of the refugees, and ever have the chance to have the taste of their own medicine.

哈哈哈⋯⋯你太好笑了！

法國死了 200 人，全世界都在哭，幾百萬個敘利亞難民迫切的需要幫助，而這些人選擇關起大門。看看那些在臉書使用者的法國國旗大頭貼照片，這種雙重標準讓我覺得噁心。那些人最好祈禱他們永遠不會成為難民，也永遠不會有機會嘗嘗自己對難民做法的滋味。

Glossary 髒話大解

❶ **mother fucking** 在此為形容詞，是 Wendy 為了強調她的憤慨而添入用來形容接下來的 redneck，可解釋為幹他媽的。

❷ **redneck**，名詞，原本是形容住在南方比較低階級的白種人，因為需要靠勞力工作，長期日曬，因而脖子後面紅紅的，通常用來指一個人素養低，可解釋為鄉巴佬。

❸ **egocentric**，形容詞，自我中心的意思，指那些只想到自己，而不會多替他人著想的人。無法接受有其他更好的辦法的可能性，緊抓著自己的想法不肯改變的可悲之人。

❹ **pathetic**，形容詞，可悲的意思，用來形容那些蠢到讓你覺得他們很可憐的人。

Chapter 07

怪胎（一）

Trumbull 高中學生餐廳裡，Bill 坐在靠牆的一張桌子，Jim 走了進來看到 Bill，就朝他走過去。

Jim: Hey Bill!

嘿，Bill！

Bill: Hi Jim! Check out this new hoverboard design I came up with over the weekend. I think this time we'll actually be able to levitate between 5 to 7 feet high, if my calculations are correct.

嗨 Jim！看看我這週末畫的飛行板新設計，我在想這次我們真的可以漂浮到大概 5 到 7 英呎高，如果我的計算正確的話。

Jim: Dude! This is [1]**fucking** impressive! How did you come up with this?

老兄！這真是他媽的了不起！你是怎麼想到的？

Bill: Well... I was going over the data we've collected from the other failed attempts. I believe that I've targeted the reason for the height issue we've been having, and now I'm pretty confident on this new design.

嗯…我回去研究我們之前收集到的那些失敗品的數據，我相信我已經找到我們過去飛行高度問題的原因，所以我對這新的設計很有信心。

Emily: Hey guys! What's up?

嘿大夥！有什麼新鮮事嗎？

Jim: Hey Em! Check out this new design Bill came up with!

(While the three are excited and chatting about this newest design of the hoverboard they've been working on together, there comes a taunting laughter from a near distance.)

Steve: Well well, look at this, two ²**nerds** and a ³**nerdacholic**, how cute.

(followed with frivolous jeer)

嘿 Em！來看看 Bill 的新設計！

（正當三人很興奮的討論著這個他們一起努力完成的飛行器的新設計，不遠處傳來了訕笑聲。）

唉呀，看看這兩個書呆子跟一個書呆子狂，多可愛啊。

（跟著是輕浮的訕笑）

Glossary 髒話大解

❶ fucking 在此是用來強調修飾 impressive 的副詞，雖然是不怎麼好聽的用詞，在這裡並非罵人之意。

❷ nerd，名詞，是書呆子或怪胎的意思，在此是 Steve 用來嘲笑 Bill 跟 Jim 的用詞。

❸ nerdacholic，名詞，是 Steve 用來嘲笑 Emily 的用詞，任何字加上字尾-holic 就有為某件事發狂、上癮的意思，像 alcoholic 就是指酒精上癮的人，這裡 nerdacholic 是指 Emily 是上書呆子癮的狂人。

怪胎（二）

  Track 08

對於 Steve 的挑釁，Emily 首先做出了反應……

Emily: Excuse me?

你說什麼？

Steve: You heard me.

你聽到我說什麼了。

Jim: Laugh all you want, Steve. But allow me to remind you something, people you are making fun of right now are the ones that are most likely to make life changing inventions that will radically change the world. The computer and smartphone you are using are invented by nerds, which are people like us. [1]**Jocks** and normal people like you have no claim to civilization except for being the hard labor. We are the people who actually do the thinking, so [2]**fuck off** and go eat your steroids.

盡量笑吧，Steve。但是讓我提醒你，你現在嘲笑的人很可能會是未來做出大大改變世界的發明的人。你現在用的電腦跟智慧型手機都是我們這些書呆子人種發明的。像你這種頭腦簡單四肢發達的笨蛋還有普通人，除了做苦役以外，是對人類文明沒有貢獻的。我們這些人可是動腦的，所以你他媽趕快滾去吃你的類固醇吧。

Bill: Nerds, [3]**dolts**, and norms all have their niche, and all have something to contribute to this great world of ours. It's fun to laugh and draw out stereotypes,

書呆子、呆子、一般人都有他們的安適之所，而所有的人都擁有可以為我們這個偉大世界貢獻之處。

but keep in mind that unless proven; otherwise, everybody has value.

用既定印象嘲笑，把人歸類固然好玩，但是要記住，除非另有證據，所有的人都有他存在的意義。

(Emily and Jim both gave Bill a round of applause with exertion, as Steve walked away silently.)

（Emily 跟 Jim 兩個都給 Bill 很用力的鼓掌，Steve 則默默地走開。）

Glossary 髒話大解

❶ jock，名詞，是指頭腦簡單四肢發達的笨蛋，通常是風雲人物，很自戀、自大、粗魯、愛欺負弱小。

❷ fuck off 為片語，fuck 是動詞，off 是離去的意思，兩個合在一起就是叫 Steve 他媽的趕快滾的意思。

❸ Dolt，名詞，是指反應遲緩、愚笨糊塗之人，也就是呆子。不見得真的是指智商有問題的人，凡是做蠢事的或是說了什麼蠢話的人都可以用這個字來稱呼他。

Chapter 09

魔戒 vs. 星際大戰（一）

Tanner 跟 Dan 都是大二學生，同時也是室友。今天他們決定到 Olive Garden 吃午餐，因為 Dan 生日的時候收到餐廳的禮品卡做禮物，這會兒正坐在餐廳的某張桌子上。

Tanner: Dan, look.

(Holding up a sliced black olive from his salad, looking at Dan through the hole of olive with a serious look on his face)

Tanner: One ring to rule them all.

(Dan shook his head.)

Dan: (laugh) And you wondered why no [1]chick wants you.

Tanner: I could get a chick if I wanted!

Dan: Who are you kidding? You can't get nobody you [2]mook.

Tanner: What do you know? I turn down chicks all the time!

Dan，你看。

（從他的沙拉裡舉起一個黑橄欖片，穿過橄欖圈，一臉嚴肅的看著 Dan 說）

魔戒至尊引眾戒。

（Dan 搖搖頭。）

（笑）而你還想為什麼沒女人要你。

我想要女人隨時就有好嘛！

你想騙誰？你誰都得不到你這個廢物。

你又知道了？我常常拒絕女孩子的示好！

Dan: Uhh, I know you're a huge ³**fucking nerd** that's into Lord of the Rings, and no chick digs that.

啊！我知道你他媽是個迷魔戒的大怪胎，沒有女孩子會喜歡那個。

Tanner: (chuckles) You're wrong. Chicks dig Lord of the Rings.

（Tanner 暗笑）你錯了，女孩子們超喜歡魔戒。

Dan: Yah, the kind of chicks that are into swords and elves and ⁴**shit**. I wouldn't even want to be near them.

是啊，那種喜歡劍、妖精那些狗屁的女孩子，我連靠近都不想。

Glossary 髒話大解

❶ chick，名詞，是指年輕的女性，本身不具有貶義，但是因為通常是男人討論女人比較輕浮的用法，所以有女孩子不喜歡被用這個字眼稱呼。

❷ mook，名詞，是指一個人很笨、很無能的意思，在此是 Dan 用來嘲笑 Tanner 的用詞。

❸ fucking nerd，fucking 是他媽的的意思，用來形容 nerd 的形容詞，nerd 在上一篇提過是書呆子的意思，但是其實書呆子這個解釋有點狹隘，nerd 英文普遍用法是對某種事物有莫名狂熱的人，因此常常被認為是怪胎，在此 fucking nerd 就解釋為他媽的怪胎。

❹ shit 在這是名詞，在此解釋為狗屁，是 Dan 用來概括那些他認為魔戒裡很怪的事物。

魔戒 vs. 星際大戰（二）

 情境對話  *Track 10*

Tanner 到底有沒有女人要的爭論仍在激烈的上演著……

Dan: You don't even have a girlfriend, stop arguing with me.

你連個女朋友都沒有，還是別在跟我爭論了。

Tanner: Who said so? I do have one.

誰説的？我有一個。

Dan: Have you guys ever had sex before?

你們上過床了嗎？

Tanner: (carefully whispering in a low volume) Ashley said there's a troll in her vagina, its name is [1]**Pillowpants**, and if we have sex before she turns 21, Pillowpants will bite my penis off.

（Tanner 很小心地小聲的説）Ashley 説她陰道裡住著一隻小怪物叫做 Pillowpants，如果我們在她滿 21 歲前發生性行為的話，Pillowpants 會把我的陰莖給咬下來。

Dan: (with a shocking facial expression) And you believe that crap? Man, you're hopless, wait to be the last virgin left on earth.

（Dan 一臉驚訝）而你相信那些狗屁？老兄，你沒希望了，等著做地球上最後一個處男吧。

Tanner: Shut up! You Star Wars [2]**geek**!

閉嘴！你這星際大戰怪胎！

Dan: Oh, now I'm the geek? You [3]**fucking moron.**

喔，我倒成了怪胎了？你真他媽的白目。

(Slamming his fists on the table.)

（猛的用拳頭重擊在桌面上。）

Tanner: Dude, chill, you're crazy!

冷靜點，老兄！你瘋了！

Glossary 髒話大解

❶ Pillowpants，名詞，指住在女性陰道裡的小怪物，父母為防年輕女孩未成年發生性行為，而放在女孩陰道裡，專門把男人陰莖咬掉的小怪物，當然是騙小孩的話，據說女孩子滿 21 歲的時候 Pillowpants 會被尿出來，但是根本說不通，因為尿是從尿道出來的，又不是陰道，所以會信以為真的真的是蠢到沒藥救了。

❷ geek，名詞，通常是指對電腦很厲害的人，geek 跟 nerd 兩種中文解釋有時候會讓人困惑，兩個都是指對某件事有狂熱的人，但是又有個不成文的規定，nerd 智商比較高，geek 則是以有朝一日成為 nerd 為目標的人。但是兩個說起來都是怪胎。也有以身為 geek 為榮的人，所以是否帶貶意因人而異。

❸ fucking moron 的 fucking 解釋一樣是他媽的的意思，這次是用來形容 moron 這個名詞，也就是白目的意思，用來指智商有問題的人。

門廊上的猴子（一）

 情境對話　 *Track 11*

Kayden 到比薩店上班遲到了……

Ashlyn: Do you know what time is it? Now get in here and start helping!

(After taking the order from the black couple at the front counter, Ashlyn turned around to the kitchen window, whispering in an angry tone.)

Ashlyn: Hey, I know this is your last day here, but while you're still on the clock, can you at least pretend that you care about this job?

Kayden: (talking loudly from the open kitchen) Sorry, ran into a [1]**jerk** I know from high school right down there in the parking lot. He kindly reminded me that I'm a [2]**fucking failure** after seeing my uniform and I just had to go somewhere else to blow off some steam.

Ashlyn: Oh come on, grow up!

你知道現在什麼時間了嗎？現在立刻進來幫忙！

（在幫櫃檯前的一對黑人夫妻點完餐以後，Ashlyn 轉身到廚房窗戶，小聲地罵。）

嘿，我知道今天是你最後一天上班，但是在你還在值班的時候，可以至少假裝你還在意這份工作嗎？

（大聲的從廚房回話）抱歉，剛剛在外面停車場碰到以前高中認識的混蛋，看到我穿的制服以後，他很親切地提醒我，我是一個他媽的失敗者。

噢！拜託！成熟點！

Kayden: (talking as he passes out the orders to Ashlyn) Hey, I don't mind if people make fun of this stupid uniform I have to wear, but I'll be damned if I let some self-righteous lucky [3]**turd** come up to me and treat me like some [4]**porch monkey**.

Ashlyn: Kayden!

(Turning right back to the black couple in front of her)

Ashlyn: uhh... I... I umm... I'm sorry, he...

Tamicka: He didn't really just say what I was thinking?

（邊說邊把餐點傳給 Ashlyn）喂，我不介意人家笑我這身愚蠢的制服，但我該死的不會讓那些自以為是的幸運屎類到我面前來，把我當門廊上的猴子對待。

Kayden!

（回過頭來面對她面前的黑人夫妻。）

哦…我…啊我…我很抱歉他…

他剛剛說的不會是我所想的吧？

Glossary 髒話大解

❶ jerk，名詞，這邊解釋為混蛋，通常是指不為他人著想、自私、自以為了不起的人。

❷ fucking failure 的 fucking 解釋一樣是他媽的的意思，這次是用來形容 failure，解釋為失敗者的這個名詞。

❸ turd，名詞，為糞、屎的意思，罵人的用詞，跟 shit 是同義。

❹ porch monkey，名詞，這詞是四零年代開始被用來蔑稱黑人的用詞，因為常常看到他們不工作，整天坐在屋前的門廊上混時間，由此而來。

Chapter 12 門廊上的猴子（二）

情境對話 Track 12

Kayden 語出驚人死不休，再接再厲……

Kayden: What? Porch monkeys?	啥？門廊上的猴子？
Ashlyn: What is wrong with you?	你到底有什麼問題？
Tamicka: I want my money back, right now!	我要退錢，現在！
Ashlyn: Of course. You know what? Take these on us.	當然，這樣吧？這些都免費。
(Putting the money along with the food they ordered on the counter in front of the couple.)	（把錢跟食物一起放到櫃台上，那對夫妻面前。）
Tamicka: Oh! No, no, I'm not eating the food prepared by some racist [1]**douchebag.**	喔不不，我不吃種族歧視混蛋準備的食物。
Kayden: What racism? Porch monkey? No, it's not. My grandma used to call me that all the time. That's no racism. [2]**Nigger**, [3]**coon** and [4]**jigaboo**, these are racial slurs, but porch monkey is not.	什麼種族歧視？門廊上的猴子？那才不是，我祖母以前常那樣叫我。那不是種族歧視。Nigger、coon、jigaboo 才是種族歧視的詞，但門廊上的猴子才不是。

Ashlyn: What is your problem?!　　你到底有什麼問題？！

Tamicka: That's it. I'm gonna write a paper about this and ya'll gonna get fired!　　夠了，我要去寫一篇關於這件事的報導，而你們都準備被開除吧！

(Grabbed her husband and walked out in an angry manner.)　　（抓了她先生就生氣的走出去。）

Ashlyn: Are you out of your fucking mind?!　　你他媽的瘋了嗎？！

Glossary 髒話大解

❶ douchebag，名詞，解釋為惡棍、混帳，原意是指女性清理私處或是灌腸的用具，現在常被用來做罵人的字眼。

❷ nigger，名詞，黑鬼的意思，18-19 世紀從法國、西班牙那邊傳開的蔑稱黑膚人種的詞，極度不禮貌，黑人彼此會開玩笑的互稱 nigga 或嚴肅的時候用 nigger，但是其他人種千萬不能用，就算是開玩笑或好玩也不行，除非你想被揍。

❸ coon，名詞，在北美是 racoon 浣熊的簡稱，但非正式用語是指黑人，而且也是帶著歧視意味的用詞。一開始是指跟浣熊一樣在晚上活動的宵小、強盜類，因為有著認為黑人窮，只會做這些壞事的刻版印象，後來就被用來蔑稱黑人。

❹ jigaboo，名詞，也是用來蔑稱黑人的用詞，雖然聽起來滿好笑的，但其實很瞧不起人，指那些居住環境很差，生活水準很低的黑膚人種。此字據說是 1900 年早期由 jig 跟 bugaboo 兩個字合用以後形成的，jig 解釋有很多，其中一個就是用來蔑稱黑人，bugaboo 是讓人害怕的事物。

老闆很糟糕（一）

 情境對話  *Track 13*

Sandra 跟她的男朋友 Rob 正在一間日本料理店享受他們的晚餐約會，這時她的手機響起了屬於她老闆的鈴聲。

Sandra: Ugh... not again! I'm sorry baby, just give me a minute. It'll be quick.(Then she picks up the phone and answers) Sandra speaking... yes, yes sir, don't worry, I'll take care of it right away.

喔…別又來了！寶貝我很抱歉，給我一分鐘，很快就好。（然後她接起電話回道）我是 Sandra，是，是的，先生，別擔心，我馬上處理。

Rob: (raises his eyebrow and says) Babe, it's almost 9 p.m. on a Saturday! What does the [1]**hymie** want this time?

（皺起眉頭）寶貝，現在已經差不多星期六晚上九點了！那個猶太人這次想幹嘛？

Sandra: His credit card was stolen. I need to contact the bank for him and get it replaced by Monday morning, so he can go off to his business trip in China.

他信用卡被盜，我得幫他聯絡銀行，在星期一早上前拿到替換的卡，這樣他才能到中國出差。

Rob: Why can't he take care of it himself? You need to let that [2]**damn** [3]**kike** know that you are not on call 24/7! It's about what? Fourth time this week? 3 a.m. on

他自己沒辦法解決嗎？你得讓那個該死的猶太人知道你不是一天 24 小時一星期七天隨傳隨到的！這

Friday, midnight on Tuesday, and 6 a.m. on Wednesday!	已經是什麼？這星期第四次了？星期五凌晨三點，星期二半夜，還有星期三早上六點！
Sandra: Baby, you and I know very well that I can't say that to him.	寶貝，你跟我都很清楚我不能對他那樣說。
Rob: Next time, do me a favor. Just don't pick up.	下次，幫我個忙，就別接。

Glossary 髒話大解

❶ hymie，名詞，是用來蔑稱男性猶太人的詞，極度沒有禮貌，現在比較少人用，八零年代早期時美國黑人開始使用這個詞來稱呼猶太人，後來其他人種也開始使用。

❷ damn，形容詞，該死的的意思，用來形容接下來的名詞 kike。

❸ kike，名詞，也是種族歧視意味濃厚的詞，也可拼作 kyke，據說是因為早期移民美國的猶太人普遍是不會拉丁字母的文盲，當他們簽移民文件的時候，移民官會在表格上需要他們簽名的地方會畫一個「X」，但是對猶太人來說「X」代表基督的十字架，所以會拒簽（因為猶太教跟基督教勢不兩立），因此需要為他們在簽名處畫「O」而非「X」。猶太人通用的意第緒語裡，代表圈圈的字為「kikel」，後來就簡稱為 kike。

Chapter 14

老闆很糟糕（二）

 情境對話  Track 14

跟老闆的通話結束以後，Sandra 繼續跟 Rob 討論老闆問題。

Sandra: If I don't pick up, he'll just keep on calling and calling until I do. One time, the part-time employee who I supervise wasn't picking up his phone, despite the fact it was his day off. It turned out he was hanging out at the beach, again it was his day off, and his phone was out of range, our boss was livid.

如果我不接，他就只會繼續打，直到我接為止。有一次，我底下的兼職員工沒接他的電話，儘管那天他放假，而後來我們知道他去海邊玩，再次強調那天他放假，而且他的電話收不到訊號，我們老闆的臉色可鐵青的哩。

Rob: Why are you scared that [1]**hebe** is going to put a [2]**sheeny curse** on you or something?

你幹嘛怕他會詛咒你窮一輩子不成或什麼的？

Sandra: (rolls her eye) No, I'm worried that I would lose my job. Remember that time when I had to go back to Ohio because my grandma was dying? I was receiving almost hourly emails, texts, and calls. I was unable to answer or reply through cellphones when even I was at the hospital. I was berated for having my priorities out of whack.

（翻白眼）不是，我擔心我會失業。記得我上次因為我奶奶病危回去俄亥俄州？當我因為在醫院而無法使用手機回覆時，我幾乎每小時都會收到電子郵件、簡訊跟電話。我因不懂事情的輕重緩急被訓斥了一頓。

Rob: Baby, let's be clear here. Your boss is completely, 100% over the line, an unreasonable and deluded [3]jerk. Did you knowingly sign up for this? When you were hired, were you told that you'd be expected to be on-call 24/7? I bet not! This is not reasonable! I think it's time for you to get a new job.

寶貝，咱把話說清楚，你老闆已經完全，百分之百越界了，他是個不講理、搞不清楚狀況的混蛋。你當初是明知如此還加入的嗎？你被錄用的時候，他們有跟你說你得一天 24 小時一星期七天隨傳隨到？我賭沒有！這簡直不可理喻！我想你是時候換新工作了。

Glossary 髒話大解

❶ hebe，名詞，指希伯來裔的人，後來被用來蔑稱猶太人，也有人會故意拼錯拼成 heeb，也是一樣的意思。猶太人普遍就是以小氣出名，所以也可以用來罵小氣的人。

❷ sheeny，名詞，也是蔑稱猶太人的詞，19 世紀被用來稱呼不可信任的猶太人。sheeny curse 是指猶太人的詛咒，會讓被詛咒的人窮愁潦倒衰到不行，當然這是玩笑話，不可能是真的。

❸ jerk，名詞，指那些不懂得尊重女性，自私自立，為所欲為的混蛋。

Chapter 15 失戀（一）

 情境對話  Track 15

Sandy 剛剛跟男朋友在很糟糕的情況下分手，所以為了讓她振作起來，Emma 決定帶她去滑雪。她們剛領了租來的器具，在置物櫃前正準備把她們的東西鎖起來。

Emma: Hey, put your stuffs in the back first. I don't want anything pressing on these new [1]**kick-ass** boots.

嘿，先把你的東西放裡面，我不想有任何東西壓在這雙超讚的新靴子上。

Sandy: K... Em, I'm really not in the mood for this.

好…Em，我現在真的沒心情做這事。

Emma: I know honey, but once you start going down that slope, you'll feel better right away, trust me! (With a huge grin on her face.)

我知道親愛的，當你開始順著坡往下滑的時候，你馬上就會覺得好很多了，相信我！（咧嘴笑著。）

Sandy: I don't know, I really miss him, and I know this is [2]**stupid**, but I really want to call him right now.

我不知道，我真的很想他，而且我知道這很蠢，但是我現在真的好想打電話給他。

Emma: Oh! Don't you [3]**dare**! If you ever call that cheating [4]**scumbag** again, our friendship would be over. You deserve

喔！你敢！如果讓我知道你又打電話給那個腳踏兩條船的爛人，我們的友情

better, and you know that!

就結束了。你值得更好
的，你知道的！

Glossary 髒話大解

❶ kick-ass 為形容詞片語，雖然照字面上的意思看來好像是踢屁股，但是其實在這裡是指一雙靴子很酷、很棒的意思。任何讓人覺得很讚的，不管事人、事、物都可以用 kick-ass 來形容。

❷ stupid 在此為形容詞，指 Sandy 覺得她想打電話給前男友是件很蠢的事，所以並不是在罵誰，而是有自嘲的意思。

❸ dare 在此為動詞，意思就是有勇氣做某件事的意思。Emma 說 "don't you dare"，就是「你敢這麼做給我試試看」的意思，在此有脅迫的感覺。有時用來作挑釁時也可以用，例如："I dare you to do (something)"，就是「你敢不敢做（某件事）」的意思。

❹ scumbag，名詞，卑鄙小人的意思，指一個人很沒有良知道德，是個自私、不顧慮他人感受的爛人，男女皆適用。

Chapter 16

失戀（二）

  **Track 16**

Emma 一聽說 Sandy 還在想那個腳踏兩條船的爛男人，氣憤的以友情威脅她放棄打電話給前男友的企圖。

Emma: Promise me you won't call that [1]**douchebag!**

答應我你不會再打給他。

Sandy: (Sigh...) Ok, I promise.

（嘆氣…）好，我答應。

Emma: Good! Alright then. Let's go have some fun now, shall we?

很好！那現在我們可以去玩了，可以吧？

Sandy: Sure, let's go.

當然，走吧。

Emma: Aww... don't give me that face, like I did you wrong or something!

喔…別給我那張臉，好像我對不起你似的！

Sandy: No Emma, I'm just... I just need some time to adjust. That's all.

不是的 Emma，我只是…我只是需要些時間來調整而已。

Emma: A [2]**rebound** is what you need right now. Let's see what we have here today. (Searched around for potential target.) Hmm... no luck, what's up with

你現在需要的是讓別的男人來陪你，來看看我們這裡今天有些什麼貨。（到處看，搜尋著。）唉…運

all the [3]**chuds** here today? Let's just get going and hit the slopes.

氣不好，搞什麼哪來一堆醜男聚在這？我們還是趕快去滑雪吧。

Glossary 髒話大解

❶ douchebag，名詞，解釋為惡棍或是混帳，原意是指女性清理私處或是灌腸的用具，近來常被用來做罵人的字眼。混蛋等級超越 jerk 跟 asshole，跟 scumbag 可以並駕齊驅。其實很多翻譯成混蛋的英文詞都是為男人而生的，但是近年來這些詞用的性別分界沒那麼清楚，所以女生被這些字眼罵也是有可能的。

❷ rebound，名詞，就字面的意思是彈回、復原的意思，但是用在這個故事裡的情況裡，Emma 說 Sandy 需要一個 rebound 的意思是指她需要另一個男人陪她度過這分手難過的期間，並非認真交往，純粹是為了不想寂寞要個人陪的狀況。

❸ chud，名詞，在這是醜男的意思。除了指一個人的樣貌醜到讓人退避三舍之外，也可以用來指某人在某項專業裡面的專業程度很低、很不成功的意思。

淘金女（一）

  Track 17

Kyle 走進酒吧裡，看見 Dan 坐在他常坐的位置上。

Kyle: Yo! Danno man! What's with the face, brother?

呦！丹老兄！幹嘛這張臉，兄弟？

Dan: Don't even mention it.

別提了。

Kyle: Why? Come on, tell me!

為啥？來嘛，告訴我！

Dan: (Sigh...) It's Crystal, last night I got home from work. The house was basically empty, and all the cash in the safe was gone, too.

（嘆氣）是 Crystal，昨晚我下班回家後，家裡基本上被搬空了，保險箱裡的現金也都不見了。

Kyle: [1]**Fuck**! I knew this is bound to happen sooner or later, probably ran off with her next target, that [2]**gold-digging bitch**!

幹！我早就知道這種事遲早會發生，八成跟她下一個目標跑了，那個淘金賤貨！

Dan: Hey, watch it. She's my girl.

喂，注意點，她是我的女人。

Kyle: WAS! I've warned you multiple times man, but you never listen. I could

曾經是！我早就提醒過你很多次了，但你總是不

sense there's something wrong with that
[3]**skank** from the moment I met her.

聽。從第一次跟那爛貨碰
面我就知道她有問題。

Glossary 髒話大解

❶ fuck 為感嘆詞，在此解釋為「幹」，「幹」這個字大家都耳熟能詳，就
不多做解釋。

❷ gold-digging bitch 裡的 gold-digging 為形容詞，淘金的意思，用來形
容後面的名詞 bitch，也就是賤人的意思，連在一起就是指為了錢啥事
都做的出來的拜金賤女人。

❸ skank，名詞，在此是指 Crystal 是淫亂的女子，一開始是常常用在窮困
的白人身上，但是近來也被廣泛用在其他社會階級，指低俗、令人不愉
快的人，比較少被用到的解釋是指一種牙買加雷鬼音樂舞蹈。

淘金女（二）

Dan 的女人捲了他的東西跑了，相較於 Kyle 的氣憤填膺，Dan 雖然傷心，反應倒是冷靜的不太正常。

Dan: (Sigh...) yah, I probably should've known better.

（嘆氣…）是啊，我可能早該知道。

Kyle: So what's your plan now? Did you call the police?

所以你現在的計畫是什麼？打電話給警察沒？

Dan: No, and I don't know.

沒有，我不知道。

Kyle: What do you mean you don't know? You can't just let this go! Let's get back at this [1]**whore**.

什麼叫你不知道？你不能就這樣算了！我們來對那妓女復仇。

Dan: I really don't want to talk about this anymore, Kyle.

我真的不想再談了，Kyle。

Kyle: Fine, but little Miss [2]**Snake eyes** better run far enough and sleep with one eye open from now on. Once I get my hands on her, she's [3]**doomed**.

好，但是蛇眼小姐最好跑得夠遠，還有從現在起晚上睡覺得睜一隻眼睡，等我逮到她，她就死定了。

Dan: Dude, I appreciate your concern,

老兄，我很感謝你的關

but this is between me and her.

心，但是這是我跟她之間
的事。

Kyle: Fine then, suit yourself.

好吧，那隨便你。

Glossary 髒話大解

❶ whore，名詞，指從事性工作的女子，也就是妓女，也可以用來稱呼淫
亂的女子。

❷ snake eyes，名詞，逐字翻譯為蛇眼的意思，但其背後的意義在此是指
Crystal 是卑鄙虛偽、陰險狡詐的女人。其他意思有像是在玩骰子遊戲時
拿到兩個一點，因為機率很低，所以也有人用來稱呼壞運氣的人。

❸ doomed 為動詞 doom 的過去式，指某人將會受到某種不幸的傷害或死
亡的制裁，再次解釋為 Crystal 小姐死定了。

掰 Felicia！（一）

 情境對話  *Track 19*

Darrel 跟 Harry 坐在屋前的長廊上抽菸，這時 Chantelle 上前來。

Chantelle: Hey Darrell, what's up?

嘿 Darrell，你在幹嘛？

Darrell: Nothing, what do you want?

沒什麼，你想幹啥？

Chantelle: I need to borrow your car real quick.

我想跟你借用一下車。

Darrell: What kind of [1-1]**shit** is that? Most people go to their neighbors to borrow sugar or salt, and you want to borrow my car? [2-1]**Hell** no!

搞屁啊你？大部分的人到鄰居家就是借糖借鹽巴，而你想跟我借車？門都沒有！

Chantelle: Well, let me borrow a [3]**joint** then.

那借我抽一根大麻吧。

Darrell: You need to borrow a job with your [4]**broke ass**. Always trying to smoke up somebody else's [1-2]**shit**. Get the [2-2]**hell** out of here!

你這窮鬼需要去借個工作來做。老是想從別人那裏撈東西來抽。從這裡滾出去！

Chantelle: I'm going to remember that.

我記住了喔。

Glossary 髒話大解

❶ shit，名詞，shit 是大家都知道是屎的意思，shit 在此是 Darrell 想表示 Chantelle 這個要求很令人生氣，所以用這個詞來代替她的要求。第二個 shit 是指東西，指 Chantelle 常常要別人的東西抽，不自己買。

❷ 第一個 hell 為感嘆詞，hell 是地獄的意思，所以帶有負面的意思，在此 Darrell 為了強調自己不想借 Chantelle 車，在 no 前面加上 hell 來增強語氣。第二個 hell 也是一樣的用法，只是不同在要 Chantelle 滾，叫她 get the hell out 而不是 get out。

❸ joint，名詞，在這邊不是關節的意思喔，是一根大麻的意思，大麻像菸草一樣是散的、乾碎的葉子，用香菸紙捲起來以後的成品就叫做 joint。

❹ broke ass 的 broke 是形容詞，破產的意思，ass 雖然是屁股的意思，但是兩個字聯在一起絕對不是破產屁股的意思，而是指一個人很窮的狀況。

掰 Felicia!（二）

Chantelle 到 Darrel 家想借些東西用用，很不幸地碰壁了，但是仍然不肯放棄，企圖想威脅 Darrel，但卻不管用……

Darrell: Remember it! Write it down! Take a picture! I don't give a [1]**fuck**!

記住！寫下來！照相存證！我他媽的不在乎！

Chantelle: (turned to Harry and asked) Harry?

（轉向 Harry 問）Harry？

Harry: (Without any hesitation, replied) [2]**Bye Felicia.**

（毫不猶豫的，Harry 答道）掰，Felicia。

Chantelle: Who's Felicia?

誰是 Felicia？

Harry: Exactly [3]**bitch**. Buh bye!

正是你這爛女人，掰掰！

Chantelle: Can I just borrow a dollar? I promise I'll pay you back.

那可以借我一塊錢吧，我保證我一定還你。

Darrell and Harry: (both replied at the same time) Bye Felicia!

（Darrell 跟 Harry 兩個同時回答）掰，Felicia！

Chantelle: I promise!

我保證！

Darrell and Harry: (Again, Darrell and Harry yelled out even louder this time) BYE FELICIA!

（再一次的，Darrell 跟 Harry 同時更大聲的罵道）掰，Felicia！

Glossary 髒話大解

❶ fuck 在此為帶有感嘆詞性的名詞，指 Darrell 他媽的不在意 Chantelle 記恨與否。

❷ Bye Felicia 是美國著名喜星 Ice Cube 在一部電影裡使用而出名的詞。Chantelle 的名字並非 Felicia，但是因為不喜歡她，所以故意叫她 Felicia。當你不喜歡的人離開的時候，你如果說 Bye, Felicia，其他人就會知道你不喜歡那個人。如果你不介意給對方當面打臉的話，當著那人的面說也行，就像這篇故事裡的情形。

❸ bitch，名詞，賤人的意思，並非 Chantelle 做了什麼不守婦道的齷齪事，純粹是因為討厭所以這樣叫她。

Chapter 21

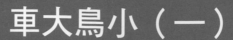

車大鳥小（一）

 情境對話  *Track 21*

Sue 跟 Peg 正站在公車站，一台大卡車經過從排氣口排出大量的廢氣，兩個女人一不小心吸進了廢氣而開始咳嗽。

Sue: [1]**Damn** it! What the [2]**fuck** is that guy's problem?

該死的！那傢伙他媽的搞什麼？

Peg: I know, that [3]**asshole** knew we were standing here. He probably did that on purpose!

對吧，那混帳知道我們站在這。他八成是故意的！

Sue: I hate people that drive those large trucks. Oh they think they are so tough.

我討厭那些開大貨車的人，喔他們好像覺得自己很厲害。

Peg: I heard the reason a man drives a big truck is because he has a small [4]**dick**!

我聽說開大車的男人是因為他們那話兒很小！

Sue: Hahaha! I believe it. His cock is probably so tiny that he can't satisfy a woman.

哈哈哈！我相信，他的鳥八成小到無法滿足一個女人。

Peg: I'll bet he doesn't even like women.

我賭他根本不喜歡女人。

Glossary 髒話大解

❶ damn 為驚嘆詞性的動詞，該死的意思，在基督教的信仰裡，damn 的意思是被上帝懲罰，打入地獄永無止境的受罪。現在通常用來表示氣憤、震驚、挫折與無奈。

❷ fuck 是 Sue 為了表示氣憤而加入句中的感嘆詞，正常問句應該是 "what is that guy's problem?"。

❸ asshole，名詞，混帳的意思，是指那個開卡車經過的男人。

❹ dick，名詞，指男人的小弟弟，一般也有男性取名為 Dick，也是 Richard 的簡稱，所以不見得是罵人，書面上最容易的分辨方法就是頭一個字母大小寫，大寫就是人名，小寫就是在罵人。至於為什麼 dick 會變成男人小弟弟的暱稱？不知道從何而來，而且似乎只有北美在用這個意思。

車大鳥小（二）

Sue 跟 Peg 對卡車男的謾罵仍然持續當中……

Sue: Hahaha! He's probably a [1]**fag** and only likes [2]**cock**. That would explain a lot. His dick is small, and it fits nicely into a tight [3]**asshole**.

哈哈哈！他八成是同性戀只喜歡男人的鳥。那就解釋得更清楚了。他的鳥太小，剛好可以好好插進屁眼裡。

Peg: He probably drove away so fast that he could get on his way to get [4]**fucked** in the ass by his boyfriend, hahaha!

他開那麼快，八成是趕著去給他男朋友幹他的屁眼，哈哈哈！

Sue: Hahaha! You are too funny!

哈哈哈！你真的很好笑！

Peg: By the way, I'm Peg, and you are?

對了，我叫 Peg，你呢？

Sue: Oh, Sue, nice to meet you here. Do you always take this bus?

喔，Sue，很高興在這碰見你。你都坐這班公車嗎？

Peg: Most of the time, I'm only a few blocks away, so on rare occasions, I would walk home instead.

大部分時間都是，我就住幾個街區外，所以偶爾，我會走回家。

(The bus arrives and two women get on while chatting.)

（公車到站了，兩個女人邊上車邊聊不停。）

Glossary 髒話大解

❶ fag，名詞，faggot 的簡稱，指男同性戀，歧視意味濃厚的一個字。有時候就算對方不是男同性戀，也是可以拿這個字來罵他，作為很蠢的意思。

❷ cock，名詞，也是指男人的小弟弟，一開始也不是小弟弟的意思，是指公雞，或公的鳥類，但是這個詞的意義轉變比較說的通，dick 就比較讓人想不通了。

❸ asshole，名詞，而這次就真的是字面上的意思了，指的就是屁眼。這個字做為混帳或是屁眼兩種意思都很常聽到，看狀況需求使用。

❹ fucked，動詞被動式，為發生性關係的動作，在這裡是指卡車男被某人上的意思。

Chapter 23

我把別人的肚子搞大了（一）

Adam 兩星期以後將要跟他的未婚妻 Ellie 搬到佛羅里達州去，現在他正站在 UPS 的後門，跟他最要好的好朋友 Charlie，一起抽菸休息。

Adam: I'm having some second thoughts.

我開始有別的想法了。

Charlie: About your sexuality?

關於你的性向？

Adam: About going to Florida.

關於去佛羅里達。

Charlie: Yeah right, why now all of the sudden?

最好是，為什麼這麼突然？

Adam: Sara's pregnant. I'm the father.

Sara 懷孕了，我是孩子的父親。

Charlie: How the fuck did you father a child with a [1]**chick** that's not your fiancée? When did this happen?

你他媽的怎麼會讓不是你未婚妻的人懷你的孩子？什麼時候發生的？

Adam: We had sex after work one night, a few weeks ago.

我們有一天晚上下班後發生了性關係，幾個星期前。

Charlie: How the [2]**fuck** do you always

你他媽的怎麼總是有兩個

have two good-looking girls who want you? You're the most [3]**hideous fucking chud** I've ever met, and you always have a pair of girls fighting over you!

美女要你？你是我見過最他媽的可笑醜男，而你總是有一對女孩為你爭風吃醋！

Glossary 髒話大解

❶ chick，名詞，本身為新生的雛鳥的意思，但在此解釋為女人的非正式用語。本身不是髒話，但是也不是多正經的用語，所以有些女性可能會不喜歡被稱為 chick，會覺得不受尊重。

❷ fuck 為形容詞性語助詞，在這裡是他媽的的意思。Charlie 想要藉此來表示他對整個事件得不解跟驚訝。

❸ hideous fucking chud 裡的 hideous 是醜得很可笑的意思。fucking 為形容詞，解釋為他媽的，用來形容之後的 chud。chud 為名詞，指又笨又醜的人。這三個字合起來就是為了強調 Charlie 認為 Adam 長這樣還這麼多女人要，真是沒天理！

Chapter 24 我把別人的肚子搞大了（二）

  **Track 24**

Adam 把自己上司的肚子搞大了，雖然兩個星期後他將要跟未婚妻搬到佛羅里達州去生活，現在他正處在兩難之中。

Charlie: What did Sara say?

Sara 怎麼說？

Adam: She says she wants to have it.

她說她想生。

Charlie: [1]**OMG**, so she wants you to break it off with Ellie and marry her?

老天，所以她想你跟 Ellie 分手，然後跟她結婚？

Adam: No.

不是。

Charlie: Wait a second... then what's the problem?

等等⋯那你到底有什麼問題？

Adam: Are you seriously that [2]**dense**?

你真的有這麼蠢嗎？

Charlie: I'm serious! If Sara isn't busting your [3]**balls** about it, then what's the big deal? You could still go down to Florida and live happily ever after.

我是講真的啊！如果 Sara 沒有想要整你，讓你難受的話，那到底有什麼問題？你還是可以下去佛羅里達過從此幸福快樂的生活。

Adam: Knowing that I have a love child up here in Connecticut?

知道我在康乃狄克州有個因愛而生的孩子？

Glossary 髒話大解

❶ OMG 感嘆詞，其實就是 **Oh My God** 的簡寫，我的老天爺啊的意思。現在年輕人盛行傳簡訊，有時候可能因為懶就只打三個字的起首字母，有時候連說話都用簡訊方法說。

❷ dense，形容詞，本意是密度很高的意思，但是非正式用法是指一個人很蠢、很白目的意思。

❸ balls，名詞，在此並非指球，而是指男人的睪丸。**busting your balls** 字面上的意思是把你的蛋蛋打爛，能想像會非常痛，但是 Charlie 想表達的意思是讓 Adam 心理上很煩惱痛苦，而不是生理上的疼痛。

Chapter 25 監獄同樂會（一）

  *Track 25*

Dave、Matt 還有 Don 在酒後駕車還有超速被逮捕之後，現在正坐在警察局的監獄裡。

Matt: Jail cell design hasn't changed much in centuries, has it? Maybe it's time they brought in the laser bars or something.

監獄設計幾百年來幾乎沒怎麼變，對吧？是時候他們該引進雷射柵欄之類的了。

Dave: Or they can make a hard plastic cage like the ones for Magneto!

或是他們可以做成像給萬磁王的塑膠監牢那樣的！

Matt: Come on, dude. Let's keep it in the real world, all right? What do you think Don?

拜託，老兄，現實一點好嗎？你覺得呢，Don？

Don: (charged at Matt and grabbed his neck, shouted) I think I'm going to kill you! You ruined my life! I can't believe you I've finally got my [1]**shit** together. I'm that close from getting out of here and really starting my new life, and you somehow figure out a way to obliterate all that and reduce me to a convict!

（Don 衝向 Matt，抓著他的脖子叫道）我覺得我想要殺了你！你毀了我的人生！我簡直不敢相信，我好不容易讓我的人生步入正軌。我差不多要離開了，開始我新的人生，而你卻有辦法把這一切都抹煞掉，還把我降級成為罪犯！

Matt: (While pushing Don off himself) Oh yeah, it's my fault that your life is [2]**fucked up**. I'm the engaged guy who [3]**knocked up** my boss.

（Matt 把 Don 推開的同時）是喔，你人生亂七八糟都是我的錯，我是那個訂了婚還把自己上司肚子搞大的男人。

Glossary 髒話大解

❶ shit 都是名詞，但是不是大便，而是指某樣東西的意思，在這裡是指 Don 他的人生，是因為他正在很生氣的狀況，所以用 shit 來代表。

❷ fucked up 為片語，某人或某事造成某個程度的傷害的意思。可以用在各種狀況，像是身理、精神、道德、美學觀點、行為表現，甚至是假設的狀況。至於情況的輕與重，就是以說的人的語氣來定奪。有時甚至可以用幽默開玩笑的語氣來說。在這裡是 Matt 用諷刺的口吻對 Don 說：「是啊，你人生一團糟都是我的錯啦」。

❸ knocked up 為片語，是指某人讓某人懷孕了，通常是指沒有計畫、不想要、不被人期待的懷孕。當然語氣也很重要，如果是朋友之間開玩笑用這個詞也是可以的。在這裡 Matt 意有所指的說他自己訂了婚還把自己上司的肚子搞大了。

監獄同樂會（二）

Dave、Matt 還有 Don 在警察局的監獄裡，Matt 跟 Don 吵到已經要打起來了。

Don: Shut up, Matt. You're chaos incarnate, man. Ever since I met you, you've been getting me into trouble and holding me back.

閉嘴 Matt，你就是個混亂的集合體。自從認識你以後，你就老是給我製造麻煩還有拖累我。

Matt: Oh, I'm holding you back? How exactly do I hold you back?

喔，我拖累你？怎麼個拖累法？

Don: Scraping by with the bare minimum, and I'm tired of that! If that's all you want out of life, then have at it, but I refuse to let your [1]**shit** [2]**taint** the rest of mine.

總是安於最低標準，而我真的很累了！如果那是你想要的人生，那儘管去，但是我拒絕再讓你那些狗屁事汙染我接下來的人生。

Matt: Wow, you should have told me this earlier then I wouldn't even bother to throw you this farewell party! If I knew you were just going to [3]**flake** on me later, I wouldn't even be bothered by you in the first place.

哇嗚，你應該早點跟我說的，這樣我根本就不會費心思給你策畫這個歡送會！如果我知道你就只會這樣不講義氣，我一開始就不會理你。

Dave: Jesus, why don't you two just get it over with already? [4]**Faggots.**

老天，你們兩個可以結束了嗎？蠢貨。

Don: (turned to Dave and said) Why can't you ever say something useful for a change?

（Don 轉向 Dave 說道）你就不能說些有用的話？

Glossary 髒話大解

❶ shit，名詞，是人生過程發生的事，這次是指 Matt 帶來的狗屁倒灶事，是因為 Don 正在很生氣的狀況，所以用 shit 來代表。

❷ taint 在此是動詞，汙染、玷汙的意思。Don 表示他不想 Matt 的狗屁倒灶事來汙染他的人生。這個字做為名詞的話除了汙點，還有另一個意思，指的是男或女性的生殖器到屁眼中間那塊空間的皮膚，有人說是因為那塊空間的皮膚，男人的睪丸或是女人的陰道才不會沾上糞便，所以叫它 taint。

❸ flake 在此是動詞，臨時改變主意的意思，在此是指 Don 是個沒義氣、不講信用的人。也可以做為名詞，譬如說你約個朋友吃飯，他臨時爽約，你可以說 "he's such a flake"，意思是他是個不守信用的人。

❹ faggot，名詞，這個字本意是指綑在一起拿來燒的乾柴，後來衍生變成罵男同性戀的字眼，但是並不是每次都是用來罵誰是男同性戀，有時候只是用來表示對方很蠢是個 loser，像在這裡 Dave 罵 Matt 跟 Don 兩個是 faggot，不是罵他們是男同性戀，而是罵他們兩個是蠢貨。

糟糕室友（一）

Colleen 在學校圖書館碰到 Amanda，於是走了過去想跟她閒聊，順便抱怨一下惡室友。

Colleen: So my horrible roommate is moving out, you know that right?

Amanda: Yah, you told me about it a few days ago.

Colleen: We had a huge fight last night. She insisted that some stuffs are hers even though I was the one who bought them from TJ-max. After I showed her the receipt, she told me that I can't prove the stuffs are mine because the items were listed as home décor, not glass vase, or wooden bowl, or such. When I asked her to show me her receipt, she said she didn't keep it. Then she locked those stuffs in her room and left the house.

Amanda: Wow... that's crazy.

我那很糟糕的室友要搬走了，你知道的吧？

對啊，你前幾天有告訴我。

昨晚我們大吵一架，她堅持有些東西是她的，雖然其實是我從 TJ-max 買回來的。在我給她看收據以後，她告訴我那不能證明東西是我的，因為發票上寫的是家庭裝飾品，而不是玻璃花瓶、木碗或那類的名字。當我要她給我看她的收據的時候，她說她沒留著，然後就把東西鎖在她房間裡，出門去了。

哇……那真的是很神經病。

Colleen: The other day, I asked her to give me money for the utilities, and by the way, she hasn't really paid me those for a few months. She told me she doesn't have money, while she was sitting on the floor in her room, drinking vodka from the bottle and smoking [1]**pot**! I mean, if you have money for those [2]**shits**, why can't you pay me the [3]**fucking** utility bills first!

某天，我跟她要水電瓦斯費，還有對了，她有好一陣子沒給我那些錢了。她告訴我她沒錢，當她正坐在她房間地上，拿著伏特加酒瓶直接灌，還有抽大麻！我說，你有錢買那些鬼東西，為啥不能先付我他媽的水電瓦斯費！

Glossary 髒話大解

❶ pot，名詞，在此不是指容器，而是指迷藥大麻，聽起來好像很恐怖，但是大麻其實在美國很常見，有些州甚至是合法的。這個詞是從墨西哥的西班牙文而來，potiguaya，指的就是大麻的葉子，後來就被普羅大眾簡稱為 pot。

❷ shit，名詞，在此不是代表糞便，而是指 Colleen 室友喝的伏特加酒還有抽的大麻，因為生氣，所以用這個詞代替。

❸ fucking，形容詞，解釋為他媽的，是 Colleen 為了表示氣憤而加上的語助詞。

 情境對話　 *Track 28*

Colleen 跟 Amanda 正坐在星巴克喝咖啡休息片刻。

Colleen: I've had enough. Excuse me for doing this, but I just can't hold it in anymore. I need to let it out!

我真的受夠了。原諒我這麼做，但是我再也忍不住了，我需要發洩一下。

Amanda: Sure, no worries. Go ahead, I'm listening.

好的，沒問題。開始吧，我聽著。

Colleen: Alright, here it goes, I want to [1]**freaking** kill my roommate!

好，開始囉，我他媽的想殺了我的室友！

Amanda: Haha... well, just think about this. She'll be gone soon.

哈哈……這麼想吧，她馬上就要離開了。

Colleen: Yah! And she still owes me the last month's rent! I don't know why I always have such bad luck with roommates! There was the [2]**JAP** two years ago. Then the [3]**psycho** who was crazy about Harry Potter, I mean really crazy, to the point where I had to get a no contact restraining order!

是啊！而她還欠我最後這個月的房租哩！我不知道為什麼我室友運這麼差！兩年前有那個猶太公主，然後是那個很瘋哈利波特的神經病，我是說真的很瘋狂，到了我要申請禁止她跟我有任何接觸的限制令！

Amanda: Maybe you just need to adjust your roommate hunting tack tick. I'll help you with the interview next time.

或許你該改變一下你找室友的方法。下次我一起幫你面試吧。

Glossary 髒話大解

❶ freaking 在此為形容詞，解釋為他媽的，是用來強調氣憤而加上的，用法跟 fucking 很類似，都是用來強調機動的情緒，像是氣憤、反感、甚至是開心、驚訝都可以。如果在不能使用 fuck 這麼不文雅的詞的場合，freaking 可以取而代之。

❷ JAP，名詞，其實是三個字的縮寫，Jewish American Princess，指那些家裡很有錢、嬌生慣養、有公主病的猶太女孩子。全世界公認最會賺錢的人就是猶太人，在美國那些被慣壞的猶太女孩就被人稱為 JAP，有蔑視取笑的意思。

❸ psycho，名詞，psychopath 的簡稱，指一個人有神經病、精神不穩定不正常，甚至有暴力傾向。

 情境對話  *Track 29*

客廳裡 Kayla 正在上網，Emily 正在看電視。

Kayla: Hey, check this funny post, [1]**sassy** / dirty valentine pick-up lines. "You're like my pinky toe, odds are I'm going to end up [2]**banging** you on a piece of furniture tonight", hahaha...!

嘿，看看這個好笑的貼文，大膽／下流的情人節搭訕話：「你就像是我的小腳趾頭，我很可能今晚會在某件家具上碰撞你」，哈哈哈…！

Emily: Hahaha... I like it, furniture, cushions... toes, do you like feet?

哈哈哈…這個我喜歡，家具、墊子…腳趾，你喜歡腳嗎？

Kayla: No, I hate feet.

不，我討厭腳。

Emily: Me too, but you know how there are people that are obsessed with feet?

我也是，但是你知道有些人對腳有種狂熱？

Kayla: Yah! How did it happen? I think it's the most revolting thing on this planet. I hate feet so much!

是啊！不知道怎麼發生的？我認為那是整個地球最令人作嘔的東西，我超討厭腳的！

Emily: I would [3]**suck** toes.

我願意吸腳趾頭。

Kayla: You would?!　　　　　　　　　　你願意？！

Emily: NO!　　　　　　　　　　　　　才不會！

Kayla: Oh! I almost believed you.　　　喔！我差點相信了。

Glossary 髒話大解

❶ sassy，形容詞，大膽的、活靈活現的意思。這個字意義可褒可貶，但是褒獎的時候居多，雖然是指某人沒禮貌，但是又是可愛的沒禮貌方式，所以當你稱某人為 sassy girl 的時候，是指這女孩很大膽奔放，雖然沒禮貌但是不討人厭的意思。

❷ banging 為動詞進行式，bang 這個字是撞擊、碰撞的意思，不小心踢到腳趾頭時說 "I banged my toe"，在這邊是指男女發生性行為時，碰撞的那個動作，其實是很下流的說法，所以想搭訕女生千萬別用這個字喔。

❸ suck，動詞，指用嘴巴吸吮這個動作。有時候可以做為很糟糕的意思，像是如果說天氣糟透了，就是 "The weather sucks!" 所以要看對話的內容，兩個意思差滿大，要注意不要想歪囉！

下流的搭訕台詞（二）

 情境對話  Track 30

Emily 對這個網站的討論內容產生了興趣，想接著看看接下來還有甚麼好玩的台詞。

Emily: Hehe... what else you got there?

嘿嘿…那還有什麼其他的？

Kayla: Hmm... let me see, oh! Here's another one, "Ayy girl, you like pie? Cuz you made my ¹**banana** ²**cream**."

嗯…讓我看看，喔！還有一個：「欸美眉，你喜歡派嗎？因為你讓我的香蕉產生奶油了。」

Emily: Eww, so gross!

噁，好噁心！

Kayla: Haha... alright, next one "There will only be seven planets left after I destroy ³**Uranus!**"

哈哈…好，下一個「在我毀滅天王星以後，將會只剩下七大行星！」

Emily: Oh my gosh! Getting wilder and wilder!

喔我的老天，越來越誇張了！

Kayla: Some guy said, "I'm not Asian, but I would still eat your ⁴**cat**."

有個男的說：「我不是亞洲人，但是我還是會吃你的貓」。

Emily: Okay, next.

好，下一個。

Kayla: This one is making me hungry, "Are your legs made of Nutella? Because I'd like to spread them!"

這個讓我覺得餓了：「你的腿是榛果醬做的嗎？因為我想抹開它們！」

Emily: Woo~ Sassy, Sassy, Sassy! But yah, I'm hungry too. Let's go eat.

哦～好敢喔！但是對啊，我也餓了，我們去吃飯吧。

Glossary 髒話大解

❶ banana，名詞，在這裡當然不是指香蕉而是指男人的小弟弟。

❷ cream，動詞，是指一個人性慾高漲的時候，性器官開始產生分泌物的狀況。

❸ Uranus，名詞，但是在這裡當然不是指天王星，Uranus 聽起來像是說 your anus，是取那個字的諧音，也就是你的肛門的意思。

❹ cat，名詞，在這裡不是貓的意思，而是指女生的陰道。陰道有另一種說法叫 pussy，這個字比較常被用，而 pussy 這個字也可以當做貓的意思。因為有亞洲人會吃貓跟狗之類的動物，所以這個人故意用 cat 這個字。

大姨媽來（一）

Rachel、Josh 跟 Amy 一起坐在學校的食堂裡。

Rachel: You know what [1]**pisses me off**?

你知道什麼事情會讓我很火大嗎？

Josh: What pisses you off, Rachel?

什麼事情讓你很火大，Rachel？

Rachel: Men's idea of [2]**PMS**. You know before you're on your period and your hormones are a little bit off, and you're a bit cranky? Well I hate when a girl is not in a good mood, and a [3]**guy** comes up and say "Are you PMS-ing?" or "Are you on your period?"

男人對 PMS 的見解。你知道在月經來之前，你的賀爾蒙會有點不正常，而你會有點情緒化？我最討厭當一個女生心情不好的時候，某個傢伙上前來劈頭就說：「你正在 PMS 嗎？」或是「你月經來喔？

Josh: Well, let me guess. Rob just said that to you?

讓我猜猜看，Rob 對你說的？

Rachel: Yah! Because apparently the only explanation that I could possibly be in a bad mood for is that I'm on my period!

沒錯！因為好像唯一可以解釋我會心情不好的原因就是我月經來了！

Amy: Just keep in your mind that if a girl is in a bad mood, the worst possible thing you can ever do is asking if she's on her period. Why would that make anything any better? Stop it!

你只要記住，如果有個女生心情不好，你所能做的最糟糕的事情就是問她是不是月經來了。難道這麼做會有任何幫助嗎？別在這麼做了！

Glossary 髒話大解

❶ piss off 在此為片語，piss 本身是撒尿的意思，但是 piss off 是讓人生氣的意思。在此是 Rachel 表示有某件事讓她很生氣。也可以在生氣的時候對你生氣的對象說 "Just piss off" 就是要對方滾的意思。

❷ PMS，名詞，指女性更年期停經以後的綜合症狀，像是發汗發熱睡不著覺等等很不舒服的徵狀，使得很多更年期女性會很容易心情不好、發脾氣，也因為這樣就常常被人用來對發脾氣的女人說，不論年齡或是她是否真的停經了，甚至有時候性別，比如說老闆剛剛臭罵你一頓，你回過頭跟同事罵說 "he's having a PMS" 的狀況也是有的。

❸ guy，名詞，一般來說是指男人，是非正式用語，但是在其他狀況下可以做為大家的意思，譬如你要準備跟一群朋友說話，男的女的都有，要引他們注意也可以用 "hey guys, listen up"，就是「嘿你們，聽這邊」的意思。

大姨媽來（二）

 情境對話　 *Track 32*

關於男人們對大姨媽的誤解，Rachel 繼續對著 Josh 跟 Amy 抱怨。

Rachel: Even if I'm in a bad mood and happen to be on my period, it's not because of my period, it is due to your [1]**stupidity**!

就算我心情不好，而且也剛好是我月經來的時候，也不會是我月經的關係，是因為你的愚蠢！

Amy: I totally get you! Guys get upset when I'm upset on my period, I mean come on! There is blood coming out of my vagina and my uterus feels like someone is punching me from the inside out, so I have absolute right to be angry!

我完全了解！我因為生理期心情不好時，男人們因此事而生氣，我說你馬幫幫忙！我的陰道正在出血，而且我的子宮感覺像是有人在裡面往外捶我，我有絕對的生氣權利！

Rachel: Exactly! Besides, PMS does not happen on your period! It stands for postmenopausal syndrome, meaning after you stop having your period, you [2]**pathetic** [3]**imbecile**!

正是！況且，PMS 不會發生在你月經來的時候！它代表絕經症候群，是你停止有月經之後的事，你這可悲的低能兒！

Josh: Why are you yelling at me for? I wasn't the one who said that.

你罵我幹嘛？又不是我説的。

Rachel: Because you are a man!

因為你也是個男人！

Josh: You seem a little flustered, are you on your period?

你看來有些慌亂，你大姨媽來了喔？

(After a few seconds of silence, three of them burst out laughing together.)

（幾秒鐘的沉默後，三個人一起爆笑開來。）

Glossary 髒話大解

❶ stupidity，名詞，指某人的愚蠢，說的是愚蠢這個特質而不是指人。

❷ pathetic，形容詞，可悲的意思，當一個人愚蠢到讓你覺得可憐時，就可以用這個字來形容他。

❸ imbecile，名詞，罵一個人是低能、笨蛋的意思，指那些只會說大話，但是其實只是半瓶水響叮噹的蠢貨。

賺錢之術（一）

 情境對話  *Track 33*

兩個股票經紀人，Matthew 跟 Leonard 正一起在一家高級餐廳吃中餐。就在他們剛點完餐點跟飲料以後，Matthew 拿出一個裝著白色粉末的小瓶子，挖出一些來，然後吸進他的鼻子裡。

Matthew: Care for some [1]**blow**?	想來點古柯鹼嗎？
Leonard: No, thank you. How are you able to do drugs during the day and function at work?	不，謝了。你怎麼有辦法白天嗑藥還能正常上班運作？
Matthew: How else would you do this job? Cocaine and [2]**hookers**, my friend.	不然你怎麼做這份工作？古柯鹼跟妓女，我的朋友。
Leonard: Right. (Laughing politely) Well I'm honored to be a part of your firm. You have some impressive clients.	是是。（禮貌的笑著）那個我很榮幸能夠成為你們公司的一員，你們有些很厲害的客戶。
Matthew: [3]**Screw** the clients. Remember, the number one rule of Wall Street is this, nobody knows whether the stock is going up, down, sideways, or in circles. Your job is to take the client's money and	去他媽的客戶。記住了，華爾街最重要的規則就是沒有人知道股票會往上、往下、往旁邊走，還是繞圈子。你的工作就是拿客

re-invest it in more stocks, then we, as the brokers, take home cash through commissions, understand?

戶的錢然後不斷地在不同的股票上做投資，而我們這些股票經紀人，就可以賺取傭金，懂嗎？

Glossary 髒話大解

❶ blow，名詞，在這裡是指古柯鹼，非正式用語裡，blow 可以做為大麻或是古柯鹼的意思，會叫做 blow，是取吸這些藥物的這個動作。

❷ hooker，名詞，在這裡是妓女的意思。另外還有其他意思，像是英式橄欖球裡其中專門鉤球的球員，或是拿來蔑稱阿米什人 (Amish) 的詞。

❸ screw，動詞，幹、去他媽的意思。作為髒話的話其實用法跟 fuck 很類似，這個字的本意做為名詞是螺絲的意思，而做為動詞是鎖螺絲的動作。

 情境對話  Track 34

Matthew 繼續傳授他精闢的賺錢之術。

Leonard: Right, that's incredible, sir. I'm excited.

是的，那真是很了不起，先生。我感到很興奮。

Matthew: You should be. There're two keys to success in the broker business. First of all, you have to stay relaxed. Do you [1]**jerk off?**

你應該的。在股票經紀人的事業裡，有兩個很重要的成功關鍵。第一，你必須要保持放鬆。你有在自慰嗎？

Leonard: Um... yeah, sure.

嗯…是啊，有。

Matthew: We deal with numbers all day, you have to find a way to stay balanced. I jerk off at least twice a day. Number two key to success is this, (he pulls out his vial) it's called cocaine. It'll keep you sharp between the eyes and ears and your fingers dialing faster, revolutions, following me you [2]**motherfucker?**

我們整天得應付數字，你得想辦法保持均衡。我每天都最少發射兩次。第二個成功的關鍵就是這個，（他拿出他的小瓶子）它叫做古柯鹼。它會讓你保持耳聰目明，手指撥得更快，這叫做革命，幹你娘的你懂嗎？

Leonard: Yes, sir. Revolutions.

是的，先生。革命。

Matthew: Make them hand in their money willingly, have those [3]suckers dreaming about getting so rich while we are the ones that benefit the most!

讓他們自願把錢交出來，給那些輕易受騙上當的笨蛋做他媽的發財的美夢，而我們才是那個受惠最多的！

(The two men laughed, clinked their glasses together, and drank their wine.)

（兩個男人笑著，碰響了彼此的玻璃杯，然後喝著他們的葡萄酒。）

Glossary 髒話大解

❶ Jerk off，為動詞片語，指的是男人自慰的動作。

❷ motherfucker，名詞，直接翻譯是連媽都幹的人，所以說是混帳的意思。但是在這邊 Matthew 雖然是對 Leonard 說，但是其實並不帶有惡意，可以說是為了表示親切而這樣稱呼 Leonard。

❸ sucker，名詞，指容易受騙上當的人，輕易相信別人的笨蛋。

好姊妹（一）

Carla 剛剛被男人給甩了，打電話給她的同性戀朋友 Marven 想找他過來喝酒聊聊女人間的體己話。當 Marven 到的時候，Carla 早已喝得爛醉拿了廚房的刀準備自殘。

Marven: What are you doing? What in the world do you think you are doing?

你在做什麼？你究竟以為你在做什麼？

Carla: Do you think he'll ever come back to me?

你覺得他會因此回來我的身邊嗎？

Marven: Keep dreaming my dear, "Romeo! Romeo! Wherefore art thou Romeo!" Translation? Desperate! Desperate! I am really desperate!

繼續做你的美夢吧！親愛的，「羅密歐！羅密歐！你在哪啊羅密歐！」翻譯？我好饑渴！我好饑渴！我真的很饑渴！

Carla: I really thought there was something special between us.

我真的以為我們之間會不一樣。

Marven: You were [1]**roofied** and didn't even realize it. Look at your life. Look at your choices. Have you even slept with this guy?

你被下了迷藥還搞不清楚狀況。看看你的人生，看看你做過的選擇。你有跟這男的睡過嗎？

Carla: I did. (Said with a smile on her face)

我有。（臉上帶笑著說。）

Marven: (gave her a big hard solid spank on her butt and said) You big [2]**slut**! Good for you! Now come on you stupid [3]**biatch**, get yourself into the bathroom and wash up, we're going out for some mid-night snacks.

（Marven 結實的一掌打在她屁股上然後說道）你這大蕩婦！好樣的你！好啦現在你這白癡婊子，給我去浴室梳洗一下，我們要出去吃點消夜。

Glossary 髒話大解

❶ roofied 為過去式動詞，roofie 是 Rohypnol 一種迷藥的簡稱，近來常常被人用來做約會強姦藥，roofie 本身是名詞，但是在這裡 Marven 把它做為動詞來用，意思是 Carla 被下迷藥。

❷ slut，名詞，蕩婦的意思，指隨便跟人睡的女人。在這裡 Marven 其實是不帶惡意的說這個字，因為跟 Carla 感情好所以才用，跟不熟的朋友千萬別開這種玩笑。雖然不會用在男人身上，但是凡事都有例外，如果是同性戀男人互罵可能也會用這個很不 man 的詞。

❸ biatch，名詞，婊子的意思。這個字其實就是 bitch，有時候聽到有人開玩笑地用 bitch 的諧音 biatch 來稱呼好朋友，也不是真的罵對方，純粹是好玩這樣叫。

好姊妹（二）

 情境對話  Track 36

吃完消夜回到 Marven 的住處，Carla 又開了瓶酒喝得爛醉。

Carla: I love him!

我愛他！

Marven: You love him? You met him Sunday. It's barely Thursday morning, slow down, crazy, slow down.

你愛他？你星期天認識他的，今天還不到星期四早上欸，慢點，你這個瘋子，慢點。

Carla: Love makes you crazy.

愛會使你瘋狂。

Marven: Face it, Carla, Mr. Romeo slept with your roommate last night.

面對現實吧，Carla，羅密歐先生昨晚睡了你的室友。

Carla: That was after he broke up with me.

那是我們分手以後的事情。

Marven: Save it, [1]**Patty Hearst**! I'm not buying any [2]**Stockholm Syndrome** today, thank you.

省省吧，Patty Hearst！我今天可不買任何人質情節的帳，謝謝你。

Carla: I'm a grown woman, and I can decide what I want to do with my life.

我是個成熟的女人，我認為我可以決定自己的人生要如何過。

Marven: I think you are fourteen and you are an [3]**idiot.**

我認為你十四歲而且是個白癡。

Glossary 髒話大解

❶ Patty Hearst，為人名，全名是 Patricia Hearst Shaw，於 1974 年在加州柏克萊被美國極左派激進組織共生解放軍綁架，後來她發表聲明宣佈加入共生解放軍，並參予解放軍的非法活動。後來的心理學和社會心理學家都將她的綁架事件視為斯德哥爾摩症候群 (Stockholm Syndrome) 的典型案例。在這裡 Marven 稱呼 Carla 為 Patty Hearst 是諷刺她有人質情節，那男的背叛她，她還幫他說話。

❷ Stockholm Syndrome，為醫學名詞，人質情節的意思，就像上面敘述的 Patty Hearst 案例，是典型的被賣了還幫人家數鈔票的狀況。

❸ idiot，名詞，在這裡是罵 Carla 是白癡的意思。

Chapter 37

綠帽子

Joe 打電話約 *Tom* 到酒吧碰面，大概半個鐘頭以後，*Tom* 在 *Citrus* 酒吧找到 *Joe* 正在喝酒。

Joe: Hi, Tom. How was your day?

嗨 Tom，你今天過得如何？

Tom: It was [1]**shitty**!

爛透了！

Joe: Really? Why?

真的？為什麼？

Tom: I caught my girlfriend sleeping with another man!

我抓到我女朋友跟別的男人睡！

Joe: Oh man! What happened?

喔老兄！發生什麼事？

Tom: I came home from work and walked in to see that [2]**bitch** sucking some guy's [3]**dick** in my living room!

我下班回家進門就看到那賤人在我的客廳吸那男的屌！

Joe: What'd you do?

你做了什麼？

Tom: I beat the [4]**crap** out of the guy and told that slut we were finished!

我揍了那男的一頓，然後告訴那蕩婦我們玩完了！

Joe: Wow, I'm so sorry about that. Let me buy you another drink.

哇，我真的感到很抱歉。
讓我請你再喝一杯吧！

Glossary 髒話大解

❶ shitty，形容詞，shit 大家都知道是屎的意思，當加上-y 結尾就從名詞變成形容詞，在此是 Joe 形容他今天過得糟糕透頂而用的詞。任何的人事物，只要想表示狀況很糟，很令人生氣，都可以用這個詞來形容。

❷ bitch，名詞，賤人的意思。其實這個字本身是指母狗、母狼、母狐狸或是母獺之類的雌性動物，但是常被用來謾罵做壞事的女人。

❸ dick，名詞，指男人的那話兒，可以用來罵討厭的人。但是要注意，有時候聽到有人稱呼某人 Dick，不見得是在罵他，Dick 也是常見人名之一，舊英文裡 Dick 是 Richard 的簡稱，現在還是有人這樣用，或是直接取名 Dick。因為某個奇妙的原因，不知道什麼時候開始，變成了指男人陰莖的俗語，只能為名字為 Dick 的人掬一把同情淚。

❹ crap，名詞，廢棄物、大便的意思。在這裡 I beat the crap out of the guy 是指 Joe 打到對方屁滾尿流的意思。

Chapter 38

挑釁（一）

 情境對話  *Track 38*

Chris 跟 Don 正在一起玩一個籃球電動遊戲。

Chris: Shit! Why is LeBron on his [1]**ass** again?

該死的！為什麼 LeBron 又摔屁股了？

Don: Because LeBron is a little [2]**bitch**.

因為 Lebron 是個小婊子。

Chris: This is such [3]**bullshit**!

這簡直狗屁不通！

Don: Why'd you pick The Cavs? They [4]**suck** in this game. You should play with another team.

你幹嘛挑騎士隊？他們在這遊戲裡遜透了。你該挑其它隊來玩。

Chris: I took The Cavs to the playoffs.

我帶騎士隊進決賽過。

Don: Yeah, against the computer on easy... Ohhhh!

是啊，對電腦玩，還是調到最簡單的設定…喔喔喔！

(Don scores a point in the game. Chris and Don bumped their elbows against each other.)

（Don 在遊戲裡得分了。Chris 跟 Don 兩人的手肘互撞。）

Don: Hey you better watch that!

你給我注意點。

Glossary 髒話大解

❶ ass，名詞，屁股的意思，是不文雅的用詞。這裡說 LeBron is on his ass 是指他跌倒了，坐在地上。

❷ bitch，名詞，婊子的意思。通常是罵女人，但是在這裡 Don 故意用來罵 LeBron，是為了表示他不把 Lebron 當男人看，故意這樣消遣 Lebron。

❸ bullshit，名詞，是狗屁不通的意思，在這裡 Chris 玩遊戲輸了，不服氣，所以用這個詞表示氣憤。

❹ suck，形容詞，很爛、很遜的意思。這個詞做為動詞的時候是吸吮的意思，但是作為形容詞又不一樣，所以看狀況而定，千萬別誤會喔！

Chapter 39

挑釁（二）

 情境對話  Track 39

Chris 跟 Don 兩人繼續撕殺著……

Chris: Do not hit my elbow! You [1]**motherfucker**! This is bullshit!

你別撞我的手肘！你這幹娘的混帳！這簡直就是狗屁！

Don: Oh really? Let's watch that on the instant replay.

喔是嗎？我們來看即時重播。

Chris: Don't play that [2]**shit**, I don't want to see it.

別放那該屎的影片，我不想看。

Don: You said it was bullshit. This is why they put instant replay in the game, to see if it was bullshit.

你說那是狗屁啊。這就是他們把即時重播放在這遊戲裡的原因，看看到底是不是狗屁。

Chris: You're unbelievable.

你簡直讓人不敢相信。

Don: Yea, I wish they still had fighting in this game, so I could [3]**bitch slap** LeBron.

是啊，我還真希望這遊戲裡還有打鬥功能，這樣我就能賞 LeBron 一巴掌。

Chris: Why'd they get rid of the fighting?

他們為什麼拿掉打架功

That's the best part about the older version.

能？那是上一個版本最讚的地方。

Don: I don't know. Think some kids were hitting each other.

我不知道。我想某些小孩可能真的打起來了。

(The doorbell rings.)

（門鈴響了。）

Chris: That's the pizza. Pause the game.

比薩到了，暫停遊戲。

Glossary 髒話大解

❶ motherfucker，名詞，直接翻譯是連媽都幹的人，所以說是混帳的意思。這裡是因為 Don 覺得 Chris 故意撞他的手肘，所以罵他的話。

❷ shit，名詞，在這裡是因為 Chris 不爽看那段影片，所以稱那段即時回播的影片為 shit。

❸ bitch slap 裡面的 bitch 是形容詞，用來形容 slap 這個動詞，也就是賞人巴掌的這個動作。因為 Don 認為 LeBron 很不夠男人，所以就算打他也只要用巴掌就夠了，不需要用拳頭。當你說要 bitch slap 某人的時候，純粹是為了羞辱對方，因為覺得對方不夠格接受你的拳頭。

Chapter 40　什麼怪味道？！（一）

 情境對話  Track 40

Miranda 跟三個女朋友在墨西哥度假。淑女們正在做準備要一起出去吃一份美好的晚餐，Miranda 跟 Tracy 用同一個房間，她剛剛走出了浴室，而Tracy 正準備要接著進去使用。

Tracy: [1]**Oh my goodness**, what's that smell?

喔我的老天，那什麼味道？

Miranda: Oh yah, sorry, that's my shampoo. I can't use regular delicious smelling shampoos like every other girl on the planet, because I have a scalp condition.

喔對了，抱歉，那是我的洗髮精。我沒辦法跟世界上其他女生一樣用一般好聞的洗髮精，因為我頭皮有問題。

Tracy: [2]**Geez**, Miranda, you should have warned me. I would have taken a shower first. It smells horrible in here!

天啊，Miranda，你應該先警告我的，早知道我就先洗澡了。這裡面聞起來真的很恐怖！

Miranda: I apologize for that. From now on, you can use the bathroom first.

我為此跟你道歉。從現在開始你可以優先使用浴室。

Tracy: What did you say was the reason for all this?

你說會這樣的原因是什麼？

Miranda: I have to use this dermatology shampoo because my scalp is disgusting, it's super embarrassing and I hate talking about it, but since this happened, why not. (She walks into the shower again, takes out her shampoo bottle and shows it to Tracy.) So I have to use this therapeutic shampoo for scalp build-up control. It's so nasty, smells like tar, there're actually two versions of it, there's another kind that's black and gooey, and I [3]**swear** it is tar and smells disgusting, even worse than this one right here.

我必須要用一種皮膚科配方的洗髮精，因為我的頭皮很噁心，這真的很丟臉，我很不喜歡聊這個，但是既然這件事已經發生了，也沒差了。（她再次走進淋浴間拿出她的洗髮精瓶子，然後給 Tracy 看。）所以我得用這個醫療用洗髮精來控制頭皮組織的累積，那聞起來真的很噁心，像焦油一樣，其實它有兩種版本，另一種看起來又黑又稠，我發誓它真的是焦油，比這邊這瓶更糟。

Glossary 髒話大解

❶ Oh my goodness，感嘆詞，「喔！我的天啊！」的意思，跟 "oh my god" 之類的的詞用法一樣，用在對某件事感到驚訝的時，通常是用來做接下來要表示的驚嚇感覺的開頭。在充滿負面的感受時用 Oh my god 其實是對神大不敬的，所以有時候會聽到有人說 oh my goodness 來代替。

❷ Geez 也是感嘆詞，老天的意思，其實就是 Jesus，只是跟上面一樣，為了不要對神不敬，而說成 Geez，這樣聽起來不是 Jesus，就不會有對神不敬的感覺，但其實是一樣糟糕的。

❸ swear，動詞，發誓的意思。另一個解釋是詛咒、咒罵，可為動詞或名詞，在此是 Miranda 對 Tracy 說 "I swear" 我發誓的意思。

 情境對話  Track 41

Miranda 跟 Tracy 解釋過浴室裡為什麼會有一股異味以後，Tracy 為此感到很抱歉。

Tracy: Oh man! I'm so sorry to hear that sweetie!

天啊！甜心，我真的很抱歉聽到這些。

Miranda: Yah, me too, if I don't use this shampoo, my scalp gets super painful and itchy, and like scabby, [1]**pussy**, anyway it's disgusting, and it's truly the most embarrassing thing in the world. I swear, I've cried about it.

是啊，我也是，如果我不用這洗髮精的話，我的頭皮就會非常的痛，還很癢，而且還會結痂流膿，總之就是很噁心，這真的是全世界最讓人感到丟臉的事。我發誓，我還為此而哭過。

Tracy: Aww... I'm sorry, now I feel like a [2]**jerk** complaining. You know, it actually doesn't smell that bad after a while. I really didn't mean to be [3]**mean** about it earlier.

喔…我真的很抱歉，現在我覺得我剛剛抱怨簡直是個混蛋。你知道嗎，其實過了這麼一會聞起來也沒那麼糟了。我剛剛真的不是故意要這麼兇的。

Miranda: That's ok, no offense taken. Let's get going and get ready for the

沒事，我沒有感到被冒犯。我們趕快來為今晚的

party tonight!

Tracy: Yeah~!

派對來準備吧！

耶～！

Glossary 髒話大解

❶ pussy，形容詞，形容流膿的樣子，充滿膿的情形。pus 是名詞，膿的意思，字尾加上-y 成為形容詞。另外一個字，pussy 雖然拼法一樣，但是發音跟意思完全不同，意思為貓，或是比較不文雅的用法是指女人的性器官。pussy 做為流膿狀的意思的時候，發音是 ['pʌsi]，但是如果是指貓或是女人的性器官的時候發音是 [poo s-ee]。説的時候千萬別説錯了喔！

❷ jerk，名詞，在此為混蛋的意思。通常是指説話不經大腦、幼稚、愚蠢的人。Tracy 覺得自己剛剛小題大作，因為一些異味而抱怨，可能傷了 Miranda 的心而罵自己是 jerk。

❸ mean，形容詞，壞、刻薄的意思。注意到同一句話裡，Tracy 説的第一個 mean 是動詞，"I didn't mean" 是「我不是故意要這麼做」的意思；而第二個 mean 是形容詞，"to be mean"，「表現這麼兇，説這麼苛薄的話」的意思。又是同一個字，詞性用法截然不同。

 情境對話  *Track 42*

在 Brian 洗完他的早晨澡準備好要出門之後，他走到客廳找到 Alice 正坐在沙發上，在 Netflix 上面找節目看。

Brian: Hey baby, I'm going to the mall to pick up some stuffs, you need something?

嘿寶貝，我要去購物中心買些東西，你有需要什麼嗎？

Alice: Nah... I'm still feeling kind of icky, can you go to Trader Joe's and pick up some nice organic chicken and make me some chicken soup?

不要…我還是覺得不是很舒服，你可以去 Trader Joe's 幫我買些有機的雞肉回來煮些雞湯給我喝嗎？

Brian: Sure, but you know? I really don't like that place, I think it's overrated. It's just a [1]**hoity-toity** place for [2]**hipsters** to get groceries. I've always felt that the clerks are so [3]**snobby** and serve people with an attitude.

當然可以，但是你知道嗎？我真的不喜歡那個地方，我覺得那地方的評價過高。不過就是個給一些自以為很潮的人買菜的地方嘛。我老是覺得那些工作人員都很自以為是，服務客人的時候態度有問題。

Alice: Oh shut up, just go get it. Bye!

喔閉嘴，給我去買就對了。掰！

Brian: Okay, bye baby. (Kisses Alice on the forehead and leaves for shopping.)

好的，掰寶貝。（親了 Alice 的額頭後出門買東西去。）

Glossary 髒話大解

❶ hoity-toity，形容詞，指某事或人很假掰、自以為是的意思。

❷ hipster，名詞，就是現在人說的潮人的意思。這個字可褒可貶，看狀況，通常是指那些活在自己世界裡的人，很有自主意識，原創性很高，對主流的事物沒興趣，喜歡談論哲學、政治、藝術之類的話題。所以看個人觀點如何，有些人討厭 hipster，有些人喜歡 hipster。從 Brian 在這裡說話的內容，可以看的出來他算是不怎麼喜歡 hipster，所以在說的時候，貶的意義居多。

❸ snobby，形容詞，也是很自以為是的意思。那些眼高於頂，或是勢利的人都可以用 snobby 來形容。

 情境對話  Track 43

Brian 在購物中心買到他需要的東西之後，也順便到糖果店買一盒 Alice 愛吃的黑松露巧克力，然後在回家前到 Trader Joe's 買了 Alice 的有機雞肉。

(Brian walks into the living room and finds Alice's sister Katie visiting.)

（Brian 走進客廳裡發現 Alice 的妹妹 Katie 來拜訪。）

Brian: Hey Katie.

嘿，Katie。

Katie: [1]**Sup** man! What do you have there? (Katie gets up to help Brian bring the groceries into the kitchen and finds the box of chocholate in the bag.) Woo~ chocholate! (She takes it out and helps herself with the chocholate right away.)

沒什麼，你買了些什麼？（Katie 站起來去幫 Brian 把菜拿進廚房裡，在袋子裡看到那盒巧克力。）喔～巧克力！（她拿出那盒巧克力後馬上就開始自顧自的吃起來。）

Brian: That's for Alice! Grr... you're such a [2]**rascal**!

那是給 Alice 的！吼…你這個無賴！

Alice: Oh that's ok honey, I don't really want them right now. I would really love some hot soup for the moment.

喔沒關係啦親愛的，我現在不是很想吃那些，我目前真的很想喝些熱湯。

Katie: Hehe... see I was helping.

嘿嘿…看吧，我這是在幫忙。

Brian: (rolled his eyes and said) Alright, just [3]**fuck off**.

（翻了白眼後説）好啦，給我滾。

Glossary 髒話大解

❶ sup 其實是問句 what's up 的縮短版，懶得把 what's up 説完的人用的字，跟比較熟的人問候近來如何的時候就可以用 "what's up?" 但是在正式場合或是跟第一次見面的人這麼説其實是很沒禮貌的。

❷ rascal，在此為名詞，無賴、不擇手段的人的意思。表示 Brian 認為 Katie 隨便拿他買給 Alice 的巧克力是無賴才有的行為。

❸ fuck off 為動詞片語，叫人滾蛋的意思。當有人讓你覺得很煩的時候，這麼説人家就會知道惹到你了。這裡是 Brian 買了巧克力回來要給老婆獻殷勤，結果被 Katie 這個程咬金先搶去吃了，所以叫她滾。

Chapter 44 趕飛機（一）

 情境對話  *Track 44*

Mia 正在做緊張的行前最後一刻打包，為了這個週末要去加拿大參加她最要好朋友的單身趴。她有點接近崩潰狀態，因為她只剩下不到一個鐘頭可以打包，可是她還找不到她的機票跟護照。

Mia: Grrahh! This is ridiculous! I remember putting them on the breakfast bar two days ago!

喔啊啊！這簡直就是太荒謬了！我記得我兩天前把它們放在早餐台上的！

James: Just go finish packing your suitcase. I'll look for them, and go put on some pants.

你就趕快去打包完你的行李吧，我來幫你找，還有去穿件褲子。

Mia: I just pooped! And my [1]**ass** is hurting! [2]**Damn** that Thai food!

我剛剛大完便！而且我肛門到現在還在痛！該死的泰國菜！

James: Stop yelling at me... Ahha! Found them! They got pushed down to the side and caught between the cabinet and the breakfast bar.

別再對我鬼吼鬼叫…啊哈！找到了！他們被推到掉在櫃子跟早餐吧檯中間。

Mia: OMG! Baby you are the best! You're a life saver! (Runs up to James and gives him a big kiss and hug.)

天啊！寶貝你最棒了！你救了我的命！（衝向 James 給了他一個大大的吻跟擁抱。）

James: Wow... this is a [3]**bipolar** household. (Both laughing out loud and hugging each other.)

哇…這個家裡真的是精神失調。（兩個一起大笑出聲然後擁抱對方。）

Glossary 髒話大解

❶ ass，名詞，在這裡是 asshole 的簡稱，就是肛門的意思。

❷ damn，動詞，詛咒某樣東西去死的意思。Mia 可能因為吃完泰國菜拉肚子，所以就怪罪在泰國菜上，説 "Damn that Thai food"，指那泰國菜很該死的意思。

❸ bipolar，名詞，其實是心理學上用的詞，指情緒遊走不定，時高時低，非常兩極化，有些人稱做躁鬱症。在這裡，James 説 "this is a bipolar household" 是因為 Mia 剛剛還很生氣激動，接近崩潰狀態，馬上卻就大轉變對他又親又抱，情緒很極端，所以這麼説來消遣她。

趕飛機（二）

終於準備好要出門了，Mia 還不忘做最後重要的交代。

Mia: Okay gotta go! Oh baby, don't forget to record my shows on Direct TV or I will kill you~! (saying with a cute voice)

好了該走了！喔寶貝，別忘了幫我錄 Direct TV 上我愛看的節目，不然我殺了你喔～！（用可愛的聲音說著。）

Jame: (grabbed his car key and replied) See what I mean? Yes, I will, don't worry. But I've been wondering, how can you still be watching that [1]**crap**? It's just episodes of recaps after recaps over and over and over, never-ending, it's like a vortex of mind [2]**mush** of [3]**nonsense**, I mean what's the point?

（James 拿起他的車鑰匙回答道）看吧？是的，我會錄，別擔心。我老是在想，你怎麼到現在都還能看那亂七八糟的東西？它就只是每集一直重複之前播過的東西，一遍又一遍又一遍，沒完沒了簡直就像是一團毫無連貫性意識的瞎扯漩渦，我是說到底有什麼意義？

Mia: How dare you say such a thing about my favorite TV show! You want to be judgemental? Sure, how about getting a hair cut for a change? I can't stand it

你敢這麼說我最愛的電視節目！你想來批評是嗎？來啊，你是不是該去剪你的頭髮了？我已經受不了

anymore. It's so short on the side and too long on the top! It drives me crazy!

(James helps her carry the luggage downstairs and put her in the car first, then went to the trunk to put the luggage in, and has made up his mind to keep quiet until she forgets why she's mad.)

了，兩邊那麼短，上面那麼長！簡直把我逼瘋了！

（James 幫她把行李搬到樓下，先把她弄上車，然後把行李放進行李箱裡，並決定保持緘默直到她忘記她在生什麼氣為止。）

Glossary 髒話大解

❶ crap，名詞，廢物、廢話、指沒有用的人事或物。在這裡是指 Mia 愛看的電視節目。

❷ mush，名詞，指一團黏呼呼的東西，沒有連貫性，讓人很反感。在這裡 James 用 mush 這個字來形容電視劇的劇情。

❸ nonsense，名詞，瞎扯、無理頭、毫無意義的人事物。也是用來指電視節目劇情，James 連續用兩個意義不佳的名詞來代表電視節目的劇情，來強調他真的覺得劇情很爛。

第五類接觸（一）

 情境對話  *Track 46*

一位美國國家安全局探員跟一位一般民眾，Rhonda，正做在五角大廈的一個房間裡。

NSA Agent: Tell me what happened after you were taken.

告訴我你被帶走以後發生了什麼事。

Rhonda: I woke up in a dirty metal dome, and 40 little grey aliens watched me pee in a steel bowl. Then they took the bowl and walked out.

我在一間髒兮兮的圓頂鐵皮房間裡醒來，有 40 個灰色小外星人看著我撒尿到一個鐵盆裡。然後他們把盆子拿了就走了出去。

NSA Agent: Interesting. Could you describe them to me?

很有意思。你可不可以描述他們的樣貌給我？

Rhonda: Well, they were grey with big [1]**fat** eyes and little mouths. I don't think I was dealing with the top brass.

嗯，他們灰灰的有肥大的眼睛和小嘴巴，我不認為我碰到的是什麼重要人物。

NSA Agent: And how did they instruct you to urinate, was it telepathically?

他們是怎麼指示你排尿的，是經過心電感應嗎？

Rhonda: No, I woke up and had to pee, so I started peeing and one of the aliens pointed to the bowl, and I got the hint,

喔不，我醒來後就很想尿尿，所以我就開始尿了，然後其中一個外星人指著

so I [2]**duck-walked** over to the bowl and peed in it.

一個盆子，我懂了那個暗示，就半蹲著走去盆子上方然後尿在裡面。

NSA Agent: And when you woke up, you were clothed?

那你醒來的時候有穿衣服嗎？

Rhonda: I had the shirt I came with, but my pants were gone, so my [3]**coot-coot** was out. I was full [4]**Porky-Piggin'** it in a drafty dome.

我穿著我原本的上衣，但是我的褲子不見了，所以我的私處就這樣晒在外面。我就像 Porky Pig 一樣在房間裡光著屁股。

Glossary 髒話大解

❶ fat，形容詞，在這裡不是指那些外星人很胖，而是用來形容他們的眼睛很大。

❷ duck-walked，duck 是形容詞，walked 則是動詞過去式，指 Rhonda 原本蹲著要尿尿，結果為了移到盆子那邊，就很醜地像鴨子走路一樣蹲著走過去。

❸ coot-coot，名詞，是陰道的意思。coot 一般的意思是指水鳥，但是在這裡是 cooter 的簡稱，cooter 是指女性的陰道，比較不入流不性感的說法，像是如果要調情就不會説 coot-coot 或是 cooter，而是 pussy 這個字。

❹ Porky-Piggin' (Porky-Pigging)，是動詞進行式。Porky Pig 是華納兄弟的卡通 Looney Tunes 裡面的卡通人物，那隻豬只穿上衣，沒穿褲子，就像 Rhonda 當時的狀況一樣，所以她很風趣地把自己比喻成 Porky Pig。

第五類接觸（二）

 情境對話  Track 47

Rhonda 繼續為國家安全局的探員解釋她被外星人綁架的經歷。

Rhonda: Then I was put on a stool while the 40 grey aliens took turns gently batting my [1]**knockers**.

然後我就被放在一個凳子上，給 40 個灰色外星人輪流拍打我的奶子。

NSA Agent: Perhaps they were collecting biological data. And how did the aliens return you back to earth?

或許他們在收集物理資料。那些外星人怎麼把你送回地球的？

Rhonda: I was dropped 7 feet down on to the roof of a McDonald's. They threw out my pants separately, which landed in a [2]**frigging** pine tree.

我被從 7 英呎高的地方丟下來掉在一間麥當勞的屋頂上。他們另外把我的褲子丟了出來，該死的掉在一棵松樹上。

NSA Agent: Well, we'd like to take you for a physical examination now.

那個，我們希望現在帶你去做身體檢查。

Rhonda: Is there going to be any knocker stuff?

還要再拍我的奶子嗎？

NSA Agent: Possibly, I'm sorry.

很有可能，我很抱歉。

Rhonda: Ah don't be. Just be gentle, 'cause they're pretty [3]**banged up.**

欸不用。輕一點就行了，因為她們快被拍爛了。

Glossary 髒話大解

❶ knockers，名詞，指女人的胸部，但是是比較粗俗的說法，所以翻成奶子。

❷ frigging，形容詞，該死的的意思，用法跟 freaking 或 fucking 一樣，就是要強調說的人的情緒。

❸ banged up 為動詞片語，就是指某樣東西被不適當地使用，而造成某種程度的破壞的意思。這裡是指 Rhonda 的奶子被一堆外星人輪流拍了好久，所以被拍爛了的意思。

網路霸凌（一）

  **Track 48**

Emma 跟 Audrey 在圖書館裡，Audrey 正在很認真的讀書，而 Emma 正在一旁滑手機。

Emma: Oh I can't believe these people!

喔我簡直不敢相信這些人！

Audrey: Keep it down. We're in a library.

小聲點，我們在圖書館裡。

Emma: These [1]**haters** on Instagram are really driving me crazy! I posted a picture of me and David kissing, and I was kind of standing sideways, so I kind of looked skinnier than usual. But then look at all these mean comments saying that I am too skinny, that I'm ugly, I have no butt, I have no boobs, eww... [2]**flat ass syndrome**, gross, laughing and tagging their friends. Not that this actually makes me feel ugly, but what's wrong with all these [3]**body shamers**?

這些在 Instagram 上的酸民真的是快要讓我瘋掉了！我貼了一張我跟 David 在接吻的照片，我當時站得偏側面，所以看起來比平常瘦一些。但是看看這些惡毒的留言，説我太瘦、我很醜、我沒屁股、我沒胸，噁…扁屁症候群，噁心，大笑然後標籤他們的朋友。也不是説這就真的讓我覺得自己很醜，但是這些做人身攻擊的人到底有什麼問題？

Audrey: You post something on the Internet, there's always going to be haters out there. What do you expect?

你上網貼東西，總是會有那些酸民的。不然你以為哩？

Emma: That's not what I'm trying to say, I just don't get what exactly these people are trying to get out of it by doing such things.

那不是我想表達的，我只是不懂這些人這麼做到底想得到什麼。

Glossary 髒話大解

❶ hater，名詞，在這裡是指網路上的酸民。大家應該都有過類似的經驗，不管你怎麼做，總是有人愛留一些不好聽的話，那些人就叫做 hater，hate 是恨的意思，hater 就是那些愛表達負面情緒的人。

❷ flat ass syndrome，名詞，這裡翻譯為扁屁症候群，也不是真的有這種病，只是網路上的酸民們為了讓 Emma 不好受而這麼說她。

❸ body shame，名詞，是現在網路發達以後更加猖獗的一個負面現象，就是對某人做人身攻擊，要不嫌人家瘦，要不嫌人家胖，要不就是醜，總之就是言詞上羞辱別人的身體的現象。body shamer，指做出這種事的人。

網路霸凌（二）

 情境對話  *Track 49*

Emma 跟 Audrey 繼續討論著網路上人身攻擊的現象問題。

Emma: Body shaming should not be tolerated, everybody should love the way they are, and we should be lifting each other up and complimenting each other, not trying to bring each other down!

人身攻擊不應該被容忍，每個人都應該愛自己原本的樣貌，我們應該要彼此誇獎鼓勵對方，而不是想辦法讓彼此難受！

Audrey: I get what you're saying, but you know what? Haters are always going to be hating. Even if you are actually curvy and have bigger [1]**boobs** and [2]**bootie**, they'll still be able to think of something to say.

我懂你在說什麼，但是你知道嗎？酸民永遠都會繼續酸。就算你其實是很有曲線，擁有比較大的胸跟臀，他們還是會有辦法想其他的話來酸你。

Emma: That's what's [3]**bugging** me! Like you said, if I'm actually bigger and people are saying stuffs like eww... look at how fat she is, how gross her big [4]**butt** and stomach looks, then people would be furious about how somebody is making fun of a girl that's bigger, they would be bashing on the criticizers. But for some reason, I'm skinny, it's ok for them to do

這就是讓我受不了的地方！就像你說的，如果我現在比較胖，而有人說像是噁…看她有多胖，看她的大屁股跟肚子看起來有多噁心，那肯定一堆人會因此而憤怒，說怎麼有人這麼取笑一個胖女孩，他們會對那個批評的人進行

that? That's a double standard, and I really don't get the logic behind it.

圍攻。但是因為某種原因，因為我很瘦，所以被這麼做沒關係？這是雙重標準，我真的不懂這之中的邏輯。

Glossary 髒話大解

❶ boobs，名詞，指女人的胸部。這個字原本的意思，是指笨蛋，有聽過 booby trap 嗎？就是設來讓人受傷或是嚇一跳的陷阱，所以 booby 是指掉入陷阱的笨蛋。大約是 17 世紀末，從 bubby 延伸出 booby 是胸部的意思，bubby 據說是指嬰兒哭跟吸奶的聲音，所以後來就被做為胸部，傳著傳著就變成 booby 了。

❷ bootie，名詞，指屁股。這字本義原本也跟人的身體部位沒關係，是指被偷的貴重物品。據說是 20 世紀初，從英國的字 botty，也就是小孩子對話說的屁股，其實是童言童語，後來傳著傳著就變成 booty 了。

❸ bugging 為動詞進行式，惱人的意思。bug 本身是蟲的意思，做為動詞可以當作竊聽或是讓人很煩的意思。這裡是指網路上的酸民行為讓 Emma 很反感。

❹ butt，名詞，也是屁股的意思。buttock 的簡稱，是個很古老的字，從 13 世紀開始就被人使用，指的就是屁股那個位置那兩團肉，因為屁股有兩瓣，所以應該要說 buttocks。

難搞的病人

 情境對話  *Track 50*

Megan 在學校壘球隊練習的時候被壘球打到臉，把鼻子打斷了，現在正在醫院裡等著接受手術。她正想上廁所，護士便幫著她把點滴提進去。

Megan: Thanks, do you mind leaving the room after you get out of the bathroom? I'm a little [1]**pee shy**, and I don't really feel comfortable peeing here knowing someone else is in the room. (Then she shouted to her friend Carla who's sitting on a chair in the room) You too, girl! Need some privacy in here.

謝了，你介意離開廁所以後也走出病房，還有把病房門關上嗎？我小便的時候有點害羞，如果我知道有別人在房間裡我沒辦法自在的小便。（然後她對坐在病房裡椅子上的朋友 Carla 叫道）你也一樣，女孩！我這裡需要些隱私。

Nurse: I'll let you take care of your business in here alone.

我會讓你自己在這裡處理你的事。

Carla: You're such a [2]**weirdo**. (Talking as she steps outside.)

你真的是個怪胎。（邊說邊往外走。）

Megan: (After using the toilet, Megan realized that the sink doesn't work, so she got out and called the nurse in.) Hey! Ahh... the sink doesn't work, I'm not

（用過廁所以後，Megan 發覺洗手台不能用，所以她到外面叫護士進來。）嘿！啊…這個洗手台不能

exactly a [3]**neat freak** or [4]**germophobe**, but I need to wash my hands now since I've just used the toilet.

用，我並不是什麼多愛乾淨的清潔狂或是細菌恐懼症患者，但是我剛用過廁所需要洗手。

Nurse: Oh, I'll call someone over to fix it.

喔，我打電話叫人來修。

Glossary 髒話大解

❶ pee shy 裡的 pee 為動詞，尿尿的意思，shy 為形容詞，害羞的意思。合在一起就是指某人在上廁所的時候如果同個空間裡有其他人在就會尿不出來的狀況。

❷ weirdo，名詞，怪胎的意思。專門做些怪事的人，這裡是指 Megan 因為上個廁所，廁所門關起來還不夠，就要連病房都清空，有點誇張，所以 Carla 這樣說她。

❸ neat freak 裡的 neat 是形容詞整潔的意思，而 freak 為名詞，怪物的意思。合在一起就是指有嚴重潔癖的人。

❹ germophobe，名詞，細菌恐懼患者。其實是一個組合起來的字，germ 是細菌的意思，phobia 是對某件事有恐懼的意思，組合起來就是 germophobe。

 情境對話  Track 51

一個有趣的聖經故事討論正在一間咖啡廳裡展開。

Olivia: You know, I've always wondered, if Adam and Eve only had sons, how did they reproduce?

你知道嗎，我老是在想如果亞當跟夏娃只有生兒子，那些兒子又是怎麼繁衍後代的呢？

Connor: Well, biblically it says that the sons went out, left their father and mother, and there's others in lands that they went... (Olivia cuts Connor off before he can finish what he was going to say.)

聖經上說，他們的兒子出去，離開了他們的父親跟母親，然後去到其他土地上找到其他的人…（Olivia 在 Connor 能說完他接下來要說的話之前打斷了他。）

Olivia: That's [1]ludicrous, weren't Adam and Eve supposed to be the first people?

那也太搞笑了，因為亞當跟夏娃不是應該是人類的始祖嗎？

Connor: I get that, but the bible said they went off to other places and became one with another woman.

我知道，但是聖經上說他們去到其他地方並跟其他女人合而為一。

Olivia: That's just a bunch of [2]bollocks if

要我說那根本就是無稽之

you ask me. It would have to be their sisters or their mom,... or an animal?

談。那肯定會是他們的姊妹或是母親…或者是一隻動物？

Connor: Well there're a lot of those going on back in the day.

嗯，過去那種事滿常發生的。

Olivia: [3]Animals sex?

跟動物亂交？

Connor: No! Honey, you don't get it, it's the bible. It does not have to make sense.

不是！蜜糖，你不懂，它是聖經，它不需要邏輯。

Glossary 髒話大解

❶ ludicrous，形容詞，因為某件事很荒謬，令人感到很滑稽、搞笑的意思。雖然這字不髒，但是跟人說他說的話很荒謬、很好笑，本身就是滿沒禮貌的，更何況是說聖經的內容。

❷ bollocks，名詞，垃圾、廢話、無稽之談、一連串的謊言，這個字的意思其實用法很廣泛，除了剛剛說的那些，還有一個就是如果是複數形的時候，也可以做為男人的睪丸的意思。舊英文裡拼法是 ballocks。

❸ animal sex，名詞，指跟動物亂交這件事。

Chapter 52　上帝為我們建造了樂園？（二）

 情境對話  *Track 52*

上帝到底是不是真的替人類建造了樂園？討論持續進行中……

Olivia: If they were the perfect beings made from God's image, why would Eve even go touch those apples and be blamed for the fall of mankind for all eternity. Truth is she was so [1]**dumb** that she couldn't even tell it was a set-up because her brain was made out of rib.

如果他們真的是依照神的樣貌去創造的完美人類，夏娃怎麼會去碰那些蘋果，然後因此造就了人類的墮落，被永世唾棄。真相是她根本笨到分不清那是個陷阱，因為她的腦袋是肋骨做的。

Connor: No, God created a paradise for them, it was Satan who lured her into eating those apples.

不，上帝為他們創造了樂園，是撒旦引誘她去吃那些蘋果。

Olivia: It couldn't have been a paradise ok? Because it's full of mistakes, God planned this world in seven days, you can't plan a good themed brunch in seven days, not to mention paradise.

那不太算是樂園好嗎？因為那裡充滿了錯誤，上帝花了七天創造這個世界，你不可能花七天就計畫好一個主題不錯的早午餐，更不用說樂園了。

Connor: You're going to [2]**hell**.

你準備下地獄吧。

Olivia: I'm serious! I thought that was a total set up for Him to get away from making women suffer for child birth because he accidentally made the [3]**baby cannon** too small.

我是說真的！我認為那根本是上帝自己設下的陷阱，以避免要負擔因為祂不小心把女人的陰道做得太小，而在生小孩的時候要受苦的責任。

Connor: You are seriously going to hell and I'm not gonna go down that road with you.

你真的準備要下地獄了，而我可不想繼續跟著你胡謅下去，連我也拖下水。

Glossary 髒話大解

❶ dumb，形容詞，很笨、很蠢的意思。在這裡是指 Olivia 認為夏娃之所以會中計吃下蘋果是因為她腦袋是肋骨做的（因為夏娃是從亞當的肋骨創造出來的人）。

❷ hell，名詞，在這裡是地獄的意思。這個字做為形容詞或是感嘆詞可以用來表示很多負面的情緒。

❸ baby cannon，名詞，能想像嬰兒被像砲彈一樣發射出來嗎？基本上就是那個意境，所以這個詞指的是女性的陰道。

Chapter 53

瓦斯氣爆（一）

 情境對話  Track 53

Kaylee 趴躺在沙發上剛剛放了屁，而 Wyatt 就坐在他屁股附近的地上。

Wyatt: [1]**Holy schmutz**, baby, how about a little bit of warning? (jumps up and runs toward the other end of the room)

天啊，寶貝，可不可以給點事前警告？（跳起來跑到房間的另一頭）

Kaylee: (starts laughing) Whoops!

（大笑著說）哦喔！

Wyatt: How many times have you farted within the last hour? Like five? What [2]**the hell** did you eat this morning?

你過去一個小時以內已經放了幾次屁了？五次了吧？你搞什麼早上到底吃了些什麼？

Kaylee: I did not fart five times within the last hour!

我才沒有在一小時內放屁五次！

Wyatt: Oh I bet you did, and you just don't know you were doing it. You need to go get yourself checked. There's something wrong with your GI track. Do you remember the time when we were in L.A.? Oh my goodness, that was [3]**heinous**! Do you remember it? That I was so mad at you and I was crying in bed?

喔我賭你有，只是你不知道而已。你需要去做個檢查，你的腸胃系統有問題。記得上次我們去 LA 嗎？喔我的老天，那簡直是噁到不行！你記得嗎？我氣到在床上哭？

Glossary 髒話大解

❶ holy schmutz，感嘆詞，我的老天的意思。holy 是神聖的意思，schmutz 則是垃圾、髒東西的意思，合併起來也是一種受到驚嚇的時候，驚叫出來的詞，也是對神不敬的，因為應該只有神可被稱為 holy。

❷ the hell，感嘆詞，搞什麼鬼的意思。先前說過 hell 是地獄的意思，可以用來表達很多種負面的情緒，在這裡是 Wyatt 被屁薰到有點不爽所以說 What the hell did you eat this morning?

❸ heinous，形容詞，在此表示 Kaylee 放的屁很噁心的意思。其實這個字的本意是邪惡的意思，但是近來被年輕人大量使用在他們認為醜陋到光是存在就是罪惡的東西上面，像是人、衣服之類的。

瓦斯氣爆（二）

 情境對話  Track 54

Kaylee 想到自己之前做的「好事」，不但不懺悔還笑得更開心。

Kaylee: Hahaha! Yes! You were gagging, you [1]**poor thing**.

哈哈哈！對！你還一直乾嘔個不停，你這可憐的東西。

Wyatt: I was gagging and tears were going down my cheek! I don't know what you ate! It was like I could taste it!

我可是一邊乾嘔還一邊流眼淚！我不知道你吃了什麼！那簡直就像我可以嘗到那屁！

Kaylee: Hahaha! [2]**Farticles** in the air!

哈哈哈！空氣裡的屁微粒！

Wyatt: Poop farticles! It was like rotten egg and [3]**after-birth**, like got together and procreated.

是糞便屁微粒！那就像腐爛的蛋還有胎衣，好像它們合在一起然後交配產生的。

Kaylee: Eewwwa! Stop it!

噁！別再説了！

Wyatt: That's why we always sleep back facing each other.

這就是為什麼我們總是背對背睡的原因。

Kaylee: Hey, you've been snoring every night for the past month, and I have to wake up multiple times a night and smack you in the face.

喂，你過去一個月每個晚上都打呼，我每晚都要醒來幾次打你的臉。

Wyatt: I know, and I always feel so bad afterward.

我知道，而我每次醒來之後都會感到很抱歉。

Glossary 髒話大解

❶ poor thing 裡面 poor 是形容詞，可憐的意思，thing 是名詞，東西，所以合起來就是可憐的東西的意思，不是窮東西的意思喔！

❷ farticles，名詞，屁微粒的意思，其實是兩個字合在一起，fart + particles = farticles，fart 是屁的意思，particles 是微粒，小粒子的意思。

❸ after-birth，名詞，胎衣的意思，指的是女人生完小孩以後，接下來生出來的東西，像是胎盤臍帶之類的，總之就是噁心的東西。

Chapter 55
麥莉搖臀（一）

 情境對話  Track 55

Aubrey 跟幾個朋友正在餐廳吃晚餐，聊的是今年的熱門話題—Miley Cyrus 在 VMAs 上的表現。

Aubrey: What did you think of Miley's performance on the VMAs?

Jill: I think that was really, really disturbing. That young lady, who is what 20? Is obviously deeply troubled, deeply disturbed, clearly has [1]**low self-esteem**, probably an [2]**eating disorder** and I don't think anybody should have put her on stage. That was disgusting and embarrassing. I have two older sons. They don't think that's attractive. Nobody does actually.

Gary: If Miley Cyrus was hoping to shock the [3]**butt floss** out of people, she sure has done it. Did you guys see Will Smith and his family's reaction? I thought that

你們認為 Miley 在 VMAs 上的表現如何？

我認為那真的讓人感到很不舒服。那年輕的小姑娘，差不多 20 歲吧？很顯然地有很嚴重的問題，嚴重心理失常，很顯然地不懂得尊重自己，可能有飲食失調症，而且我認為任何人都不應該讓她上台演出。那真是噁心又丟臉。我有兩個年紀長一點的兒子，他們不認為那是有魅力的，說真的沒人那麼認為。

如果 Miley Cyrus 希望把大家嚇到掉內褲的話，她很顯然是做到了。你們有看到 Will Smith 跟他

was gold, hahaha... definitely my favorite part of the night.

家人的反應嗎？我認為那真是太經典了，哈哈哈…絕對是我整個晚上最喜歡的片段。

Glossary 髒話大解

❶ low self-esteem，low 是低的意思，self-esteem 是自尊的意思，是說 Jill 認為 Miiley Cyrus 不懂得尊重自己，其實是滿惡毒的話。

❷ eating disorder 裡的 eating 是吃東西的意思，disorder 是毛病的意思，吃東西出毛病，就是飲食失調症的意思，這裡是在罵 Miley 太瘦，八成有厭食症之類的。

❸ butt floss，名詞，指那種細到會夾在屁股中間的丁字褲，因為這種內褲能像牙線一樣有效的從隙縫周圍挖出東西，所以叫做 butt floss，滿噁心的用詞。

 情境對話 *Track 56*

Jill 還是對 *Miley* 在 VMAs 的表現抱持負面的看法。

Gary: People were totally caught off guard by her ¹**twerkathon**, hahaha...

大家都被她的搖臀馬拉松嚇到了，哈哈哈⋯

Jill: That was not funny at all, Gary. That was really, really bad for anybody who's younger and impressionable and she's really ²**messed up**. MTV should be ashamed of themselves for putting it on the air. They knew the people watching these shows are ³**tweeners** and they are promoting the sexualization of pre-teen girls!

那一點也不好笑，Gary。那真的對任何年輕一些的，還有容易受影響的人非常地不好，而她真的很胡來。MTV 應該要讓這個表演在電視上演出而感到羞愧。他們知道看這些節目的人都是半大不小的人，而他們這是在推倡青春期女孩的性物化！

Aubrey: Alright guys, I'm going to break it down real quick. Everyone is hating on Miley Cyrus right now, and everyone is talking about how much they hate Miley Cyrus right now. Guess what? You're talking about it, she wins! And guess what else? All the people that are hating Miley Cyrus right now, you know that

好了各位，我想很快地分析一下。現在大家都在罵 Miley Cyrus，大家都在說他們有多討厭 Miley Cyrus。但是你猜怎麼著？你們正在討論這個話題，所以她贏了！在猜猜看還有什麼？那些現在在

when you're alone in your car, and that song comes on the radio, you're like, "yeah we can't stop~", you are totally singing along, and you all love it.

酸 Miley Cyrus 的人，你們其實很清楚當你們一個人在車子裡的時候，而收音機開始播放那首歌，你們就開始 "yeah we can't stop~"，跟著唱，而且你們愛死那首歌了。

Glossary 髒話大解

❶ twerkathon，名詞是 twerk 跟 marathone 合在一起的字。twerk 是因為 Miley Cyrus 在 VMAs 上面的表演而出名的動作，是一個伴隨著節奏，猥褻地旋轉臀部，為的是引起看的人的性趣。marathone 是馬拉松的意思，在這是指表演當中不斷出現 twerk 這個動作的意思。

❷ messed up，形容詞片語，指某件事或人被弄得亂七八糟，這裡指 Miley Cyrus 很胡來、亂搞的意思。跟 fucked up, beaten up 有異曲同工之妙。

❸ tweeners，名詞，在這裡是指不到青少年期的，但是又不是太小的男孩女孩，就是可以看得懂電視，但是分不清是非對錯的年紀。還有別的解釋，像是不屬於任何集團的人，中立的人也叫 tweener。或是對自己的文化背景感到困惑、沒有歸屬感的人，舉例來說，如果一個白人年輕男孩學著黑人的舉止與說話方式，這讓他不管被歸類到哪邊都怪怪的，所以叫他 tweener。

惡意留言（一）

Kat 做為一個 Youtube 上的部落客在網路上有著很多的粉絲。現在她正坐在客廳裡，她的室友 Amy 也在，兩人各自在電腦跟平板上上網。

Kat: I'm checking the YouTube comments I'm getting from people for my video blog. Check out what I'm getting.

我正在查看我在 Youtube 上面的影片得到的留言。看看我得到的些什麼？

Amy: Alright, [1]**shoot.**

好吧，開始。

Kat: First of all, "U are haribile. "

首先，「你很『騷糕』。」

Amy: (starts laughing and asks) Haribile?

（Amy 開始大笑然後問）騷糕？

Kat: I think this person means horrible. Next, "Eww... what's that ugly thing it looks like a fat no life."

我想這人的意思是糟糕。下一個，「噁…那個醜得像人生沒意義的胖子是什麼東西。」

Amy: Fat? What is he talking about?

胖子？那人在説什麼？

Kat: "Yo makeup look so terrible like [2]**jizz** all over your face."

「你妝化得真恐怖，好像精液灑了你滿臉。」

Amy: How about "Yo need going back to school and retake English."?

「你需要回學校重新上英文課。」，如何？

Kat: "Oh what a silly ³goatse."

「喔這真是個愚蠢的 goatse。」

Glossary 髒話大解

❶ shoot，動詞，在這裡是 Amy 要 Kat 開始說的意思。通常是用在手槍發射之類的動作上，或是注射毒品也可以用，但是如果有人問你 "Can I ask you a question?" 你可以回答 "Shoot." 就是你願意聽，讓他們說的意思。還有就是如果不想說 shit 這不文雅的字，也可以說 shoot，這樣大家也知道你其實想要罵 shit。

❷ jizz，名詞，指男人的精液。其中一種指稱精液的俗語，跟女士說話的時候用這個字是很沒禮貌的喔，正確的醫學用詞應該是 semen。

❸ goatse 在此為名詞，這個字類似像中文說的惡作劇，但是指一種特殊狀況下。是從一個很舊的網路笑話來的，有人把一個男的用力撐開他屁眼的照片放在網路上，連結說明用其他不相關的名稱，引發別人的興趣去點閱，像是「可愛的兔子.jpg」之類的，結果等點進去看，後悔就來不及了，是一個很糟糕的惡作劇。這個字可以做為名詞或是動詞，"I've been goatse'd." 就是我被整了，現在不見得是指那張撐開屁眼的照片，可以是其他噁心的、讓人不舒服的影像。

惡意留言（二）

 情境對話  Track 58

Amy 沒碰過 Goatse 這個惡作劇，所以不知道那是什麼意思，於是發問…

Amy: What's a goatse?

什麼是 goatse？

Kat: You don't wanna know.

你不會想知道的。

Amy: Fine, I'll look it up later.

好啦，我等下查查看。

Kat: "You are such a ¹**freak** and I'm not going to subscribe to you."

「你真是個怪物，而我不再訂閱你的頻道了。」

Amy: Whatever.

隨便你。

Kat: "You're ugly ²**as fuck!**" Reading these mean comments really is entertaining. They think that they are making me feel bad, but the joke is actually on them. Their comments are making me money and they are actually helping me pay my bills.

「你真他媽的醜！」讀這些留言真是有趣。他們認為他們這麼做會讓我難受，但是笑話其實是在他們身上。他們的留言在幫我賺錢，他們其實是在幫我繳帳單。

Amy: Yah, judging from their grammar, they are obviously uneducated ³**dickheads** who probably still live in their parents'

是啊，從他們的文法上看來，他們很顯然的是沒受過教育的混蛋，八成 35

basement or garage at age 35. There's no need to mind those [4]**losers** at all.

歲了還住在他們父母的地下室或是車庫裡，根本沒必要理那些敗類。

Glossary 髒話大解

❶ freak，名詞，怪物、怪胎的意思。指那些行為舉止很怪異的人，可好可壞，看說的人的口氣。

❷ as fuck 為語助詞片語，真他媽的的意思，通常是放在句尾來強調前面說的話。在這裡是強調留言的人認為 Kat 真他媽的醜 "you're ugly as fuck"。

❸ dickheads，名詞，白目、混蛋的意思。dick 是男人的陰莖，dickhead 就可以想像成陰莖長在頭上，指那些很愛現、很沒禮貌、很討人厭的人。

❹ losers，名詞，指那些成事不足、敗事有餘的敗類。

Chapter 59 川普要選總統？！（一）

 情境對話  *Track 59*

Adam 跟 Wayne 正準備一起吃中餐，才剛點完菜，旁邊的電視新聞就開始報導總統大選的最新消息。

Adam: Who do you think is going to win?

你覺得誰會贏？

Wayne: Seriously, I hate it when people ask me about politics. It gives me anxiety, I don't even know the difference between the Democrat and Republican. I just know that I'm supposed to be a democrat or my friends will get mad at me. And when I'm around my grandpa, I have to say that I'm a Republican or he'll get all [1]**nuts** about it.

說真的，我很討厭有人問我跟政治有關的問題，那讓我感到焦慮，我連民主黨跟共和黨之間有什麼不同都不知道。我只知道跟朋友在一起的時候我應該是民主黨人，要不他們都會生我的氣。然後當我跟我祖父在一起的時候，我必須說我是共和黨人，要不他會「起肖」。

Adam: Alright then, answer me this, what do you think about Donald Trump?

好那這樣吧，回答我這個問題，你覺得 Donald Trump 如何？

Wayne: I'm like most people, when he announced that he's running, I thought it was a joke, but that was a few months

跟大部分的人一樣，當他宣布他要選總統的時候，我以為那是在開玩笑，但

ago, and he's winning, and ahh... it's not funny anymore. I think America needs to stop doing things because it's funny.

是已經過了幾個月了，他正在領先，所以啊…這已經不好笑了。我認為美國應該不要再因為好玩而做某些事。

Adam: So you don't support him?

所以你不支持他？

Wayne: [2]**Hell no! He** [3]**pisses me off!**

才不！他惹到我了！

Glossary 髒話大解

❶ nuts，動詞，為某件事瘋狂，就是台灣人常説的「起肖，發瘋」的意思。這裡是 Wayne 指他祖父如果知道他不是共和黨派的就會很生氣，所以誇張的用這個字來形容他祖父會有的反應。做名詞的時候可以做為堅果類的意思，還有也可以作為男人的蛋蛋的意思。

❷ hell 在這裡是語助詞，為了強調之後説的那個 no。這個字做為語助詞的時候可以用來強調惱怒或是驚訝，不見得是指壞事，像是有甚麼好事發生的時候很興奮也可以説 "Hell yeah!"

❸ piss off 為動詞片語，因為某件事讓某人很生氣的意思，這裡是指 Donald Trump 讓 Wayne 很不爽的意思。如果是對你生氣的對象説 piss off 則是叫對方滾的意思。

 情境對話  *Track 60*

Adam 跟 Wayne 繼續聊著這次總統大選目前的選舉情形。

Wayne: I've never cared about this election business, but now that he's winning, I have to actually get out and vote hoping that could change the situation!

我從來就不管這些選舉的事情，但是現在他領先了，我就得出門去選舉，希望可以改變現況。

Adam: Yah I agree, [1]**God forbids** if he wins, I don't even get why he's still running, I mean all the [2]**messed up** racist comments that he has made during his speeches, you would think he would be stopped a long time ago. Do you know this isn't the first time he's tried running for president?

是啊，我也同意，老天保佑他最好不能贏，我根本搞不懂他為什麼到現在還在競選，我是說那些他演講上說的很糟糕的種族歧視言論，你以為他應該早就該被阻止了。你知道這不是他第一次參選總統嗎？

Wayne: What? [3]**Get out**.

什麼？真的假的？

Adam: No, I'm serious. He actually tried running twice already, but like you said, people have thought it was a joke.

不，我是認真的，他已經試過兩次了，但就跟你說的一樣，大家都覺得那是個笑話。

Wayne: Hahaha... that's funny.　　　　　哈哈哈…那真好笑。

Glossary 髒話大解

❶ God forbids，God 是名詞，指上帝，forbid 是動詞，禁止、不允許。所以 God forbids 就是指上帝不允許某件事發生，其實是用來表示某人殷切的希望某件事不會發生，至於上帝允不允許，只有上帝知道囉。

❷ messed up，形容詞片語，指某件事很糟糕的意思。在這裡是指 Donald Trump 在總統選舉演講期間說過的話。

❸ get out，形容詞片語，在這裡並不是真的叫 Adam 滾出去，而是因為震驚於他說的消息而說的，有點像是說「真的假的？！」的意思。

情境對話  *Track 61*

Bob 正在休息室喝咖啡，Marcus 走了進來，Bob 剛好想到剛剛看到關於被駁回的變性人平權法案，於是便跟 Marcus 聊了起來。

Bob: Hey Marc, have you heard of the Houston equal rights ordinance?

嘿 Marc，你有聽説那個休士頓平等權利條例嗎？

Marcus: No, why?

沒有，為什麼問？

Bob: Apparently some people have voted against allowing transgender people access to public bathrooms of their gender identity.

很顯然地，有些人對於讓變性人進他們對自己性別認知的公共廁所投了反對票。

Marcus: Huh... interesting.

喔…有意思。

Bob: So this anti-discrimination law was voted down, because some people claimed it's just an excuse to allow guys in women's restrooms.

所以這條反差別待遇的法令被否決掉了，因為有些人認為那是讓男人進女人廁所的藉口。

Marcus: What do they think any man with a normal set of mind would go through the troubles of years of hormonal treatment, surgery, changing

他們以為任何心態正常的男人會經過多年的荷爾蒙治療、手術、改名字、換掉衣櫃裡的衣服，甚至

their name, their wardrobe, and even coming out to their family, just to watch women go to the bathroom? What kind of [1]**wacky** persons would come up with such a senseless conclusion?

Bob: [2]**Beats me!** I thought that was [3]**lame** too.

跟家人坦白一切，這些麻煩就為了看女人上廁所嗎？是什麼樣的神經病才能想到這種無意義的結論？

問倒我了！我也覺得那很白目。

Glossary 髒話大解

❶ wacky，形容詞，在這裡是古怪的、腦袋有問題的意思。wacky person 就是想法很怪的人，簡單説就是神經病。

❷ beats me 裡的 beat 是動詞，打敗、擊敗的意思，所以 beats me 就是指打敗我了，在這裡是 Bob 覺得被 Marcus 的問題問倒了，不是他被揍的意思喔！

❸ lame，形容詞，這個詞本意是指瘸腿走路走不好的意思，但是普遍被用來表示某件事很糟、很爛的意思。在這裡是 Bob 用來表示，他認為變性人不被允許使用他們對自己性向認知的廁所，是件很白目的事。

變性人平權（二）

Marcus 繼續解釋著社會大眾對女廁的敏感是件很無聊的事。

Marcus: What do they think is going on in the lady's room? There's no shirtless pillow fights or disco balls. I grew up with sisters, and trust me, it [1]**sucks** sharing bathroom with women.

他們以為女廁裡有什麼？又不是有上空的枕頭仗還是迪斯科球，我跟姊妹們一起長大，相信我，跟女人共用浴室是件很糟的事。

Bob: You've got a point! We've all had a mother, sisters or that sort in our life at some point, and we've shared bathrooms at home, I don't know why it would be such a great deal for men and women to share restrooms, not to say transgenders.

你説的很有道理！我們一生中在某個階段都有媽媽、姊妹之類的，而我們在家都是共用廁所的，我不知道為什麼男女共用廁所會事情這麼大條，更不用説是變性的人了。

Marcus: Even if for some reason a man is desperate to use a lady's room, you don't need a sex change to do it, you can just walk in! There's no [2]**bouncer**. The door is right there! Seriously, I've done it here in the office building. Last time I really needed to [3]**deficate**, but in the men's

就算因為某種原因，一個男人迫切地需要用女廁，你不需要變性就可以用了，就走進去就好啦！又沒有看門的人，門就在那裡！説真的，我就在這棟辦公大樓用過。上次我真

room toilets were out of order on this floor, I couldn't hold it till I find another one on a different floor, so I just went and used the toilets in the lady's room.

的很需要排便，但是這層樓男廁裡的馬桶不能用，我憋不到等我到別層樓找廁所，所以就進女廁用馬桶囉。

Bob: Ahh... so you were the one the ladies were complaining about.

啊…原來你就是那個女士們在抱怨的對象。

Glossary 髒話大解

❶ suck 這個字做為動詞是吸吮的意思，在此為形容詞，很糟的、很討厭的意思。在這裡是 Marcus 表示跟女人共用浴室是件很討厭的事情。

❷ bouncer，名詞，這字聽起來很有彈跳感，其實是指看門的人，特別是那些看起來凶神惡煞、高頭大馬的，在夜店門口看門的人，他們的職責是專門擋看起來有問題的人，或是把鬧事的人丟出去。

❸ deficate，動詞，指排便這個動作。以大便這個動作來說，這個詞算是文雅的，但是普遍還是說上廁所比較有禮貌，不會跟人說我要去大便或排便。

 情境對話  *Track 63*

Tara 問 Correy 知不知道關於他們的共同朋友 Summer 跟 Nora 的近況。

Tara: Did you know that Summer lost her job at the catholic school just a few days ago?

你知道 Summer 幾天前丟了她在天主教學校的工作？

Correy: No why?

不知道，為什麼？

Tara: Ok... So the school found out that Summer is [1]**gay** and is married to Nora.

因為那個學校發現 Summer 是同性戀而且還跟 Nora 結了婚。

Correy: You know, if they're going to be [2]**balls to the wall**, [3]**guns blazing**. Let's get right to the homosexual, then they should be going after anyone who's divorced, anyone who's having pre-marital sex, anyone who is living together but isn't married, anyone who's getting drunk all the time, and so on and so forth.

你知道嗎，如果他們要這樣極端的、不顧一切的去抓同性戀的人，那他們也應該去找那些離婚的、那些婚前發生性行為的、那些同居但是沒結婚的，還有老是喝醉酒的，那些有的沒有的人啊。

Glossary 髒話大解

❶ gay，名詞，同性戀，原本是指男同性戀，但是現在男女都適用，雖然這邊 Summer 跟 Nora 都是女的應該用 lesbian，但是或許是因為不太好說，講 gay 比較快，所以大部分人稱男女同性戀都說是 gay。至於帶不帶惡意完全就是看說的人的語氣了。

❷ balls to the wall，形容詞片語，推向極限的、極端的意思。一個非常活靈活現的一個詞，但是用的時候要小心，雖然它的緣由並不帶髒，但是大部分人聽到 balls 這個字最先聯想到的大概就是男人的睪丸，其實這個詞的由來是從開戰鬥機的飛行員傳出來的，這個 ball 指的是飛機油門控制旋鈕上的球型手把，把球往前推到最頂就是加速的極限，所以才有 balls to the wall 這個詞。

❸ guns blazing，形容詞片語，很用力魯莽的、不顧後果的做某件事，特別是指在辯論、吵架的時候火藥味十足的意思，所以不是真的有人拿槍掃射。

同性戀不平等待遇（二）

Tara 跟 Correy 仍然很氣憤地在談論發生在 Summer 身上的事情。

Tara: Totally agreed! There are so many other sins in the bible that are just neglected, but that's the only one that people are fired up over, which I just think is absolutely ridiculous. Not that I think being [1]**LGBT** is a sin, it's not, and there's nothing wrong with it!

完全同意！聖經裡有那麼多罪行都被忽視掉，但是這個卻是唯一讓人被開除的理由，我認為真的是很荒謬。並不是説我認為同性戀、雙性戀跟變性是罪，那不是，而且那並沒有錯！

Correy: This makes me [2]**sick to my stomach** that this kind of nonsense still exists in the world! Are they allowed to do that? I thought workplaces aren't supposed to discriminate against people's sexual orientation?

這種荒謬的事情還是存在這個世上真讓我感到噁心！我以為工作場所不能歧視個人的性向？

Tara: Well yah, except that it's a catholic school and they're allowed to do that because it is against their religious beliefs. By the way, Summer actually chose to leave the school because they were going to start an investigation on

是啊，但是那是天主教學校，所以他們被允許這麼做，因為這與他們的信仰互相牴觸。對了，Summer 其實是自願離開學校的，因為他們準備

her whole life and look into her personal life.

要開始對她的人生，甚至私生活進行調查。

Correy: That's the most [3]rabid thing I've heard this week.

這是我這星期聽到最瘋狂的事。

Glossary 髒話大解

❶ LGBT 其實是四個名詞連在一起，Lesbian / Gay / Bisexual / Transgender，分別為女同性戀／男同性戀／雙性戀／變性人，四種人都是敏感話題人物，近年來 LGBT 人權開始比較受重視，為了方便就把四個字取頭一個字母做為簡稱。但是因為還是有一部分的人反對 LGBT 的存在，所以對於這些人抱有敵意。

❷ sick to my stomach，形容詞片語，就是說讓我很想吐，讓我覺得很噁心的意思，其實滿容易聯想得到，胃不舒服，就是想吐囉。

❸ rabid，形容詞，對某件事或信仰有極端狂熱的意思。這個字一開始是指得狂犬病的動物，後來被用來形容某件事或動作是很極端、瘋狂的。

Chapter 65

生意頭腦（一）

 情境對話 ＋  Track 65

Aiden 跟 Jacob 正在談論剛剛聽到的好笑新聞，有個賓州的青少年因為對著耶穌的雕像做猥褻的動作還拍照貼在社交網站上，結果被逮捕，現在聽說可能會被關兩年。

Aiden: Kids these days are out of control. They don't know what they are doing, and posting stuff online getting themselves in trouble. Remember that other kids who took a selfie on top of the Brooklyne Bridge and got arrested after the picture was discovered by the police?

最近的小鬼頭簡直就是無法無天，根本不知道他們自己在做什麼，隨便在網路上貼東西給自己找麻煩。記得那個爬到布魯克林大橋頂端自拍的小鬼，然後照片被警察發現，結果就被逮捕了？

Jacob: Yah, but you gotta admit, we used to be just as [1]**dumb** as them back in those good old days.

是啊，但是你得承認，在那些過去的好日子裡我們也曾經那麼白目過。

Aiden: Hahaha... True, true. But that doesn't mean we should approve of what that kid has done though, I mean you gotta stop them before they get into deeper trouble.

哈哈哈⋯沒錯，沒錯。但是這不代表我們應該認同那個小鬼做的事，我是說你得在他們搞出更大的麻煩之前阻止他們。

Jacob: Nah yah, I agree. I don't approve

嘿啊，我同意，我不贊同

what that kid has done. I'm just saying that kids that age do that sort of things all the time. It's just the matter of getting caught or not. I remember when I was in high school, that "how much money would you [2]go down on a guy for" game was a [3]hit!

那小鬼做的事，我只是説那個年紀的小鬼就是會做出那些事，只是有沒有被抓到的分別而已。我記得我高中的時候，那個「給你多少錢你會願意替男人服務」的遊戲很受歡迎！

Glossary 髒話大解

❶ dumb，形容詞，愚蠢的、白目的意思。其實這個字一開始是指因為先天性耳聾而説話説不好的人的狀況，如果真的用在那些人身上是很差勁的行為，但是普遍是被做為罵一般人是蠢蛋的意思。

❷ go down on a guy 裡的 go down 是動詞，是指一個人去另一個人的下體做口交之類的動作，on a guy 就是指對男人，on 之後的人稱是可以隨需要替換的。這個 go down on someone 的説法算是比較含蓄的，但是還是很不合宜的詞，所以別在公共場合大聲説。

❸ hit，名詞，只轟動一時的人或事，在這裡是指 Jacob 提到的遊戲在他高中時期很受歡迎，不是有人被揍喔。

生意頭腦（二）

 情境對話  **Track 66**

Jacob 剛剛提到他高中時期同學間開玩笑的遊戲，Aiden 聽了有些詫異。

Aiden: (with a shocking disapproval face replied) What? Never heard of it.

（Aiden 一臉驚愕還有不甚認同的臉答道）什麼？聽都沒聽過。

Jacob: Ok, so it's basically, one of your friends would be like "Hey man, would you go down on a guy for a million dollars?", and then we would all lie and say no, hahaha...

好吧，所以基本上就是你其中一個朋友會問你：「嘿老兄，你會為了一百萬幫男人服務嗎？」然後我們都會撒謊說不，哈哈哈…

Aiden: So you would go down on a guy for a million dollars?

所以你會為了一百萬幫男人服務？

Jacob: Of course I would! A million dollars is a [1]**steal**!

當然會！一百萬是個好交易！

Aiden: Sounds like someone is part of the [2]**queer** community here.

聽起來某人是同性戀團體的一員。

Jacob: No, I'm a businessman! I used to say no to that when I was in high school,

不，我是個生意人！我高中時曾經說不，但那是因

but that was when I was living at my parents', had free food and roof over my head. I didn't need to worry about money. Times have changed man!

為我當時住在我父母家裡，有免費的食物跟房子住，我不需要擔心錢的問題。時代已經不一樣了老兄！

Aiden: I don't know man, that is some [3]**wacky** business you're talking about over there.

我不知道喔老兄，你現在說的是個很不正常的生意。

Glossary 髒話大解

❶ steal，名詞，好交易的意思，因為太好，感覺像是偷來的，所以叫做 steal，不是真的去偷東西。

❷ queer，名詞，指同性戀。原本是被用來貶低同性戀的詞，但是現在被同性戀或雙性戀者拿來自稱，算是一個自我肯定的詞，可以說是引以為傲，但是被一般人拿來稱呼其他人還是很沒禮貌的。

❸ wacky，形容詞，不正常的、瘋狂的、古怪的。是一個用來形容人或情況非常不尋常，但是同時又有點好笑的狀況。

Chapter 67 恐嚇信函

 情境對話  *Track 67*

星期四，Ariana 起床後覺得很不舒服，所以決定請病假不去上班，Ian 剛剛從藥店幫她買藥回來。

Ian: Hey baby, check this scented candle out. It smells amazing! I smelled it as I was walking by it in the store and I just couldn't resist.

嘿寶貝，來聞聞看這個香精蠟燭，它聞起來超讚！我在店裡經過的時候聞到，就無法抗拒地把它買回來了。

Ariana: Aww... hahaha... you're so [1]**sappy**. By the way, I just got a death threat email earlier.

喔…哈哈哈…你真的好噁心。對了，我剛剛收到恐嚇電子郵件。

Ian: What? Show me!

什麼？給我看！

Ariana: Here, "If you stop reading this, you will die. My name is Tereasa Fassenova. If you don't forward this to 20 more people, I will sleep with you forever."

這裡，「如果你停止閱讀這封信，你會死。我的名字叫做 Tereasa Fassenova。如果你不把這封郵件傳給 20 個人的話，我會永遠跟你睡在一起。」

Ian: Woo... [2]**Kinky**.

哦…很猥藝喔。

Ariana: Hahaha... It's not over yet, "A girl ignored this and 29 years later her mom died. I'm real, you can search me on google." I feel bad for her, what a ³loser-ass.

哈哈哈…還沒完哩，「有個女孩不理會我，29 年以後她的媽媽死了。我是真的，你可以上 google 搜尋我。」我為她感到悲哀，真是個失敗的混蛋。

Ian: Yah... I wouldn't worry about it.

是啊…是我的話不會理這個。

Glossary 髒話大解

❶ sappy，形容詞，指某件事或人很憋腳但是又同時讓你覺得很可愛、很三八得讓你想吐。

❷ kinky，形容詞，情色的、猥褻的。通常是用來形容那些有特殊性嗜好的人，這裡是因為恐嚇的人說要跟 Ariana 永遠一起睡，所以 Ian 開玩笑地說，有點像是說「哦～好色」的意思。

❸ loser-ass，名詞，罵人同時是失敗者加上混蛋的意思。

Chapter 68

電子灣是敗類灣？！

 情境對話  **Track 68**

Ariana 剛剛吃過感冒藥，現在正躺在沙發上在一本筆記本上亂塗鴉，這時 Ian 問道……

Ian: Did you order something from Ebay? There's a charge close to $400 on our credit card.

你有在電子灣上面訂東西嗎？我們信用卡上有一個將近$400 的費用。

Ariana: From [1]**Loserbay**? No, I don't like that site, better call our credit card company for it.

從敗類灣？不，我不喜歡那個網站，最好打電話告知我們的信用卡公司。

Ian: Hahaha... loserbay? Where did you come up with that?

哈哈哈…敗類灣？你從哪裡來的這個詞？

Ariana: Everybody's calling it that now. Last week Sam spent $500 on Loserbay for a laptop but got a cigar box instead, that's when I learned about that term.

現在大家都這麼叫它啊。上星期 Sam 花了$500 在敗類灣上買了一台手提電腦，結果收到一個雪茄盒，我就是那個時候學到這個詞的。

Ian: What a [2]**bungle**! Was he able to get his money back?

真是糟糕！他有辦法退錢嗎？

Ariana: He's still dealing with the seller. You should see how he [3]**lost it** on the phone in the office the other day. It was hilarious!

他還在跟賣家交涉。你該看看他那天在辦公室如何在電話上發飆的那真的很爆笑！

Glossary 髒話大解

❶ Loserbay，名詞，敗類灣，取 eBay 的 Bay 加上 Loser，因為近來 eBay 頻頻出問題，服務品質大不如前，所以開始有人這樣叫它。

❷ bungle，名詞，指很糟糕、被搞砸的狀況，通常是指因為管理不善或混亂造成的情形。

❸ lost it，動詞片語，指一個人失去理智而開始發飆的狀況，聽起還像是丟掉了什麼東西，就想像成把理智給丟了吧。

誰不愛看妹？！（一）

 情境對話  *Track 69*

Riley 正在她房間裡倒掛在床邊唱著不成調的歌，這時 *Brianna* 走了進來想問她要不要一起去海邊玩。

Brianna: Hahaha... What are you doing?

哈哈哈…你在幹嘛？

Riley: Singing, can't you tell?

唱歌啊，你看不出來？

Brianna: Singing up side down?

倒掛著唱歌？

Riley: Yah! I love singing this way. What's up with the hot bathing suite?

是啊！我愛這樣唱歌。幹嘛穿著那麼辣的泳裝？

Brianna: Going to the beach, you wanna come?

準備要去海邊，你要來嗎？

Riley: Hell yah! I love watching hot chicks on the beach.

當然要！我超愛在海邊看辣妹。

Brianna: Hahaha... You're so [1]**gay**.

哈哈哈…你很蠢欸。

Riley: You see, I believe that nobody is one hundred percent gay or one hundred percent [2]**straight**. I am straight, I like men, but when I see beautiful attractive

你看，我相信沒有人是百分之百同性戀或是百分之百異性戀。我是異性戀者，我愛男人，但是當我

women with a nice figure, I'd be like "Honey, I would lick chocolate sauce off your sexy ab, cause you are [3]**banging**".

看到身材很好、美麗、很有吸引力的女人時，我就會説：「蜜糖，我會從你性感的腹部舔食巧克力醬，因為你好辣。」

Glossary 髒話大解

❶ gay，形容詞，這詞本身是指男同性戀，因為以前對同性戀是很排斥的，所以這個字就被拿來罵人，做為形容詞的時候，是罵人很蠢、很笨的意思，其實最好是避免用這個字罵人，因為這對 gay 很不公平，好像把他們跟愚蠢畫上等號，非常的沒禮貌。

❷ straight，名詞，跟 gay 或 lesbian 相反，指異性戀者，算是非正式用語，因為是一般正常人，不是其他的「邪魔歪道」，走的是「正道」，所以是直的，正式説法應該是 heterosexual。

❸ banging，形容詞，當某件東西或人非常的棒、美好、性感的時候就可以用 banging 來形容。但是記得之前提過的，做愛的動作也可以叫做 banging，所以要注意聽對話內容，不要會錯意喔。

Chapter 70

誰不愛看妹？！（二）

 情境對話  Track 70

Riley 剛剛發表了她碰到美女時的反應，Brianna 聽了覺得搞笑又受不了，於是回道……

Brianna: Hahaha... Eww... You are so [1]**gross**.

哈哈哈…嗯…你好噁心喔。

Riley: I'm not! If you think appreciating beautiful people that are the same sex as you is gross, then you are a [2]**douche**, because you think homosexuality is gross.

我才不會！如果你認為欣賞美麗的同性是件噁心的事，那你是個壞蛋，因為你認為同性戀是噁心的事。

Brianna: That's not what I mean, I meant the chocolate licking part.

我不是那個意思，我是說那個舔食巧克力的部分。

Riley: What? It's not like I'm going to lick her [3]**poonanny** or something. I just want to show my appreciation for her to show up on my eye ball.

幹嘛？又不是說我要去舔她的陰道之類的。我只是想要為了她出現在我的眼球上，表示我的感謝而已。

Brianna: I'm alright. Don't think I'd ever see other women that way.

我還好，不認為我曾經用那樣的眼光看過別的女人。

Riley: Oh come on, don't be a liar. You've never seen a beautiful woman walking by and say "Damn! She's hot"?

喔拜託，別騙人了。你從來沒有看過一個美女從你身邊走過然後說：「該死的！她真是辣」？

Brianna: Nope!

沒！

Glossary 髒話大解

❶ gross，形容詞，指某件事或人很不吸引人、很噁心的意思。在這裡是指 Brianna 覺得 Riley 很噁心，因為她想舔其他女生腹部這件事。

❷ douche，名詞，壞蛋、惡棍的意思。之前提到過 douchebag 的簡稱，這東西原本是用來清潔女性私處的道具，後來被用來罵人，普遍是罵男人比較多，但是近年來各種分別罵男女的詞句分界已經沒有那麼清楚了。

❸ poonanny，名詞，指的是女性的陰道，正式的醫學名詞是 vagina，這個算是比較下流，但是聽說有女性認為聽起來比較可愛，所以比起 pussy 之類的接受度較高。

Chapter 71

槍械管制（一）

又一個大規模槍案發生了，Owen 跟 Eli 在整個事件上有著截然不同的看法。

Owen: If guns were as regulated as cars, you know, if it required title and tag at each point of sale, extensive training prior to receiving one, conducted written and practical tests beforehand, also required the holders to pass certain standard of mental health test, requested them to get liability insurance on each gun, and renewals and inspections at intervals, it would have greatly decreased the amount of tragedy as this one right here.

如果槍械能跟車輛一樣受到一樣的管制，你知道的，如果在買賣的時候要求要有註冊抬頭跟標籤，領取之前要求要接受深度培訓、筆試跟實際操作測試，還有要求持槍者要通過一定的心理健康測試標準，要求他們要為每支槍買責任險，還有一段時間要做更新還有檢驗，那會更有效的降低像這樣的不幸事件發生的次數。

Eli: This is why people should do research before calling for action. [1]**Stupidity** hurts everyone. Everything but the last two you mentioned has been done already. [2]**What the fuck** would I need liability insurance for? [3]**How on earth** would that help prevent gun violence? Gun permits

這就是為什麼大家應該要先做些研究考證過後再行動。愚蠢是會傷害到所有人的。除了最後兩點以外，所有你提到的都已經被執行了。我他媽的要責任險做什麼？請問那怎麼

are renewed at an interval and what the fuck purpose would an inspection serve? Again, not addressing the issue at hand.

可能會幫助預防槍支暴力？持槍許可證每隔一段時間要更新，但是他媽的檢驗槍支的目地是什麼？再次的，沒有解決這裡的問題。

Glossary 髒話大解

❶ stupidity，名詞，指愚蠢這個特質，指某人行為顯示缺乏良好的判斷力。stupid 是大家耳熟能詳的罵人是笨蛋的形容詞，而加上-ity 就是名詞了。

❷ the fuck，感嘆詞，任何問句 How / what / when / where / why 之類的加上 the fuck，目地就是要表示説的人的憤怒、震驚之類的情緒。

❸ on earth，感嘆詞，也是在問句裡加在 How / what / when / where / why 之後，雖然本身不髒，但是通常是生氣、情緒激動的時候會説的。

Chapter 72

槍械管制（二）

Eli 仍然還是為了 Owen 的提議而感到憤怒，繼續的發表他的想法。

Eli: Suggestions like this make it harder for honest, safe, law abiding citizens to maintain guns. Turning them into victims, do your research, criminals don't follow the law! If you don't want one, you don't have to have one, but stop trying to regulate those of us who do.

像這種提議只會讓誠實、安全、遵守法律的市民在維持槍枝上更加困難。把他們變成受害者，回去做點研究，罪犯是不會遵守法律的！你如果不想要，你不需要擁有，但是別再試著要監察我們這些想要有槍的人。

Owen: Wow, chill dude.

哇，冷靜點老兄。

Eli: I never take the loss of my rights or the spread of [1]**propaganda** lightly. I want them to make laws that actually help people. This isn't about guns. It's about mental illness, and we need to work on getting the [2]**psychos** off the street.

我從來不輕看我的權利喪失或是這種誤導性質的宣傳的散播。我想要他們訂定真的會幫到人的法案。這個跟槍沒有關係，這是關於精神病的問題，而我們需要做的，是別讓那些神經病上街。

Owen: I disagree, studies have shown that

我不同意，研究顯示大部

large majority of people with mental disorders do not engage in violence against others. Less than 5% of the 120,000 gun related killings were perpetrated by people diagnosed with mental illness. In fact, mentally ill people are far likely to be the victims of violence, rather than the [3]**perpetrator**.

分心理不正常的人不會有針對他人的暴力行為。120,000 件槍殺案裡，低於 5%的是由被診斷過有精神病的人犯下的。事實上，精神不正常的人更有可能成為暴力的受害者，而不是肇事者。

Glossary 髒話大解

❶ propaganda，名詞，直接翻譯成中文是宣傳的意思，特別是指散播誤導性質的信息，通常是為了某種陰謀推倡某個特定的政治觀點。在這裡 Eli 不贊同 Owen 的想法，所以把它稱做 propaganda，其實是很不尊重對方意見的說法。

❷ psycho，名詞，psychophath 的簡稱，就是指有精神疾病的人、瘋子。

❸ perpetrator，名詞，指犯了罪的人，不見得是已經被法律定罪的罪犯，也可以是做了很壞、很糟糕的事的人。像是在一群朋友裡挑撥離間的人也可以說是 perpetrator。

Chapter 73

你還要喝牛奶嗎？！（一）

 情境對話  *Track 73*

Ginny 剛剛讀了關於乳製品業的生產過程，感到極度地噁心，決定不再碰任何的乳製品，並準備跟 Dane 還有 Walter 分享她的心得。

Ginny: Guys, we need to stop buying dairy products. You have no idea what is going on behind the scenes of all the [1]**evil** dairy industry.

各位，我們必須要停止購買乳製品。你不知道那些邪惡的乳製品業背後都搞些什麼鬼。

Dane: Okay... I'm listening.

好吧⋯我聽著。

Ginny: So like all mammals, cows only lactate to produce milk when they're pregnant and have a newborn to feed. So the dairy industry artificially inseminates the cows starting at 1 year old until the day they [2]**crash** and die.

所以跟所有的哺乳類一樣，牛只會在懷孕生完小牛以後為了餵養牠們的新生兒而分泌乳汁。所以乳製品業就會從牠們一歲起不斷給牠們人工受孕直到牠們筋疲力盡而亡。

Walter: Wow that sounds [3]**nasty**.

哇！那聽起來很糟糕。

Glossary 髒話大解

❶ evil，形容詞，邪惡的、非常不道德的意思。在這裡是形容乳製品業者。

❷ crash，動詞，這個字用法很廣泛，像是撞車也叫 crash，通常比較口語化的用法是說一個人很累的時候倒頭就睡的狀況，在這裡是指母牛們被榨乾到筋疲力盡暴斃而死的情形。

❸ nasty，形容詞，一個人或事讓人感到很不舒服、很討厭。在這裡是形容乳製品業者對待動物的方式。

Chapter '74

你還要喝牛奶嗎？！（二）

 情境對話  Track 74

Ginny 繼續努力地說服 Dane 跟 Walter 也來拒食非人道生產的乳製品。

Ginny: That's not it, so to get the semen, they make a bunch of bulls [1]**jerk off**, sometimes using a hand or electro-ejaculator to help, which is basically a giant cow [2]**dildo** that goes into the anus of a cow until they [3]**blow**.

還不只那樣，所以要得到精液，他們得讓一群公牛射精，有時候是用手，或是電動發射器來幫忙，其實就是一個牛專用的超大號假陽具，拿來放到公牛的屁眼裡直到牠們洩了為止。

Walter: What the fuck? That sounds extremely unpleasant.

他媽的搞什麼？那聽起來非常的不舒服。

Ginny: Then the semen is collected and inserted into the vagina of a female cow with a long tube. Sometimes they have to put their fists right into the anus of the female cow to help loosen up the area. This job is done at this place called the "[4]**rape rack**" by the industry. See the irony of that?

然後收集到的精液就會被一個長長的管子送到母牛的陰道裡。有時候他們還得把拳頭放進母牛的屁眼裡來幫助放鬆那個部位。這件工作是在一個被業者稱作「強姦架子」的地方完成的。諷刺吧？

Dane: I think I'm going to throw up...

我想我快要吐了…

Glossary 髒話大解

❶ jerk off，動詞片語，男性自慰的動作的俗稱，醫學名詞是 masturbate。在這裡雖然公牛是被動的狀態，但是還是用 jerk off 這個詞。

❷ dildo，名詞，假陽具，就是一個被做出來的、勃起狀態的陰莖形狀的性玩具。

❸ blow，動詞，在這裡是指射精的動作，而且不要懷疑，這東西也有醫學用詞，動詞是 ejaculate，射出來的東西是名詞稱為 ejaculation，順帶一提精液本身叫做 semen。

❹ rape rack 裡的 rape 是動詞，強姦的意思，rack 是名詞，架子的意思。rape rack 這東西是很多乳牛牧場裡都有的東西，業者把母牛趕上去讓他們跑不了，然後執行人工受孕，就跟強姦一樣，所以業者們自以為風趣的把那些架子叫做 rape rack。

Chapter 75

你還要喝牛奶嗎？！（三）

 情境對話  *Track 75*

Ginny 繼續説著乳製品業的恐怖內幕，勢必要達成讓兩位朋友完全放棄食用乳製品。

Ginny: Oh that's not the worst part, they [1]**snach** the baby cow away from the mother cow so he or she wouldn't drink up the milk. And if it's a girl, she'll end up just like her mother, going through the same process till the day she [2]**collapses** and is no longer able to reproduce, then get killed for meat. Or if it's a boy cow, he'd be sent right to the [3]**slaughter house**, so we can taste the deliciousness of veal.

喔那還不是最壞的部分，他們會從母牛身邊奪走小牛，這樣小牛才不會把牛奶喝光。然後如果小牛是母的，她最後將會跟她媽媽一樣，經歷同樣的過程直到有一天她崩潰虛脫無法再生殖，然後被殺來吃。或是如果小牛是公的，他就會直接被送到屠宰場去，這樣我們才能嚐到小牛肉的美味。

Walter: That's it, I'm never touching veal again.

夠了，我再也不吃小牛肉了。

Ginny: The bond of the mother cow with her baby is so strong. She would almost always cry for days after her baby is taken away.

母牛跟小牛之間的感情聯繫是很強烈的，她幾乎總會在她的寶寶被帶走以後哭叫好多天。

Dane: Alright we get it, just stop.

好了我們知道了，別再説了。

Walter: We'll never touch any dairy products again.

我們再也不碰乳製品了。

Glossary 髒話大解

❶ snatch，動詞，很快地抓走某樣東西，以很沒有禮貌的方式，像偷東西或是綁架的時候都可以用 snatch，在這裡是指乳製品業者搶走母牛的小牛。

❷ collapse，動詞，崩潰、一個人或動物因為疾病或是受傷昏厥過去，也可以用在建築物倒塌上。在這裡是指母牛被壓榨到筋疲力盡倒下去了。

❸ slaughter house，名詞，屠宰場。slaughter 是動詞，屠殺、殺戮的意思，通常是指大量屠殺動物做為食物的時候，但是殺人的時候也有聽説用這個詞，像是 man slaughter，就是指殺人。

Chapter 76

金　厲害（一）

星期五晚間一個手無寸鐵的黑人青少年被警察槍殺，Obama 總統領著民眾進行第 50 屆阿拉巴馬州塞爾馬的民權遊行，而媒體關心的卻是 Kim Kardashian 的新髮色。

Landon: Kim Kardashian is the blackhole of media, sucking everything in around her and warping the fabric of reality itself. I think it was Terence McKenna who said "media is the spreading of darkness at the speed of light", and I can't agree more.

Daniel: The portrayed image of Kim Kardashian itself isn't her. It's just [1]**simulacrum** that any other human could be playing her part. So, we shouldn't be calling her "the blackhole of media", like she's the representation of the media and its distortions itself.

Jaden: Kim Kardashian and her family are making tons of money selling fake image

Kim Kardashian 簡直就是媒體的黑洞，吸盡她周圍的一切，扭曲現實的結構。我記得 Terence McKenna 說過：「媒體正以光速散播黑暗。」，我不能同意更多了。

那被刻畫出來的形象並不是 Kim Kardashian 本身。那只不過是捏造出來的，任何人都可以演她那個角色。所以我們不應該把她稱作「媒體的黑洞」，好像她就代表整個媒體跟媒體帶來的扭曲似的。

Kim Kardashian 跟她的家人對無知的年輕一代出

of themselves to the clueless younger generation, and we are all [2]**fags** allowing it to happen.

賣著他們自己的假形象而賺取大量的金錢，而我們都是讓這種事發生的蠢貨。

Daniel: And you're jealous, what's new? They're clearly not [3]**idiots** if they've managed to amass the wealth they have.

所以你忌妒，還有什麼新鮮的？如果他們已經成功地聚斂他們所擁有的財富，那他們很顯然地不是白癡。

Glossary 髒話大解

❶ simulacrum，名詞，指幻影、模擬物、膚淺的假象，雖說是有某樣東西的複製品的意思，但是該樣東西不一定要存在，這個概念通常涉及意識形態而不是真的有某個原創物的存在。像在這裡是指 Kim Kardashian 跟她家人的形象，他們的作為只是一種概念而不是真的存在的。

❷ fag，名詞，指那些很讓人討厭的人、蠢貨之類的。faggot 的簡稱，雖然一開始是用來罵男同性戀的詞，後來也開始被用來罵人是蠢蛋。

❸ idiot，名詞，白癡的意思，一般是拿來罵討厭的人，或是某人做了蠢事，被你發現就可以罵對方是 idiot。

Chapter 77

金　厲害（二）

 情境對話  *Track 77*

Daniel、Jaden 跟 Landon 繼續討論著他們對 Kim Kardashian 和她家人的看法。

Daniel: They've abused the flaws in our world and got rich and happy off. So technically, they're geniuses.

他們濫用這世上的缺陷因此而發財，生活得很愜意。所以技術上來說，他們是天才。

Jaden: It takes intelligence to manipulate the media and carry on ¹**milking** money off ²**silly** trivial things. I reckon it does. Else everybody would be doing it.

用愚蠢瑣碎的事來操縱媒體賺大錢是需要智慧的。我是這麼認為的。要不然大家都可以這麼做。

Landon: I think it would take genius if they in the mean time could preserve their dignity. They're just the product which is being sold. Their sellers are the geniuses.

我認為那需要一個天才讓他們能同時保有尊嚴。他們只是被販售的商品。他們的賣家們才是天才。

Jaden: Spot on, dude. She made a ³**porno**, which got her the exposure. It takes a certain mind to know what brainwashes people and what people are interested. She is still a genius in that sense.

講到重點了你，老兄。她拍了部 A 片，讓自己曝光。要知道怎麼對大眾洗腦，還有觀眾有興趣的是什麼是需要頭腦的。以某種角度來看，她還是能算是個天才。

Glossary 髒話大解

❶ milking，動詞進行式，在這裡是指賺錢的動作，milking 一般來說是指擠奶的動作，還有一種比較下流的，用法是指促使男人射精的動作，單看對話的內容是什麼。

❷ silly，形容詞，愚蠢的、愚笨的意思，不見得是罵人，有時候你覺得某人做的事很呆很無聊卻也很可愛，也可以用 silly 來形容，像是如果小狗追著自己的尾巴轉，你覺得很可愛又很蠢，就可以說 silly dog。

❸ porno，名詞，pornography 的簡稱，也就是 A 片或三級片的意思。

Chapter '78

灰狗治療（一）

 情境對話 *Track 78*

在內華達州南部，唯一一家國營精神病院，Rawson-Neal 最近被爆料給予他們的病患一種叫做「灰狗療法」的事，社評專家說這簡直就是無法讓人置信的作法。

John: Have you heard the news about the [1]**psychward** in Nevada? It's so messed up.

你有聽說關於內華達州的那間精神病院的新聞嗎？那真的很糟糕。

Ariel: No, what is that?

沒有，是什麼事？

John: So this place called Rawson-Neal is said to be discharging their seriously ill patients too soon, and supplying them with a one-way bus ticket out of town.

那間叫做 Rawson-Neal 的醫院被爆料說，他們提早讓那些有著嚴重疾病的病人出院，然後提供他們一張單程巴士票給他們出城。

Ariel: Geez! That's insane! What were those people thinking? You can't just put people you'd rather not see on a bus to another city.

老天！那真是瘋狂！那些人在想什麼啊？你不能就這樣把你不想看到的人放到巴士上送到其他城市去。

John: [2]**Beats me**, this is not the worst,

問倒我了，這還不是最糟

I've also heard that approximately two million mentally ill people go to jail every year. That means there're now ten times more psychologically ill people behind [3]**bars**, than State funded psychiatric treatment facilities.

的，我還聽説每年大約有兩百萬名精神患者被送進監獄。這也就是説十倍以上的精神病患者現在正在監牢裡，而不是國營精神病治療設施。

Glossary 髒話大解

❶ psychward，名詞，指精神病院，比較不好聽的詞，一般來説是講 psychiatric institute 或 psychiatric hospital。

❷ beats me 裡的 beat 是動詞，是説的人講「我被打敗了」的意思，不是説真的打架打輸人，而是被問題問倒了。

❸ bars，名詞，監牢的意思，在這裡跟酒吧是沒有關係的，監牢都是有鐵欄杆的，那些鐵欄杆就叫做 bars，所以説讓某人去坐牢也可以説 put someone behind bars，字面上的意思就是把人放到欄杆後面，也就是讓他去坐牢的意思。

❹ 特別説明上面説的灰狗治療，英文是 Grey Hound Therapy，美國有一間規模比較大的巴士公司叫做 Grey Hound，就是灰狗巴士，這裡他們説把病人放到巴士上就不管了，所以叫做灰狗治療。

Ariel 對於這件新聞感到很不可思議，也繼續跟 John 討論著美國近年來對於精神病患缺乏照顧的狀況。

Ariel: That just sounds terrible; using the criminal justice system to treat the mentally ill isn't just ineffective. It's expensive! Our whole system for dealing with the mentally ill definitely needs a massive overhaul.

那聽起來真的是很糟糕，用刑事司法系統來治療精神病患不只是缺乏效率，還很花錢！我們整個應付精神疾病患者的系統需要來個大翻修。

John: Medicaid which is supposed to be the public safety net for the mentally ill, works differently across the States. There isn't really any clear uniform guideline. And there are eight federal agencies who administered over a hundred programs that in some ways touch on mental health, and the social services agencies in each of the fifty States, so basically, the whole system is a [1]**clusterfuck**.

政府的醫療救助系統 Medicaid 本該是精神病患的安全網，每個州的做法卻完全不一樣，並沒有一個清楚的統一指導條文。而八間聯邦機構管理的一百多個程序方案或多或少都有接觸到心理健康治療，還有五十個州裡各自的社會福利機構，所以基本上，整個系統就是一團混亂。

Ariel: More like a [2]**friggin'** [3]**cluster-**

比較像是該死的一團阿嚕

dryhump of some kind.

吧之類的。

John: Hahaha... We as a society needs to figure out how to fund the programs that are actually useful and work.

哈哈哈…我們的社會需要想辦法資助那些真的有實質幫助的方案。

Glossary 髒話大解

❶ clusterfuck，名詞，一團混亂的意思，一開始是軍隊裡的用詞，指戰況上很糟一團亂的意思，現在則普遍被用來指大規模的混亂。

❷ friggin'，形容詞，也就是 frigging，用來強調或表達憤怒、懊惱、蔑視或是驚訝，用法跟 fucking 一樣，在不能說 fucking 的場合的時候就可以用這個字，但是其實是一樣的意思。

❸ cluster-dryhump 裡的 cluster 是一團東西的意思，因為上面 John 用 clusterfuck 這個字，所以 Ariel 風趣的在 dry hump 前面也加上 cluster。dryhump 或 dry hump 指的是像是阿嚕吧的動作，穿著衣服磨蹭性器官的動作，在這裡是名詞，也可以做動詞用。因為英文 fuck 可以做為性交的意思，John 說 clusterfuck，雖然跟性沒有關係，但是 Ariel 因為認為政府的政策措施根本沒做到效用，就像 dryhump 一樣穿著衣服磨蹭根本不是來真的，所以說 cluster-dryhump。

 情境對話  Track 80

美國已經正式成為全世界囚犯人數最多的國家，有近 1% 的人口正在坐牢，這表示有超過了百萬的人正深陷囹圄。

Jackson: The only thing we have more than China now is our prison population, how wonderful, isn't it?

Aaron: Our prison population has exploded for a number of reasons, from our broken mental health system, to mandatory minimum sentenced laws, to of course [1]**drugs**. Half the people in federal prison are there on drug charges, which is vacuous! They should just be [2]**fined** instead of being in there provided with free food and shelter, costing us tax payers' money.

Jackson: Actually, we are not taking care of them at all. Government has become progressively more [3]**thrifty** toward prison food spending, so I've heard there are times when prisoners aren't actually

我們唯一比中國多的就是我們的監獄人口，真是美妙不是嗎？

我們的監獄人口暴增的原因有很多，從我們破碎的心理治療系統，到最低強制判刑，然後當然就是毒品藥物了。聯邦監獄裡一半的囚犯是因為毒品控告，說真的很沒有意義！他們應該被罰款而不是在那裡面被供給免費的食物跟庇護所，花我們納稅人的錢。

其實我們並沒有在照顧他們。政府對於監獄牢飯的花費變得越來越小氣，所以我聽說有時候囚犯根本沒飯吃，或是有過在食物

getting food or have instances like maggots found in their food.

裡有蛆的例子。

Aaron: Eww... that sucks.

噁…那真糟。

Glossary 髒話大解

❶ drug，名詞，在這裡是指非法藥物或是毒品，特別是那些有麻痺效果或讓人興奮的藥劑，常見的就是安非他命、古柯鹼、大麻之類的。

❷ fined，動詞被動式，被罰款的意思，fine 可以做為名詞是罰金的意思，所以不是只有 I'm fine, thank you 的時候才會用到喔。

❸ thrifty，形容詞，在金錢使用上很小心、節儉的意思。但是 thrifty 不是指一個人有節儉美德的意思，而是比較類似小氣，當你看到一個人老穿舊衣，就可以說他很 thrifty。但是最近因為一首流行歌，Machlemore 跟 Ryan Lewis 的 Thrift Shop 的關係，thrifty 變得有點酷，thrift shop 就是當鋪的意思，而從當鋪買來的二手舊衣跟首飾本該是很醜很跟不上流行的，但是因為歌裡面歌手們把當鋪買來的東西穿得很潮，所以現在 thrifty 也可以是滿酷的意思。

監獄人口氾濫（二）

 情境對話  Track 81

Jackson 跟 Aaron 繼續討論著美國監獄管理失調的問題。

Jackson: I've also heard how the prison health care is pretty [1]**jacked up**, too. Government has cut their budget so much that they can't afford to have sufficient amount of prison staffs, 50 people died in eight months in an Arizona prison back in 2013, another prison I've heard, put sugar into a woman's C-section.

Aaron: That's just depressing, I understand that prisons are for bad people, but at the end, they are all human beings just like us, the whole system just seems fundamentally [2]**wacked up**.

Jackson: It's a fact that needs to be spoken more, America's prisons are pretty [3]**screwed up**. It's a hard truth about incarceration. Prison is needed for

我還聽說監獄裡提供的醫療也被搞得很混亂，政府過度縮減預算導致他們無法負擔起雇用足夠的監獄工作人員，2013 年的時候亞利桑那州的監獄在八個月內死了 50 個人，我還聽說另一個監獄在一個剖腹產的女人傷口上灑糖。

那真是讓人感到憂愁，我了解監獄是給壞人待的地方，但是說到底，他們跟我們一樣都是人啊，整個系統基本上看來就是壞掉了。

這是個需要被討論的事實，美國的監獄真的很糟糕。這是個關於監禁很難讓人接受的事實，文明社

a civilization, but we can't just lock those people away and forget about them. What we need to do is figuring out a way to help them get back on their feet and become a functionable member of the society.

會是需要監獄的，但是我們不能只是把那些人關起來然後就把他們忘了。我們需要做的是找出幫助他們回歸正常生活的方法，讓他們能夠成為社會上有功能的一員。

Glossary 髒話大解

❶ jacked up，形容詞片語，指某件事不太對的意思，大致上是指混亂的狀態，常常用在 to jack someone / something up，讓某人或事變得很混亂、很糟糕的意思。有些時候意思可能會不一樣，因為 to get jacked 也可以是被打受傷或因藥物很興奮的意思，所以單看對話內容而定。

❷ wacked up，形容詞片語，單看 wacked 通常是指頭部被重創的意思，所以被重創以後的事當然就是很糟糕了，所以 wacked up 就是指某人或事被搞得很糟糕的意思。用法很類似 messed up。

❸ screwed up，形容詞片語，指某件事被搞得很糟或人心裡上出問題，用法跟 fucked up 一樣。screw 跟 fuck 兩個字其實是一樣的意思，所以替換著用也是行的通的，像是 fuck you 也可以說成 screw you。

自以為（一）

 情境對話  Track 82

美國的保釋系統越來越精彩，現在連電視節目都有了，Assad 跟 Chase 剛剛看完一集賞金獵人電視真人秀⋯

Assad: America's bail system has proven itself to be better for the reality TV industry than it is for the justice system. I strongly believe that law enforcement should be left to professionals.

美國的保釋系統已經證實了它比較適合電視真人秀業界，而不是司法系統。我強烈的認為執法應該留給專業的人。

Chase: I totally agreed on that too. Those guys on TV are just [1]**thugs** without any real training or authority.

我也完全認同。那些電視上的傢伙們不過是群沒有接受過正式訓練，也沒有實權的惡徒。

Assad: What is with this country and its fascination with weaponry? Cops want to act like the military and have tanks and ATVs. Civilians want to act like cops and carry tasers and guns, a stiff population of people are religiously against gun control, federal defense budget is higher than the next 10 countries' combined, and you have the highest stockpile of nuclear weapons in the world. All of

這個國家跟它對於兵器的迷戀到底是有什麼問題？警察想要跟軍人一樣有坦克和全地形車，一般民眾想要跟警察一樣有電擊器和槍，還有一堆死硬派的人很篤信地反對槍械管理，聯邦國防的預算比後面排名接下來十個國家加起來的都要多，而你們還

these is because the ^{2}**obtuse** society elected a party of ^{3}**insane** people.

有全世界最多的核子武器庫存。這些全部都是因為這愚鈍的社會選出一黨派的瘋子的關係。

Glossary 髒話大解

❶ thug，名詞，惡棍，指那些有暴力傾向的人，通常是罪犯。這個字的來源是從印度來的，19 世紀初印度有一群由強盜跟刺客組成的宗教組織，是女神 Kali 的信徒，這些惡徒會搶劫旅客並以一個制定的儀式殺害他們的受害者，後來在 1830 年左右被英國政府控制住。現在常常被用來稱呼流氓之類的人，也有白人用來蔑稱黑人用，因為不想要因為說 nigger 這個字被抨擊，所以改說 thug。

❷ obtuse，形容詞，愚鈍的、令人感到厭煩、遲鈍的意思。也可以用來罵胖子，因為 obtuse angle 指的是大於 90 度，不超過 180 度的鈍角，可以說是 big fat angle，又大又肥的角度，所以也被用來嘲笑胖子用。

❸ insane，形容詞，指那些無法正常思考運作，有嚴重精神病的意思。

自以為（二）

Chase 對於 Assad 對自己國家的評價感到不是很高興，所以予以反擊…

Chase: I beg to differ. America is not the one with the problem. We lead the world in innovation and have provided a template for democracy for other countries to use, which by the way is something that your country still needs to work on.

我不同意。美國不是那個有問題的。我們引領世界的創新，並為其他國家提供民主的樣本，附帶一提，是一件你的國家還需要學習的事。

Assad: Excuse me, but you gotta admit, this country is fucked up in many aspects. Like how you came off as a [1]**pompous snot** just now. Ironically, this is how Americans are perceived in a lot of countries. You should be trying to debunk that [2]**stereotype**, not reinforce it.

不好意思，但是你得承認，這個國家很多方面都一團糟。就好像你剛剛表現得像是個自大傲慢的勢利鬼。很諷刺的，這是很多國家對美國人的看法。你應該要試著洗刷那刻板印象，而不是強化它。

Chase: My apologies. The way you commented on this country also came off that way and was the reason for my [3]**snobby** response.

我道歉。你對這個國家的評論方式也是一樣的表現，所以我才會也那樣傲慢的回應。

Assad: Fair enough. I'm sorry if you misunderstood me. Cheers.

很公平。對於你的誤解我感到抱歉。乾杯。

Chase: Cheers.

乾杯。

Glossary 髒話大解

❶ pompous snot 的 pompous 為形容詞，自大的，用來形容後面的 snot，但是其實 snot 指的就是高傲自負的人，所以前面的 pompous 算是累贅，但是也是 Assad 強調他認為 Chase 真的太高傲。snot 本身是鼻涕的意思，可以想成是跟鼻涕一樣討人厭。

❷ stereotype，名詞，指對某種人或事物的刻版印象，通常是過於籠統簡單的概念，不能做為標準，像是黑人一定都很壞、很恐怖，或是亞洲人數學一定很好，還有 Assad 在這裡說的美國人都很傲慢之類概括的想法。

❸ snobby，形容詞，自以為是、勢利的意思。形容那些自認為是專家，還有喜歡表現自己高人一等、不尊重他人意見的人。

 情境對話  *Track 84*

Kevin 站在一家工資日貸款公司外面，猶豫著要不要進去借點現錢來付他的修車費，*Joey* 剛好從旁邊經過，看到 *Kevin*，於是決定上前去打招呼。

Joey: Hey Kevin! What's up man? How's it going lately?

嘿，Kevin！你在幹嘛啊？最近過得如何？

Kevin: Oh hey, Joey! Good to see you, I'm just here to get some cash for my car repair. Some mechanical issue that's going to cost me $2000, if I don't pay for it, I can't get my car back, and I need it to go to work.

喔嘿，Joey！看到你真好，我只是來這裡借點現金修車。機械上出了些問題，要花我美金 2000 元，如果我不付的話，車拿不回來，而我需要它去上班。

Joey: And you were going to go in there to borrow money? Gosh I'm glad I [1]**bumped into** you before you have done that. Those places are [2]**evil**. I worked for a short time for Quik Cash. They would continually tell us we were providing a service to people, but I could see first-hand how it was ruining people's lives.

而你準備要在這裡借錢？老天，我真高興我在你做這件事之前碰到了你。這些地方很惡劣的。我之前幫這種快速借款的地方工作過一小段時間，他們不斷地告訴我們是在為民眾提供服務，但是我親眼見到那是在摧毀那些人的人生。

Kevin: But I need the cash to pay for my car repair.

但是我需要現金付我的修車費。

Joey: Don't worry man. I'll ³**hook you up.**

別擔心，我可以借你。

Glossary 髒話大解

❶ bumped into，動詞片語，bump 本身是碰撞的意思，當你說 bump into someone 的時候是指你遇到那個人，而不是真的肢體上有接觸。

❷ evil，形容詞，非常邪惡的、惡劣不道德的的意思。

❸ hook you up，動詞片語，借你某樣東西的意思，在這裡講的是 Joey 願意借 Kevin 錢，另外其他時候像是如果你幫某人個忙之類的也可以說 hey, I'll hook you up，不一定是有實質上的物品交換。要注意，hook someone up 跟 hook up 的差別，hook up 可以是接管線之類的動作，但是也可以做為跟某人發生性關係的意思，通常是指一夜情的那種，不是情侶之間的性關係，hook you up 跟 hook up with you 意思差很多，所以千萬別說錯喔！

Chapter 85

合法高利貸？！（二）

Kevin 對於 Joey 願意大方的幫忙感到非常感激，連忙保證會盡快還錢。

Kevin: Geez, thanks for doing this man, I'll get the money back to you as soon as my next paycheck comes in.

老天，真是感謝你願意這麼做，我下個薪水支票進來的時候我會立刻把錢還你。

Joey: No problem, just remember, don't ever attempt to go to these places again. Payday loans put a staggering amount of people in debt. They're [1]**godawful**, and nearly impossible to regulate. Do you know that some places even put out 1900% APR?

沒問題，只要記住，別再試著進這些地方。這些工資日貸款讓很大量的人負債。他們非常糟糕，而且基本上沒有辦法監控。你知道有些地方甚至會發給 1900%的年利率？

Kevin: What?! Not even the [2]**Mob** has 1900% interest rates! And that's legal? There're no regulations defining annual interest rates greater than, say 70%, as [3]**loan shark**, which is illegal?

什麼？！連黑手黨都沒有 1900% 的利息！而且這是合法的？難道沒有法規訂定年利率不能高於，就說 70%吧，像放高利貸一樣是違法的？

Joey: Because using an APR as a way to compare would mean that you're directly

因為用年利率來算的話，就表示你是直接在比較一

comparing a loan with a due date of 2 weeks to a loan with a due date of 20 years. They're totally different. These loans also are typically being taken by people who couldn't afford the loan in the first place and took it out anyway.

個還款期限兩個星期跟一個還款期限 20 年的貸款。他們是不一樣的。會貸這些款項的人通常就是那些根本付不起的人，但是還是貸下去了。

Glossary 髒話大解

❶ godawful，形容詞，指某個人或事物很猥瑣、太可怕了、非常糟糕的意思，其實跟 awful 意思一樣，只是更上一層樓、神等級的可惡。

❷ mob，名詞，一開始是義大利西西里島來到紐約的 Mafia 黑手黨最有名，現在基本上只要類似的非法組織都叫 mob。另外如果街上群眾暴動也可以叫 mob，只要是一群人，特別是指胡作非為、製造麻煩或暴力的都可以稱作 mob。

❸ loan shark，名詞，放高利貸的人或組織。

 情境對話 ┼  *Track 86*

Ron 因為超速被警察攔車，正好當時車上帶著準備去買另一台車的 $20,000 現金，警察先生堅持那是跟毒品相關的錢所以全部沒收。現在 Ron 正在跟他的朋友 George 討論這件事。

George: Remember, when a cop asks if you have cash or other items of interest in your car, YOU DO NOT HAVE TO ANSWER. If they ask you to step out of the car, say "Are you detaining me, officer?" If they say no, ask "Am I free to go?" If they insist on the questioning, say "May I contact my attorney?" You have rights, use them.

記住，當一個警察問你車裡有沒有現金或其他特殊物品，你沒有必要回答。如果他們要你下車，就說：「你準備要拘留我嗎，警察先生？」，如果他們說不，就問：「我可以走了嗎？」如果他們執意要審問你，就說：「我可以打電話給我的律師嗎？」你是有權利的，善用它們。

Ron: We have no rights. Even if you do all that, they can just shoot you and claim you deserved it.

我們根本沒有權利。就算你真的做了那些事，他們還是可以開槍射你，然後說那是你自找的。

George: You have an unhealthy level of [1]**paranoia**, my friend. I've dealt with many

你有著很不健康程度的妄想症，我的朋友。我遇過

cops, I have yet to encounter one that was [2-1]**bigoted** or even [3]**barbaric**. I do acknowledge that such police exist. However, please do not look at a random cop you see as a murderer. A very small percentage of cops are like that. Don't hate them all, hate individuals, not groups. That would make you the [2-2]**bigot**.

很多警察，但是還沒碰過一個持過度偏見或甚至是野蠻的。我知道有那樣的警察存在。但是別看到任何一個警察都當作是殺人犯。那樣的警察佔得百分比是很小的。別仇視所有的警察，仇視個體，而不是團體。要不你就是那個偏執的人。

Glossary 髒話大解

❶ paranoia，名詞，妄想症，一種精神疾病，特點是誇大自身的重要性，老是認為自己會被迫害，毫無理由的懷疑他人，嚴重點的會跟社會脫節。

❷ 第一個 bigoted 為形容詞，第二個 bigot 則為名詞，指那些對他人充滿偏見，容不下自己認知裡所謂的「正常」以外的意見，特別是指那些歧視其他種族或同性戀的人。

❸ barbaric，形容詞，這裡是用來形容殘忍野蠻的警察，但是也可以用在生活方式很原始未進化的人身上。

Chapter 87

壞警察（二）

Ron 仍然為了發生在自己身上的事感到非常氣憤，所以繼續發表著他對警察的偏見。

Ron: Any of them can be murderous on any given day. It varies depending on what [1]**color** you are. The government is the one arming them and training them, they won't hold them accountable so we're the ones to get [2]**fucked over**. The [3]**KGB** was at least trying to keep their stuff secret, but the US police don't care if they do the same thing in broad day light. They have the tendency to terrorize the people into submission. It's all about intimidation and fear.

他們當中任何一個在任何一天都有可能殺害某人。情況的不同跟你的膚色有關係。政府是給予他們武器還有訓練他們的，他們才不會追究他們的責任，所以我們只能坐著等死。克格勃至少還會秘密進行，但是美國警察根本不擔心在大白天做一樣的事。他們有威嚇民眾讓他們服從的傾向。這全是關於恐嚇跟恐懼。

George: Unless they have a search warrant or probable cause, they cannot touch you or your property, but once you open the door of consent, they can do almost whatever they want. Don't lose your temper. Don't make sudden movements. And don't panic. Be calm, speak clearly, and don't be intimidated.

除非他們有搜索證或是合理的理由，他們不能碰你或是你的所有物。但是一旦你開啟了同意的大門，他們幾乎可以做任何他們想做的事。別發脾氣，不要有突然的動作，還有別慌。保持冷靜，口齒清晰，還有別被唬住了。

Glossary 髒話大解

❶ color，名詞，在這裡是指皮膚的顏色，任何有色人種都可以叫做 colored person，colored 是形容詞，皮膚有顏色的意思，其實這麼稱呼人是很沒禮貌的事，是以前白人對有色人種的一種蔑稱方式，現在可能也還聽得到，但是會這麼說的通常就是有種族歧視，瞧不起人。

❷ fucked over，形容詞片語，被不公平的對待、被佔便宜、被整很慘的意思。

❸ KGB，名詞，Komitet Gosudarstvennoy Bezopasnosti 的簡稱，蘇聯的中央情報局，活躍於 1954 至 1991 年，有人稱克格勃，類似美國的 CIA，是蘇聯秘密警察的組織，他們以手段殘忍為名，使用酷刑和處決的方式來解決蘇聯的問題。

國會選舉（一）

國會中期選舉正在接近中，最近州議員們通過了許多法案，但是有人發現這當中，有些法案是議員們由 ALEC 抄襲而來的，雖然如此，選舉仍然照常舉行。

Carol: What's ALEC?

什麼是 ALEC？

Pam: It stands for American Legislative Exchange Council. So it's basically a conservative bill mill that brings State lawmakers, conservative think tanks and corporate interests together, to introduce legislations to State Houses and get them passed across the country.

那是美國立法交流委員會的縮寫。所以基本上那是個將州議員、保守派智庫跟大公司權益結合在一起的保守派的法案工廠，將法案介紹給州議院，然後讓他們在國家裡通過。

Carol: That sounds so [1]**bizarre** and [2]**shady**! So you're telling me that the elected congress men aren't even doing their job? They're paying someone else to do their job? That's just wrong.

那聽起來好詭異、好可疑喔！所以你是在告訴我那些選上的議員們根本沒在做他們的工作？他們花錢請人做他們的工作？那是不對的。

Pam: Well... I wouldn't say all of them are like that, one Minnesota law maker was confronted by his colleague about a

嗯…我不認為他們全都是那樣，有一個明尼蘇達州的立法者就因為一個看起

bill that looks exactly the same as the one on ALEC's website.

來跟 ALEC 網站上一模一樣的法案，而被他的同事當面對質。

Carol: That's just [3]**pathetic**.

那真是可悲。

Glossary 髒話大解

❶ bizarre，形容詞，形容詭異的、不尋常的、奇怪的事物，比較常用在有趣的事物上，像是滑稽可笑的衣服就可以叫做 bizarre clothing，怪異的行為舉止就是 bizarre behavior。在這裡是指國會議員讓別人幫他們寫法案是件很詭異可笑的事。

❷ shady，形容詞，在這裡是指國會議員做的事是可疑、偷偷摸摸、不誠實的意思。也可以用來形容很陰暗、很沒有存在感的人，a shady person。

❸ pathetic，形容詞，很可悲的、遺憾的意思。通常是因為某件疏漏或悲傷的事所造成的遺憾感。在這裡是因為覺得議員無能到讓人感到悲哀。

國會議員被爆料這種醜事，但是社會關切度卻不高，實在讓人感到憂心，
Pam 為此而有感而發。

Pam: This sort of lack of accountability behavior is making the Congress the [1]**frat house** of democracy. And yet nobody is paying attention to this madness.

這種缺乏責任感的行為使國會成為民主的聯誼會所。然而還是沒有人對這亂象表達關注。

Carol: Well... I'll make sure to pay more attention now before I go in to vote on Tuesday.

嗯…我星期二去投票之前會特別注意一下的。

Pam: I'm afraid it's too late, sweet heart. Because an estimated 30% of the candidates are running unopposed. Their sole political asset is that they exist. And they're going to win. Remember the [3]**midget** tossing guy on the news a few days ago? And the woman who has an interesting theory about black prison population? The Islamic cancer guy? They are all going to win because they have no opponent!

甜心，恐怕已經太遲了。因為大約有 30%的競選者是沒有競爭對手的。他們的存在就是他們唯一的政治資產。而他們會贏。記得前幾天那個丟侏儒來玩的男的嗎？還有那個對黑人監獄人口有著有趣的理論的女人？那個稱回教是毒瘤的男人？他們都將要贏得競選，因為他們沒有競爭對手！

Carol: [3]Boy! I wonder what the Congress is going to turn out to be like in the next several years.

哦喔！我懷疑接下來幾年國會會變成什麼樣子。

Glossary 髒話大解

❶ frat house，名詞，fraternity house 的俗稱，fraternity 是兄弟會，指的是大學裡男學生組成的聯誼會之類的組織，通常這些人住在一起，或是有個屋子一起活動，那屋子就叫做 fraternity house，通常會以二到三個希臘字母取名，這些人平常沒事就喜歡搞秘密集會，然後計畫一些很愚蠢瘋狂的事，辦很瘋狂的派對，通常只要不要太誇張，就不會有人管，所以在這裡 Pam 會把國會比喻成兄弟會的聚會場所，因為他們做了這麼多的壞事，可是還是沒人管。

❷ midget，名詞，侏儒，身材比一般人小很多，但是比例算正常，是侏儒們不想被稱呼的詞，比較正面的詞就是 dwarf、little person 或是 person of short stature 之類的。

❸ Boy! 在這是感嘆詞，Carol 不是在稱呼誰，也不是在叫誰，而是在表示驚訝，通常說 "Oh boy!"，但是 "Boy!" 單獨意思也是一樣的。

 情境對話  *Track 90*

大考將至，學生們開始感到有壓力了。在紐約南哈德遜谷，很多學校回報有超過 25%的學生選擇以不去參加考試，來表示對基測的不滿。

Isabella: Did you know that the entire class [1]**boycotted** the test today in Adam's class? Adam's teacher told me that there were kids crying and throwing up during tests because of the pressure! In fact, this happens so much. There is an official guideline for the test administrators on how to handle the situation.

你知道今天 Adam 班上所有的學生全部一起抵制參加考試嗎？Adam 的老師告訴我，曾經有小孩在考試期間因為壓力哭出來，還有吐了的哩！事實上，這種事太常發生，現在有了一個正式的指南教主考官如何應對這個狀況。

Alex: Something is obviously wrong if we have to assume a certain number of students are going to throw up during their test. That "No Child Left Behind" policy had increased the amount of mandated tests by three fold. After Obama took office, he added his own educational initiatives like the "Common Core" that feature a logo of snails [2]**sixty-nineing**.

這很顯然地就是有問題，如果我們需要假設有一定數量的學生會在考試期間嘔吐的話。那個「不讓任何孩子落後」的政策已經給國家指定考試的數量增加了三倍。Obama 選上總統以後，還加上他自己的教育提倡，像是那個有個兩隻蝸牛口交標誌的「共同核心」。

Isabella: Hahaha... You know they meant well. The problem is how they implement. You should hear what Amy's kids had on their test last week, the content is full of [3]**fatuity.** I don't even know how they got there in the first place.

哈哈哈⋯我知道這些本意是好的，問題是在實行的方式上。你該聽聽上星期 Amy 的小孩考了些什麼，那內容充斥著愚蠢，我壓根兒不知道它們怎麼會出現在那。

Glossary 髒話大解

❶ boycott，動詞，抵制的意思，這個字的起源於 19 世紀末有個叫 Captain Charles Boycott 的愛爾蘭退休軍人，因為代替當時的某個地主去收房租，還有把繳不出房租的住戶趕走，當時正因為飢荒還有戰爭，正是大家生活得很困苦的時候，農民們團結起來形成一個聯盟，Boycott 因此被抵制，他家的僕人全部辭職不幹，所以他的田地沒人照顧，作物全部都爛光光，這件事很快地傳開，因此他的名字就成了這種抵制抗議策略的代名詞。

❷ sixty-nineing，動詞進行式，sixty-nine，也就是 69，是從法文的 "soixante neuf" 直接翻譯來的，字面上的意思就是來做 69，69 取的就是 6 跟 9 剛好就是彼此顛倒的形式，就是指兩個人同時為對方做口交時的動作。

❸ fatuity，名詞，用來罵愚蠢的事或人。用法類似 stuipidity、imbecility 之類的。

基本能力測驗（二）

Isabella 跟 Alex 討論著基準測驗的弊端，現在正準備要跟 Alex 分享她從 Amy 那裡聽來的愚蠢考題內容。

Isabella: Almost thirty different questions have now been declared invalid, because they are confusing and have errors all over the place. One of the bizarre questions includes a talking pineapple. This is how it goes. A pineapple challenges a hare to a race, and other animals figure it has a trick up its sleeves, but the hare wins and the animals eat the pineapple at the end.

幾乎有三十個不同的問題已經被宣告無效，因為它們太撲朔迷離而且錯誤百出。其中一個詭異的問題包括一個會說話的鳳梨。題目是這麼問的：有個鳳梨對一隻兔子挑戰賽跑，其他動物們都認為它有什麼預藏的詭計，但是兔子贏了，然後動物們最後就把鳳梨吃掉了。

Alex: That's [1]**absurd**!

那真是荒謬！

Isabella: I've even heard, the Pearson Company, you know, the company that made all the exams, posts ads on Craigslist to find people to grade the exams.

我還聽說皮爾森公司，你知道的，那間出這些考題的公司，在 Craigslist 上面登廣告找改試卷的人。

Alex: They look for graders the same way people buy second hand [2]**garbage** and

他們在那個大家買二手垃圾，還有找不用負責的手

[3]**no strings attached** [4]**handjob? That's just great.**

淫的網站上找改試卷的人？那真是好極了。

Glossary 髒話大解

❶ absurd，形容詞，用來形容荒謬的、荒唐的人或事。

❷ garbage，名詞，垃圾、沒用的東西，在這裡是 Alex 指在 Craigslist 上買到的二手物品都是垃圾，其實是有些誇張啦，但是也相差不遠。

❸ no strings attach，形容詞片語，字面上是沒有線牽連著，所以解釋成在做某件交易的時候沒有限制，不用負責任，沒有附帶條件的意思。也可以用在幫別人忙不求回報，或是男女交往沒有互相限制，還同時跟其他人交往之類的狀況。Craigslist 這個網站是專門讓人貼廣告，看物品上的買賣、找室友、徵人，甚至有找一夜情對象的，有很多不入流的事發生，所以 Alex 才會說居然在那種可以找到不用負責的性交易的網站上找改試卷的人。

❹ handjob，名詞，手淫、打手槍，可以是幫別人打手槍 give a handjob 或你得到這項服務 get a handjob，所以這邊才會說可以在網路上找不用負責任的打手槍服務。

 情境對話  Track 92

現在大學生畢業，十個裡面有七個負債，目前全美大學生的學貸總金額高達一兆美元。

Susan: My word of advice is the opposite of "pay it off immediately". I support the "income based repayment plan", once you give them all your information on how much you actually make and how much you pay in rent your payment can be as low as zero dollars a month! After enough decades paying whatever they deem is appropriate, your debt will be wiped clean.

我的建議跟「立刻付清」剛好相反。我奉勸各為用「收入基準的還款計畫」，只要把你的資料給他們，像是你一個月實賺多少還有你付多少房租，你每個月的付費可以低至零元！過足幾十年，在你支付過他們認為合適的數目以後，你的負債就可以抹清了。

Nathan: Awesome [1]**rebuttal**. (Turned to Samantha and Emma) Don't listen to her.

很棒的反駁意見。（轉向 Samantha 跟 Emma）別聽她的。

Susan: No, I was serious, I haven't been paying my student loan for the past three years and they haven't come to bother me, but there was another reason behind it. The loan company called me a couple

不，我是認真的，我已經三年沒有繳我的學生貸款了，而他們也還沒有來煩我，但是這背後另外有原因就是了。貸款公司打電

of times asking me to pay them more each month, and I told them I can't afford to pay more, it's not like I'm ²**splurging** or anything. I live in a bad neighborhood. I'm a white girl and I know white ³**crack** smells like, that's how bad it is!

話給我幾次，要我每個月多付他們一些，而我告訴他們我付不起更多，又不是說我亂花錢還是怎樣，我住在很不好的區，我是白人女孩，而我知道古柯鹼菸聞起來是什麼味道欸，知道有多差了吧！

Glossary 髒話大解

❶ rebuttal，名詞，反駁、通過相反的建議來反對的意思。通常是在辯論的時候，有一方先表示意見，然後另一方就會有反駁對方的意見，那個反駁的意見就是 rebuttal，類似 disagreement。也有玩遊戲時起死回生的意思，如果有一隊快要輸了，另一隊讓他們一次給他們扳回一城的機會。

❷ splurging，動詞進行式，大量的亂花錢、噴錢的意思，還有一個用法就是做為名詞的時候可以指射精的動作。

❸ crack，名詞，抽的古柯鹼，一般的古柯鹼是吸進鼻子裡的粉末，crack 則是指參了一點水跟蘇打，然後燒來抽的古柯鹼，所以有煙味，Susan 才會說她知道 crack 聞起來是什麼味道。

學生貸款（二）

 情境對話  Track 93

Susan 繼續跟朋友們分享她拒繳學生貸款發生的過程。

Susan: After telling him about my living situation, the guy on the phone told me I should [1]**prostitute** my way out of it since I can probably find that sort of clientele easily in that neighborhood. I [2]**flipped** and told him to go [3]**fuck** himself then hung up. They have never called me again since then.

在我告訴他我的居住狀況之後，電話上那男的告訴我，我應該出賣我自己來走出那裡，畢竟我住的區應該很容易找到那種客戶。我翻臉叫他去死然後掛電話。從此他們沒有在打給我過。

Nathan: Wow... Someone must've got [4]**shit-canned** after that.

哇…有人在那之後肯定被炒魷魚了。

Samantha: It's kind of sad that I consider myself lucky that I'll only be $20,000 in debt when I graduate.

這其實滿悲哀的，我覺得我自己算幸運的，畢業以後我只會有$20,000 的債務。

Emma: Do you think I should even go to college? I don't want to be in debt for the rest of my life.

你們覺得我該不該去上大學？我不想要一輩子負債。

Nathan: I had no problem paying off my

我付完了我的兩年專科學

two year college degree. Avoid the for-profits, they have a lot of hidden traps, poor job placement programs, and in some cases the degrees are not considered official. It all depends on what work you are aiming for.

位也沒甚麼問題。避免那些以營利為目的的，他們有很多隱藏的陷阱，很糟的就業安置計畫，而且有些時候學位甚至不被認為是正式的。完全取決於你想做什麼工作。

Glossary 髒話大解

❶ prostitute，動詞，在這裡是指電話上那男的叫 Susan 把自己當妓女賣了的意思。

❷ flipped，動詞，發飆、翻臉的意思，在此是指 Susan 跟電話上的男人翻臉的意思。

❸ fuck，動詞，是 Susan 因為生氣，所以叫那男的去 fuck himself。如果你是對著某人罵的話，就是說 go fuck yourself!

❹ shit-canned，動詞過去式，被炒魷魚的意思。shit-can 本身是名詞，字面上的意思是裝屎的罐子，也就是馬桶。做為動詞的時候就想像被丟進馬桶裡沖走，也就是公司不要你了，讓你滾蛋的意思。

 情境對話  Track 94

新聞記者採訪一位住在賭場附近的婦人，她敘述著自己如何常常要去買菜，卻兩手空空的回家，因為買菜錢全輸在超市裡的電子撲克機上。

Jack: I just can't feel sorry for that [1]**bitch** who spends her grocery money on video poker. It's not the state's fault if you can't manage the most basic of adult responsibilities.

我真的無法為那把菜錢花在電子撲克上的賤貨感到抱歉。如果你不能管理最基本成年人的責任，那不是州政府的錯。

Andy: But wouldn't you say it's the state's fault for not only letting this happen, but encouraging it by funding poker machines?

但是你不認為那是因為州政府的錯，不止是讓這種事發生，還有以資助撲克機器來助長它？

Jack: No, a responsible adult can play video poker without spending all of their money. It's self-discipline. The state has no responsibility to protect someone from their own [2]**capriciousness**.

不，一個有責任感的成年人可以在不輸光他們所有錢的情況下玩電子撲克。那是自我約束。州政府沒有責任要為了他們自己的任性保護某人。

Andy: It doesn't, but does that mean it's entitled to encourage and exacerbate irresponsibility via the media like what

它是不需要，但是難道那就表示它有資格經過媒體助長跟加劇這種不負責任

we just saw on TV?

Jack: McDonald's has commercials on TV too, but I wouldn't blame them if I ate there too much and got heart disease. [3]**Gambling addiction** is a thing, but so is [4]**alcoholism**, we don't ban alcohol to protect the people with the problem.

的事，就像我們剛剛在電視上看到的？

麥當勞在電視上也有廣告，但是我不會因為我太常吃然後得心臟病而怪他們。賭癮是一件事實，但是酗酒也是，我們沒有因為那些有問題的人而查禁酒。

Glossary 髒話大解

❶ bitch，名詞，賤貨、婊子，在這裡是因為 Jack 討厭電視上被採訪的那位婦人而這麼稱呼她。

❷ capriciousness，名詞，個人的任性、任意妄為，通常是指不好的事。

❸ gambling addiction，名詞，指賭癮這件事而不是人，上癮的人叫 addict，gambling 是賭博的意思，addiction 是指對某件事上癮，如果是酒癮就是 alcohol addiction，對非法藥物上癮的就是 drug addiction，以此類推。

❹ alcoholism，名詞，指酗酒這件事，酗酒的人叫 alcoholic，算是一種慢性疾病，因為依賴酒精反覆過度使用。

Chapter 95

賭癮（二）

 情境對話  *Track 95*

Jack 跟 Andy 在他們州政府設立賭場，還有合法化的賭博機器上抱持著不同的看法。兩人繼續討論著這個社會問題。

Andy: You're saying we don't ban it because it's too widespread and therefore difficult to remove. So we, as a society, should ¹**thwart** at a chance to improve ourselves because we are too lazy?

你是説我們不查禁它，是因為它散佈的範圍太廣，因而太難移除。所以我們這個社會，就因為我們太懶惰了，所以應該阻撓一個可以改善我們自己的機會？

Jack: In a free country, freedom comes with the chance you will ²**abuse** it. Alcohol is widely available, and it will cause problems with some. Same with unhealthy food and video poker. Others will practice restraint and enjoy the occasional beer, cheeseburger, or game of video poker. Part of being an adult is to maintain a balance. We can't punish the many for the faults of a few ³**degenerative gamblers**. Besides, history proves if you ban something people want it will be criminals who pick up the ⁴**slack**.

在一個自由的國家，隨著自由而來的就是能夠濫用它的可能性。酒精到處都有，而且它會對某些人造成問題。這跟不健康的食物還有電子撲克是一樣的。其他人會實踐克制，偶爾享受啤酒、起司漢堡或是電子撲克遊戲。維持平衡是做為成年人的一部分。我們不能因為少數墮落賭徒的錯而懲罰大多數的人。況且，歷史證明如果你查禁某樣大家都想要的東西，罪犯將會拾起這個漏洞。

Glossary 髒話大解

❶ thwart，動詞，對某件動作造成阻礙、防止實現某樣目地、阻撓某樣計畫。

❷ abuse，動詞，在這裡是濫用的意思，不正當地運用自由的權益。其他時候可以做為虐待的意思，physical or verbal abuse 就是身體或言語上的受虐，domastic abuse 就是家庭暴力，以上這些都是名詞，這個字可以做為動詞或名詞。

❸ degenerative gambler，名詞，指那些墮落到無法自拔的賭徒。degenerative，形容詞，是墮落、退化、腐敗的意思，gambler，名詞，就是賭徒。

❹ slack，名詞，在此是漏洞、疏漏的地方的意思，這個字本身是指繩子沒拉緊的部分，或是地面、山岳之間凹下去的地方。

萬聖節（一）

萬聖節即將到來，剩下的時間不多了，大家準備好你們的裝束了嗎？

Debra: The bit about Halloween costumes being sexy [1]**pisses me off** every year. My sister and I went through puberty early, by the time we were about nine, we had the bodies of adults. I wanted to be Hermione Granger, but all the costumes in my size were "sexy witch". What nine year old wants to show off her [2]**tits** and [3]**ass**? Why does everything need to be sexy? People in our hypersexualized world don't seem to realize it, but not everything needs to be sexy.

萬聖節服裝過於性感這點每年都讓我感到不快。我姊妹跟我提早經歷了青春期，在我們大概九歲的時候，我們的身體已經跟成年人一樣了。我想當妙麗・格蘭傑，但是所有我穿得下的尺寸的裝束都是「性感女巫」。試問有哪個九歲的女孩會想展現她的胸跟屁股？為啥所有的東西都需要是性感的？在我們這個高度性物化的世界裡，人們好像不了解不是所有的東西都一定要性感才行。

John: Why does everything come down to how sexy it is? Easy, because sex sells. Always has. Always will.

為什麼所有的東西最終都要歸結於它有多性感？很簡單，因為性有賣點。過去是，以後也是。

Evan: [4]Boohoo... something doesn't revolve around you and your sister. Deal with it.

唉唷討厭…有東西不是繞著你們姊妹轉的。接受現實吧。

Glossary 髒話大解

❶ piss off，動詞片語，當有事情讓你感到火大時說的，piss me off 就是讓我很生氣的意思，或是如果你在生氣想叫某人滾就說 piss off。

❷ tits，名詞，指女性的胸部，比較不文雅的用詞，正常應該說 breast。這個字本身是指小型的雀鳥類。還有一個用法是指很令人討厭的人。

❸ ass，名詞，在此是指屁股的意思，看狀況跟說法，也可以做為屁眼來用，還有當然就是用來罵討厭的人囉。

❹ boohoo，動詞，裝哭的聲音，通常用來諷刺嘲笑對方，這裡 Debra 剛剛抱怨完，Evan 就很假地裝哭說 Boohoo，但是其實一點也沒有為 Debra 感到不平，有點像中文的「唉唷～討厭啦～」那種很機歪感覺。

Chapter 97

萬聖節（二）

  **Track 97**

對於 Evan 的嘲諷，Debra 可是一點也沒在怕的，立刻反擊回去⋯⋯

Debra: Terror from the [1]**brony**, I'm so scared.

小馬兄在威脅我耶，我好怕喔。

Evan: [2]**Salty**, much?

生氣啦？

Debra: There's a time and place where [3]**scanty**, sexy clothes that leave little to the imagination are called for, and appreciated. Then there are times where it's out of place and pointless. Especially in October, when it's usually cold [4]**as fuck** on Halloween night.

有時候這些布料很少，很性感，不留遐想空間的服裝是被需要的，也會被賞識的。但是也有時候是不適當也沒意義的。特別是在十月份，萬聖節晚上通常很他媽的冷的時候。

John: Parents like to dress up their kids in ways that emulate adults. Look at kid's clothing, especially girls' clothes age two to seven. You're going to see a lot of it designed to emphasize or at least use optical illusions to make it appear that she has more breast and hips than the boys do, even though boys and girls bodies at that age are inherently the same basic

家長們喜歡把自己的孩子裝扮成大人的模樣。看看小孩的衣服，特別是二歲到七歲女孩子的衣服，你會看到很多設計是來強調或至少是用視覺效果來讓它看起來好像她有比男孩子大的胸或臀，雖然那個年紀的男孩跟女孩身體本

shape. Mommies and Daddies want their kids to look like themselves, or at least, what they'd like to look like.

質上是同樣的形態。媽媽跟爸爸們想要他們的小孩看起來更像他們自己，或至少是他們希望自己能看起來的樣子。

Glossary 髒話大解

❶ brony，名詞，用來嘲笑那些喜歡看彩虹小馬卡通的男性，是 bro + pony 合成的字，bro 就是 brother，兄弟的意思，pony 是小馬。也不是說 Evan 真的是 brony，只是因為他剛剛用 boohoo 這個很女性化的假仙哭法嘲笑 Debra，所以 Debra 才會這樣給他罵回去。

❷ salty，形容詞，形容生氣、被惹毛的狀況。在這裡是 Evan 明知道 Debra 被惹毛了，還這樣回她，像是說：「這樣就生氣啦？」的意思。

❸ scanty，形容詞，不足的、微薄的，在這是形容衣服布料很少。

❹ as fuck，形容詞片語，真他媽的的意思，對某件事感到不滿的時候加上的語助詞。

  *Track 98*

香菸製造公司早至 1950 年末就已經知道菸對人體的危害，甚至會引發癌症，一直到近年，美國政府才開始實行比較嚴格的管制。

Sophia: It's funny how cigarettes used to be the corner stone of American life, and movies and TV shows always like to portray them as an essential after sex element. They knew all along that it could cause infant deformity and cancer and yet, they are legal.

這真是挺有趣的，香菸曾經是美國生活的基石，而電影跟電視劇總是喜歡把他們描繪成性愛過後的必要元素。他們早就知道那會造成胎兒畸形還有癌症，但是他們還是合法的。

Sophia: My thoughts on the matter boil down to "If tobacco is legal, so should every other drug that is currently illegal. If other drugs are illegal, for example, [1]**marijuana**, then tobacco should be illegal as well." Consistency is all I ask, not double-standards nor [2]**hypocrisy**, just an even playing field for all whatever the end result happens to be. If you're not willing to let your local convenience store sell [3]**meth**, then there's no reason tobacco should be sold there either, because it is

我對這件事想法的歸結就是「如果菸草是合法的，那其它目前非法的藥物應該也要是。如果其他藥物是非法的，例如大麻，那菸草應該也要是非法的。」我想要的是一致性，而不是雙重標準或是偽善，只是給予那些結果相同的東西一個公平的競爭環境。如果你不想要你當地的便利商店賣安非他

similarly harmful, just in different ways.

命的話，那應該也沒理由在那裡賣香菸，因為它一樣是有害的，只是方法不同。

Glossary 髒話大解

❶ marijuana，名詞，大麻，常常被人拿來當作興奮劑的藥物，用過大麻後的效果常常聽到的有兩種，"high" 情緒高昂興奮的狀態，還有使用夠份量的時候的效果 "stoned"，就字面上的意思好像被石頭打到，不會痛，但是會暈暈的兩眼發直，通常瞳孔會放大，眼球會充滿血絲，反應變遲緩。

❷ hypocrisy，名詞，指假意、偽善的事。如果要罵一個人偽善、表裡不一就是 hypocrite。

❸ meth，名詞，methamphetamine 的簡稱，指安非他命這個毒品藥物，他會刺激人的中樞神經系統，給予用藥的人滿足感，但是很容易上癮，算是常見的刺激性藥物。在美國有醫生會給有 ADHD 的過動兒開這個處方做為治療，但是常常聽到醫生為了達到治療效果過度給病人施打藥物，結果造成更嚴重的後果。

 情境對話  *Track 99*

Emily 跟 Sophia 繼續討論著香菸跟其他藥物管制的問題。

Emily: The people who want to smoke should be able to, but even I, as a smoker, agree that no one should be lured in. I would not want my kids to smoke, but I do believe making something such as smoking illegal is wrong. And I don't think you should compare tobacco with marijuana or meth.

想吸菸的人應該要能夠吸菸，但是做為一個抽菸的人，連我也同意沒吸過菸的不應該被誘騙進去。我不會想要我的孩子吸菸，但是我相信讓吸菸這種事違法化是不對的。而且我不認為你應該拿香菸跟大麻還有安非他命相提並論。

Sophia: Explain to me please, how tobacco is less harmful than Marijuana while the [1]**mary-J** does not, explains why mary-J does not and the context, the specific effects that make the [2]**pot** worse. I'll give it to you that maybe meth is much more harmful than tobacco, but explain to me why tobacco gets this privileged place of legality when we know that it's just as [3]**bullcrap** as all the drugs we've decided are too much.

請你解釋給我聽，香菸是怎樣比大麻有比較少的害處，值得合法化，而大麻卻不行，解釋這前後的背景，讓大麻比較糟的具體影響。我可以同意或許安非他命是比菸草藥有害得多，但是給我解釋一下為什麼香菸可以獲得合法性這個特權，而我們都知道其實它跟其它我們認為太過的藥物一樣糟。

Glossary 髒話大解

❶ mary-J，名詞，另一種稱呼大麻的用詞。marijuana 的 j 其實是氣音，說的時候應該是像 h 的發音，不發 j 的音，之所以會是氣音是因為這個字是從墨西哥的西班牙文來的，西班牙文裡的 j 大部分都是發 h 的音，跟英文不一樣，筆者以前跟哥倫比亞來的朋友聊 MSN 的時候，對方每次打 hahaha 都是打成 jajaja，滿好玩的。但是這裡稱 Mary-J，那個 J 就是直接唸 J 這個字母。

❷ pot，名詞，又是另一個稱呼大麻的用詞，也是從墨西哥西班牙文來的字，potiguaya 或是 potaguaya，指一種有泡大麻苗的酒，傳到美國來以後就變成大麻的暱稱。

❸ bullcrap，名詞，字面上的意思是指牛大便，bull 是公牛，crap 是指廢棄物或糞便，用來表示很糟糕的事物，這裡是 Sophia 說香菸跟其他非法藥物一樣有害、一樣糟糕。這個字跟 bullshit 其實是一樣的意思。

Chapter 100

愛德華・斯諾登（一）

 情境對話  *Track 100*

有記者到俄國採訪 Edward Snowden，在新聞播放採訪過程以後，記者們也在紐約街頭採訪民眾對 Edward Snowden 的看法，但是很多人都不知道他是誰或做過了什麼。

David: It's sad how [1]**ill-informed** U.S. citizens are, myself included. I admit I did not understand the full ramifications or information of who Edward Snowden was or what he did. The only reason I even knew his name was because he was brought up a few times during the presidential debates. I knew that people were calling him a [2]**Benedict Arnold** and that he released valuable information, and some people thought he was doing good. That's it. It was a [3]**hyperbole** to say that about 40-50% of population knows about the issue, but as the two years have passed we are still immobile, about the NSA constant surveillance relying on sacrificing "little" freedom for safety.

美國居民的消息不靈通真的是很可悲，我自己也包括在內。我承認我是不知道整個細節或關於 Edward Snowden 是誰，還有他做過了什麼的資訊。我會知道他名字的原因是因為他有幾次在總統大選辯論會上被提到。我知道有人罵他是 Bennedict Arnold，還有他洩漏了有價值的資訊，而有些人認為他是在做對的事。就這樣。如果説 40 - 50%的民眾知道這個問題是誇張了，但是在經過了兩年以後，我們還是對 NSA 所謂的，為了安全犧牲「一點」自由的，不斷監視束手無策。

212

Dieter: How can Americans, even New Yorkers not know who Edward Snowden is? Back in Germany, every 4th Grader knows who he is, how about watch some news? The Americans do not care about national security of their own country?

美國人怎麼可能會，甚至是住在紐約的人都不知道誰是 Edward Snowden？在我的國家德國，每個小學四年級的學生都知道他是誰，也該看看新聞吧？美國人難道不在意自己國家的安全嗎？

Glossary 髒話大解

❶ ill-informed，形容詞，ill 通常是指生病，但是在此是狀況很差的意思，informed 就是被告知的意思，所以被告知的狀況很差就是消息不靈通。

❷ Benedict Arnold，名詞，在此是指 Edward Snowden 是大叛徒的意思。Benedict Arnold 是以前在美國革命戰爭期間的將軍，他在戰爭途中叛離美軍加入英軍，所以後來只要是出賣自己隊伍或國家，然後加入另一邊的叛徒就會被罵是 Benedcit Arnold。Edward Snowden 是個前中央情報局電腦專員，將大量的國家安全局機密提供給記者，目前逃亡到俄國，有人認為他是英雄，也有人罵他是叛徒。

❸ hyperbole，名詞，指某個說法過於誇張、不切實際。

Chapter 101
愛德華・斯諾登（二）

情境對話 Track 101

Dieter 對於美國人民的無知感到驚訝，David 則繼續接著解釋目前美國媒體的現象。

David: You saw why in the news segment. In the U.S. news and entertainment have been combined in order to keep the general population as uninformed as possible. So the average American cares more about Justin Bieber getting arrested in Florida than they do about the U.S. government slowly eroding our freedom and security for no reason other than they want to and they can.

你剛剛在新聞片段上看到了是為什麼。在美國，新聞跟娛樂圈被合併起來以確保一般民眾知道得越少的可能性。所以一般美國人比起關於美國政府沒理由地逐漸地侵蝕我們的自由還有安全，只因為他們想而且他們可以這麼做，反而比較關心 Justin Bieber 在佛羅里達州被逮捕。

Dieter: Sounds like U.S. media [1]**doesn't give a crap** about important news. They don't care about how the government propagandized people and leave them in [2]**apathy** and [3]**oblivion**. [4]**Ignorance** is a bliss? I would say it's the beginning of terrorism.

聽起來美國的媒體根本對重要的新聞漠不關心。他們不關心政府對民眾做不實的宣傳，而把他們留在冷漠跟遺忘當中。無知就是福？要我說那是恐怖政策的開始。

Glossary 髒話大解

❶ don't / doesn't give a crap，片語，意思是漠不關心，crap 跟 shit 是一樣的意思，大便或廢棄物，所以連屎都不想給，就是懶都懶的理、管都不想管的意思。I don't give a _____ 空格裡這個字可以用很多不一樣的字，crap、shit、fuck、damn 之類的都是一樣的意思，我根本懶的理。

❷ apathy，名詞，冷漠、對於大家都覺得有趣或感動的事物完全沒有熱情的表現。

❸ oblivion，名詞，在此是遺忘的狀態，也可以做為被遺忘的狀態，或是可以做為被完全毀滅或滅絕的狀態，if we don't preserve their habitat, the entire species will pass into oblivion，就是說如果我們不保存他們的生存環境的話，整個物種將會步入毀滅。

❹ ignorance，名詞，指缺乏知識、無知的狀態。

Chapter 102

報稅（一）

  **Track 102**

報稅的季節又到了，這大概是一年當中大家最討厭的時刻。

Mackenzie: If you need to visit the IRS office this year, prepare to wait. I got a warning letter and had to stop in yesterday, and guess how long I was there for? From seven to four!

如果你今年需要去國稅局，準備漫長地等待吧。我收到一封警告信函，所以昨天得過去一趟，猜猜看我在那等了多久？從七點等到四點！

Faith: It's always a [1]**dread war** around this time of the year. I think I'll just call them on the phone. I don't need to go in for anything.

每年到了這個時間總是要打場硬仗。我想我就打電話給他們就行了，我沒必要進去辦什麼事。

Machenzie: Well good luck my dear, I've heard there's only a total of four working phone lines nationwide and currently the "[2]**courtesy disconnect**" overload system is at a count of five million so far.

那祝你好運了親愛的，我聽說全國總共就只有四條打得通的電話，而目前那個所謂的「禮貌上斷線」的超載系統目前統計總數是五百萬。

Faith: I've always wondered why everyone hates the IRS so much. They're just doing their job. I don't understand why people are [3]**taking it out** on the IRS so much.

我總是在想為什麼大家都那麼討厭國稅局。他們只是在做他們的工作。我不懂為什麼大家都那麼愛拿國稅局出氣。

Glossary 髒話大解

❶ dread war 裡的 dread 是形容詞，恐怖的意思。war 是名詞，戰爭的意思，所以兩個字合在一起就是指很恐怖、很難打的戰爭，也就是硬仗。當然在這裡不是指真的有戰爭，而是指因為應付國稅局跟報稅是很令人頭痛的事，就像打仗一樣。

❷ coutesy disconnect，名詞，指電話系統如果響太久都沒接通的話就會自動掛斷，掛電話本來是很沒禮貌的事，虧國稅局想得出來，聲明他們是「禮貌性的」掛你電話。

❸ taking it out，動詞片語，對某人或物發洩脾氣的意思，如果你心情不好，去揍布娃娃之類的，就是在 taking it out on the doll，對布娃娃發洩你的不滿，當然不一定是有動手的狀況，只是對某人發脾氣也算。

報稅（二）

 情境對話  *Track 103*

Faith 對人們都非常討厭國稅局感到一頭霧水，但是該討厭的人到底是誰呢？

Faith: Not just regular citizens. Even State governors are publically [1]**demonizing** them. I've even heard our governor comparing them to the [2]**Gestapo**.

並不是只有一般民眾這樣，連州政府官員都公開惡魔化他們。我甚至聽我們的州議員拿他們跟納粹秘密警察來做比較。

Machenzie: Why do we hate them? Well... Dealing with them is obligatory. It often functions badly, and it involves two things we hate the most, someone taking our money and math.

我們為什麼討厭他們？嗯…應付他們是義務性質，它常常功能很差，而且它涉及到我們最討厭的兩件事，有人拿走我們的錢還有數學。

Faith: If you are angry about the amount of tax you're paying, that has nothing to do with them. That's determined by a voting Congress. And if you are angry about the tax codes that are too complicated, that's the Congress' fault, too. The fact is, blaming the IRS because you hate paying your taxes, is a bit like

如果你是對你繳稅的金額生氣，那跟他們沒關係，那是由被選出來的國會決定的。而如果你是為了稅法太複雜所以生氣的話，那也是國會的錯啊。事實上，因為你討厭繳稅就把責任歸咎於國稅局，有點

[3]slapping your check out clerk at the supermarket because the prices of eggs have gone up.

像是因為蛋的價格上漲了對超市的收銀員賞巴掌一樣。

Glossary 髒話大解

❶ demonizing，動詞進行式，把某個人或物惡魔化、魔鬼化的意思。demon 是惡魔的意思，加上 –ize 字尾就可以把名詞變動詞。

❷ Gestapo，名詞，是納粹統治期間，德國的秘密警察，於 1933 年組成，臭名昭彰、手段殘忍，現在被用來罵壞警察，或是像在這裡，州議員把國稅局比喻成 Gestapo，算是誇張的説法。

❸ slapping，動詞進行式，slap 是用手掌拍打的動作，在這裡是賞人巴掌的意思。

他們到底算不算是美國人？！（一）

 情境對話  Track 104

一百多年前美國最高法院通過決定不給予美國維爾京群島、波多黎各、關島以及北馬里亞納群島境內的居民身為公民同等的權益，讓他們至今仍然不能在議會上派有代表。

Joseph: Do you know that there are U.S. citizens that are not eligible to vote for president?

你知道有美國公民沒有權利選總統嗎？

Thomas: Never heard of it. Where is this happening?

聽都沒聽過，這在哪裡發生的？

Joseph: I met a guy the other day at work. Just moved here with his family from Peurto Rico. We were chatting about the presidential election and that's how I found out. They are considered as a belonging to the United States, but not a part of the State. Basically, when we took over their land, the judges of the Supreme Court had declared that the new territory is inhabited by [1]**alien races**, any they may not be able to understand [2]**Anglo-Saxon** laws. Therefore, the constitution doesn't apply to them.

有天我在工作上碰到一個男的，剛剛跟他的家人從波多黎各搬來，我們在聊總統大選的事，而我就是這麼得知的。他們被認為是美國的所有物，但是不是美國的一部分。基本上當我們占領了他們的土地，最高法院的法官們聲明說外來種族居住在新領地上，而他們可能無法了解盎格魯—薩克遜的法律。所以，憲法章程不會施行在他們之中。

Thomas: Wow... even I find that [3]condescending.

哇…連我都覺得那很沒禮貌。

Glossary 髒話大解

❶ alien races，名詞，指的是外來的種族，不是外星人種族喔！alien 這個字除了做外星人以外，指的就是外來的民族，諷刺的是這些人跑到人家土地上，然後說當地人是外來種族，其實他們自己才是。對於那些覺得外國人都應該滾出美國的白人種族，就可以回他們說，那他們應該也要滾回英國去，把土地還給印地安人。

❷ Anglo-Saxon，形容詞，盎格魯-薩克遜人的，歷史上是指從薩克遜跟南丹麥入侵日耳曼還有英國的種族，在北美現代人的用法裡指的是有英國血統的人，或是指說的話很低俗的意思。

❸ condescending，形容詞，有表示自我的優越感，讓人覺得沒禮貌的意思。

 情境對話  Track 105

Joseph 跟 Thomas 聊到關於美國政府對本土外的海島領地內的國民們給予他們不平等的投票權，認為這應該是幾十年前就該不再存在的問題了。

Joseph: (started speaking in a British accent) I do so wish we could explain the concept of voting to them, but their [1]**savage** little coconut brain would probably just collapse.

（開始用英國腔說話）我真的希望我們能對他們解釋選舉的概念，但是他們野蠻的小巧椰子腦袋大概會崩潰。

Thomas: Hahaha, they sure were the ones invented [2]**patronizing** [3]**bigotry**.

哈哈哈，他們的確是發明自大偏執的人。

Joseph: It's been about 140 years already. You would think our government would be working on making some changes already. It's like over a century, America computer is saying "An update to your country is available," and we've been clicking "Remind Me Later", again and again and again.

已經過了 140 年了，你認為政府會做些改變。那好像是過去一個多世紀了，美國電腦顯示「你的國家有項更新」，然後我們就一直在點「稍後提醒我」，一遍又一遍又一遍。

Thomas: Voting rights in this country are still very much a working progress it sounds like. It is an unsettling fact that I'm sure the congress knows about but choose not to think about.

聽起來選舉權在這個國家仍然有很多進度需要趕。我相信那是個國會知道卻選擇不去想的，令人不安的事實。

Glossary 髒話大解

❶ savage，形容詞，野蠻的、未開化的、殘暴的意思。也可以做為名詞，罵人是野蠻人或是沒人性的人。

❷ patronizing，形容詞，表現出自己高人一等的樣子，這裡是 Thomas 説英國人就是發明這種最自以為是態度的民族，眼高於頂，蔑視其他人種。

❸ bigotry，名詞，偏執，不容許別人有不同意見的狀態或行為，如果要罵那個人的話是用 bigot。

戰區翻譯不是人幹的（一）

 情境對話  *Track 106*

在阿富汗跟伊拉克戰區裡，幫美國軍隊翻譯的當地居民其實是冒著生命的危險在做這份工作的，但是美國移民局的繁文縟節，讓這些工作人員大部分都幾乎無法安全離開戰區。

Ray: Have you ever tried to plug in some sentences into Google translate and copy the translated sentences right back, and it doesn't turn out to be the same at all. And it's usually funny and [1]**stupid as hell**.

你有沒有在 Google 的翻譯網頁上打些句子，然後把翻譯好的句子再貼回去，結果出來會完全不一樣。那通常都很好笑而且蠢的要命。

Jack: Bad translation can be a lot of fun, when the [2]**stacks** are low. But if you are in a [3]**warzone**, accurate translation can be the difference between life and death. Do you know that many good local translators in Afghanistan and Iraq have saved countless American lives?

不好的翻譯可以很好笑，如果代價不高的話。但是當你在一個戰區當中，準確的翻譯可以決定生或死。你知道在阿富汗跟伊拉克有很多很好的當地翻譯救過無數的美國人性命嗎？

Ray: Sure, sounds cool.

是啊，聽起來很酷。

Jack: Ask any veterans. Their translators risked their own lives working for us, yet

問問任何一個退休軍人，他們的翻譯人員冒著自己

we have failed to provide the least we can do, provide them and their family safety, [4]**red tape** is making it impossible for many of them to leave.

的生命危險在幫我們工作，但是我們卻無法做到我們至少能做到的，提供他們跟他們家人的安全，繁文縟節讓很多的那些人根本無法離開。

Glossary 髒話大解

❶ stupid as hell，形容詞片語，stupid 就是很蠢、很笨的意思，as hell 是指跟地獄一樣，誇飾的方法，所以笨到地獄等級就是笨的要命的意思。as hell 其實可以加在很多形容詞後面，做為誇飾的用法來強調語氣，不一定是負面的意思，像是某人很聰明，讓你很佩服，就可以說 You are smart as hell!

❷ stacks，名詞，指一疊東西，像是錢、撲克牌、書之類的，在這裡是指所要付出的代價、後果的意思。stack 還有一種比較低俗的用法是指一千美元，one stack 就是一千美元，five stacks 就是指五千美元，通常是黑人或是窮人在用的說法。

❸ warzone，名詞，在這裡是指真正在打仗的戰區，但是這個字可以用在派對、酒吧、夜店之類的，指有些地方醜男醜女太多。

❹ red tape，名詞，指那些阻塞性的官方程序，費時的官僚機構處理事務的過程，在這裡是指美國移民局的申請過程。

 情境對話  *Track 107*

Jack 剛剛提到，在阿富汗跟伊拉克戰區幫助美軍的本地翻譯就因為一些無聊的移民程序，無法安全地離開他們的國家來到美國，Ray 感到好奇問道…

Ray: How so?

Jack: Because of what they are doing, they are permanent target for [1]**insurgents**. Even though they have applied for visa to come here, they're often stuck in [2]**bureaucratic limbo**. Through the Afghan Allies Protection Act, we should have been giving out about 1,500 special immigrant visas in 2009, but only 3 were issued.

Ray: You know why? Because Americans are afraid of anything related to Muslims or Islam, even the Muslim people that help them to fight [3]**terrorists**, would also be considered "potential threats". They were just purely [4]**racist** and let fear get the best of their judgment.

怎麼會？

因為他們所做的事，他們成為叛亂者的目標。雖然他們已經申請簽證來這裡，他們常常會卡在官僚體系的邊緣地帶。透過阿富汗盟軍保護法，我們應該在 2009 年發出一千五百多個特殊移民簽證，但是只有三個被頒發出去。

你知道為什麼嗎？因為美國人很怕任何跟穆斯林或是伊斯蘭教有關的事，就連那些幫助他們打擊恐怖份子的穆斯林人，也會被認為是「潛在威脅」。他們不過純粹就是種族歧視的人，讓恐懼勝過他們的判斷力。

Glossary 髒話大解

❶ insurgent，名詞，像政府或其他執法人員執行武裝抵抗，叛亂、引發暴動的人，美軍在伊拉克跟阿富汗境內稱呼恐怖份子的詞。

❷ bureaucratic limbo 裡的 bureaucratic 為形容詞，政府機構辦事的行事方式，也就是官僚體系的意思，通常是用來諷刺它們辦事很沒效率，limbo 為名詞，指某個人或事被遺忘的狀態，因為在政府機構裡需要通過層層的考察，有時候因為時間久了或哪裡出了問題卻沒人管，可能被忘記了，所以叫做官僚體系的邊緣地帶，因為是很容易被遺忘掉的部分。

❸ terrorist，名詞，恐怖份子，指的是那些用恐怖武力手法來達成目地的人，大部分是指伊斯蘭教派的激進派份子。

❹ racist，名詞，有種族歧視觀念的人。

Chapter 108

破爛到不行（一）

  *Track 108*

Emma 跟 Chloe 剛剛從一間餐廳吃完午餐出來，正在抱怨著餐廳老舊的廁所。

Emma: I like the food here, but the bathrooms are [1-1]**ghetto as hell**.

我喜歡這裡的食物，但是那廁所真的是破爛到不行。

Chloe: So ghetto, oh my gosh.

真的很破爛，我的老天爺。

Emma: They still have those double faucet sinks.

他們居然還有那種雙水龍頭的水槽。

Chloe: I hate that, what year is it? Please, [2]**get it togetha**!

我恨死那個了，都什麼年代了？拜託，認真點！

Emma: Right? And on the way here I took an UberX and the driver picked me up in a [3]**busted-ass** Toyota. And his wife was [4]**literally** in the front seat. So ghetto. So Chloe, how's your living situation?

對吧？而且我來的時候搭的是 UberX，但是司機卻是開一台破爛豐田來接我。而且他的太太還真給我坐在前座。真是有夠爛的。所以 Chloe，你的生活狀況現在如何？

Chloe: Oh, it's so ghetto. I'm still living with that family in low-income government housing.

喔，那真的是很糟。我還是跟那個政府輔助的低收入戶家庭住在一起。

Emma: You mean literally in [1-2]the ghetto. That sounds really awful. I'm sorry.

你是說你真的住在貧民區裡。那聽起來真糟糕。我很抱歉。

Glossary 髒話大解

❶ ghetto as hell，形容詞片語，指真的破爛到不行的狀況，as hell 之前提過是用來誇飾的詞。the ghetto，名詞，指的是貧民區。Ghetto 這個字可以做為名詞指貧民區，也可以做為形容詞形容跟貧民區一樣很破爛、很糟糕的狀況，像這裡被用來形容廁所的裝潢，Uber 司機載著老婆做生意，而且車子還很破爛，還有 Chloe 的生活狀況。

❷ get it togetha，形容詞片語，正確說法是 get it together，指的是人事物失去控制，很需要好好整頓一番的意思，基本上只要你看不順眼的，就可以跟他們說 "get it together!"，意思是要他們認真點，別再亂七八糟給自己丟臉。

❸ busted-ass，形容詞片語，形容物品很破爛，人長得很醜，就是比較負面的狀態。

❹ literally，副詞，就是指字面上的意思。這個字想特別解釋是因為在這個句子裡其實根本不用出現，意義不大。literally 現在被年輕人濫用，好像是想要強調誇飾語氣，但是常常用在不對的地方，像是 "I literally dies of embarrassment."，說這句話的人不可能真的像字面上的意思，因為羞愧而死，所以用在這裡是錯誤的，figuratively 會比較恰當。

破爛到不行（二）

 情境對話  Track 109

Emma 跟 Chloe 接著聊到 Chloe 最近的居住狀況。

Chloe: Also, my roommate Mr. Ollie lost his job again, so he doesn't have his part of the rent for the millionth time and now he's back to selling pot again, so now our apartment is always full of [1]**randos.**

還有我的室友 Ollie 先生又失業了，所以他已經第 N 次付不出他那一份的房租，現在他又回去賣鍋子了，所以我們的公寓總是充滿著亂七八糟的人跟東西。

Emma: You need to move out of that place. Why do you live there?

你需要搬出那個地方。你為什麼要住在那裡？

Chloe: Because it's only 3 blocks from the train station. I'm in the city in under an hour. Oh, and they have the best [2]**franks.**

因為它離車站只有三個街區。我一個小時內就可以到市區內。喔，還有那裡有最讚的熱狗。

Emma: Oh, I love franks!

喔，我愛死熱狗了！

(A random man in dirty clothes who is pushing a shopping cart interrupts the two women.)

（某個穿著髒衣服的男人，推著購物車打斷兩個女人的談話。）

Man: Excuse me, is one of you Chloe?	抱歉，你們其中一個是 Chloe 嗎？
Emma: [3]**What the heck** is that?!	那是什麼？！
Chloe: Oh, that's my [4]**Uber cart**. Gotta go. I'll see you later!	喔，那是我的 Uber 推車。得走了。以後再見了！

Glossary 髒話大解

❶ rando(s)，名詞，random + people，指隨機式出現的人，通常是會讓人感到很奇怪，放錯地方，不該出現在那的陌生人。像是如果派對裡沒被邀請卻出現的人就可以稱做 rando。

❷ franks，名詞，不是人名喔，是 frankfurter 的簡稱，指一種用牛肉或是牛肉跟豬肉混合做成的，來自德國的熱狗，比一般的熱狗大支。

❸ what the heck，驚嘆詞，跟 what the hell 是一樣的用法跟意思，只是因為沒有提到 hell 所以比較不髒。

❹ Uber cart，名詞，用超市推車來接送人的 Uber，其實是不存在的東西，只是因為想要表示 Chloe 的生活方式真的很 ghetto，才會這樣説。美國街頭看到的遊民很多會推著從超市偷來的推車，裝著他們的所有物在街上晃。

臉書大掃除（一）

 情境對話  *Track 110*

Fidel 正在一邊喝下午茶，一邊跟朋友 *Jeremy* 還有 *Wendy* 聊到他很氣憤於因 *Manny Pacquiao* 公開發起的，在臉書上表示反對同性戀的文章。

Fidel: I'm really amazed that it took a [1]**homophobic** bigot like Pacquiao to unveil the ugly sentiments of some of my so called "friends" and "relatives" in my list of contacts on Facebook. I didn't realize that being bigoted and intolerant were Christian values.

我真是感到吃驚，有了像 Pacquiao 這樣排斥同性戀的偏執狂，才揭穿那些在我臉書聯絡人清單上自稱是我「朋友」跟「家人」的人的醜陋情緒。我都不知道偏執跟不寬容會是基督徒的價值觀。

Jeremy: That said, FB pre-spring cleaning is in order for us. I've already removed 20 of these [2]**pests** and it feels fantastic! Though my natural inclination was to bite their heads off, I've promised myself that I wouldn't allow these illiterate [3]**douched mops** to increase my blood pressure and give me wrinkles.

那就説了，我們的臉書春前大掃除即將就緒。我已經刪除 20 個這些討人厭的害蟲，而那感覺好極了！雖然我的自然反應是把他們的頭咬下來，我已經向自己保證過絕不讓那些沒知識的混蛋使我的血壓上升，還有讓我長皺紋。

Fidel: Oh if I see any "holier-than-thou",

喔如果我看到任何的「我

bible thumping, hate-filled, intolerant, anti-gay post on my feed, just go "Click" and they're gone, [4]**bishes**!

比你神聖」、拿聖經砸人、充滿仇恨的、不寬容的、反對同性戀的貼文出現在我的版面上的話，就只要「點擊」，然後他們就會消失了，爛貨！

Wendy: No need to stoop down to their level, my dear.

沒必要降低到他們的等級，親愛的。

Glossary 髒話大解

❶ homophobic，形容詞，排斥同性戀的意思，homo 是 homosexual 的縮減版，phobic 就是對某件事有恐懼、排斥、討厭的感覺，像是 clusterphobic，就是對擁擠感到恐懼或討厭的意思。

❷ pest，名詞，通常是指對農作物有害的害蟲，在這裡是 Jeremy 用來罵那些在臉書上公開反對同性戀的朋友。

❸ douche mop，名詞，douche 是 douchebag 的簡稱，原指女性私密處的盥洗用品，但是常常被用來當做罵人是混帳的意思，mop 是拖把，是 Jeremy 因為生氣所以把兩個一般不會想碰的骯髒物品合在一起用來罵人。

❹ bish，名詞，其實就是 bitch，通常是朋友之間用來說笑的說法，沒有帶有殺傷力的，還有如果是在不能說 bitch 的狀況下，就可以用這個字，像是工作場合。

臉書大掃除（二）

 情境對話  *Track 111*

Fidel、Jeremy 還有 Wendy 繼續討論著他們對於仍然有人敢公開表達對 LGBT 的厭惡的人感到不可思議。

Wendy: I can't believe there are still people who are bigoted against LBGT people, I mean, come on, it's 2016!

我不敢相信現在還有人會對 LBGT 抱有偏見，我是說，拜託，都 2016 了欸！

Fidel: Exactly! Their religion is taking them back to the dark ages!

就是！他們的信仰把他們送回黑暗時代。

Jeremy: I've told myself numerous times not to let those [1]**religious maniacs** get to me. They are ignorant and don't know any better, but if we hate them back, then we are no better. Forgiveness and tolerance is the key, and yes, I'm still working toward it myself.

我告訴自己很多次了不要讓那些宗教狂熱份子影響到我，他們是愚昧的，而且不知道怎樣才是對的，但是如果我們也對他們還以仇恨，那我們也沒好到哪去。寬恕與容忍才是關鍵，還有對，我自己也仍然在朝那個方向努力。

Fidel: I'm way over it! I used to entertain these [2]**buffoons** but not anymore. I've learned to click and delete and get rid of

我已經過了那個階段了！我曾經會去娛樂討好那些愚蠢的混蛋，但是不會再

these [3]bible thumping [4]morons, bub bye!

發生了。我已經學會了點擊，然後刪除，擺脫那些拿聖經砸人的白目，掰掰！

Glossary 髒話大解

❶ religious maniac，名詞，指對宗教有狂熱的危險份子，maniac 就是罵人是瘋子的一種説法。

❷ buffoon，名詞，通常是用來稱呼小丑的詞，但是也可以用來罵人很白癡、很愚蠢的意思。

❸ bible thumping，形容詞片語，thumping 有槌打的意思，聽起來像是説會拿聖經砸人的基督徒，其實是抽象地形容那些激進派的基督徒。

❹ moron，名詞，白目、蠢蛋的意思。是被用來罵那些愚蠢、缺乏良好判斷力的人，這個字曾經在心理學裡，也算是用在輕微智障的人身上的專業用詞，但是已經不再是了，因為被認為太具有攻擊性，很沒禮貌。

 情境對話  *Track 112*

新聞剛剛播報了國會議員對立法要求公司給予女性員工帶薪產假的投票結果，但是很可惜的大部分的議員都投了反對票。

Marcus: Disgusting. Seeing all the senators who voted against that legislation had campaign ads blathering about how much they love their mothers on Mother's day. Bunch of [1]**fuckwit.**

真噁心。看到那些議員們對那項條款投反對票，而在他們競選期間的母親節時，大放厥詞地說他們有多愛他們的母親。真是一群他媽的頭殼壞掉的白癡。

Joe: What's disgusting is your [2]**sexism.** Men have been held financially accountable for the choice to have children, either voluntarily as a breadwinning husband or involuntarily for child support for millennia and no one has ever had a problem with this. But when women are held financially accountable for the choice of choosing to have children, you call a "Mommy Tax" and demand the employers and tax payers be forced to remedy this injustice.

噁心的是你性別歧視的態度。男人們為了生小孩在經濟上被追究責任，不管是自願地養家糊口，還是非自願地子女撫養費已經幾千年了，也沒人對這有過抱怨。但是現在女人要為了生小孩在經濟上負責，你們就提議要有「媽咪稅金」，還要要求雇主們跟納稅人們被迫來彌補這項不公。

Marcus: Dude, I don't think we can act like we know better considering we don't push living human beings out of a small hole in our body.

老兄，就我們不用從我們身上的小洞擠出活生生的人來說，我不認為我們可以擺出我們才是對的的態度。

Joe: What the living fuck does that have to do with anything?

那他媽的跟什麼有關係了？

Marcus: Wow... You are clearly not a ³sexist individual at all.

哇…你很顯然地完全不是一個有性別歧視的人。

Glossary 髒話大解

❶ fuckwit，名詞，fucked + halfwit，指那些不會從失敗中學取教訓，不斷地做著愚蠢的事情，讓人很討厭。halfwit 就是智商只有別人一半的意思，fucked 是指 fucked in their head，腦袋有問題的意思，所以 fuckwit 就是「他媽的腦袋壞掉的蠢蛋」。

❷ sexism，名詞，基於性別而產生的歧視態度或想法，男女都有可能是性別歧視的受害者。

❸ sexist，名詞，指有性別歧視的想法的人。

Chapter 113 該不該有帶薪產假？！（二）

 情境對話  Track 113

Joe 剛剛發表了他對女人想要有帶薪產假的要求的看法，Marcus 諷刺過他 以後，他又繼續回擊…

Joe: Yep, I'm sexist because I don't let women get away with the delicate little [1]**damsel** act. You [2]**phony** [3]**sack of shit.**

是啊，我是有性別歧視，因為我不讓女人用嬌滴滴女的假掰形象來討便宜。你這袋虛偽的狗屎。

Marcus: Tell me the last time that you were pregnant because you clearly know how it feels.

告訴我你上次懷孕是什麼時候，因為你很顯然地知道那感覺如何。

Joe: So what, I have to believe everything women say about being women, regardless?

所以呢？我就不論如何應該要相信所有女人說過身為女人的話？

Marcus: The difference is that nearly the entire world agrees that women should get time off work after pregnancy. That is because women need to get pregnant in order to forward the species, and it's not an easy task.

不同的地方就在差不多全世界都同意女人應該要在生產完後休公一段時間。那是因為女人需要懷孕才能繁衍後代，而那不是件容易完成的任務。

Joe: The world can go to hell. The whole

全世界都可以下地獄去。

world used to be [4]**misogynist** and oppressive to women, so the world's opinion doesn't mean shit.

全世界也曾經是厭惡女人，還有打壓女人，所以這世界的意見連屎都不算。

Glossary 髒話大解

❶ damsel，名詞，曾經是用來稱呼年輕美麗的閨女，特別是貴族出生的，現在被降格用來稱呼妓女或是醜化女人的稱呼。

❷ phony，形容詞，指一個人很努力地要表現出不是自己原本的樣子，很虛偽、很假仙的意思。這裡 Joe 用 phony 來形容 Marcus 是因為覺得他自命清高地幫女人說話。

❸ sack of shit，名詞片語，sack 就是麻袋、袋子的意思，sack of shit 就是裝了一袋滿滿的大便，是 Joe 用來罵 Marcus 的話。

❹ misogynist，名詞，用來稱呼會仇視、排斥、瞧不起女人、虐待女人的男人，這個字是從希臘文的 misogynes "woman-hater" 來的。

 情境對話  *Track 114*

對於 Joe 偏激的發言方式，Marcus 也一再地表示不認同，兩人的唇槍舌戰繼續如火如荼的發展。

Marcus: I bet that your mother has great love and respect for you. And I bet that once you have a daughter, if any women have a low enough self-esteem to mate with you, you will change your mind.

我打賭你的母親一定給了你很大的愛與尊重。我也打賭你一旦有了自己的女兒，如果有女人的自尊夠低到願意成為你的伴侶的話，你會改變你的想法。

Joe: My mother, like my father, understood parenthood was a responsibility, which is why they married. My father's employers didn't give him a raise because he was keeping the human race going. When men make sacrifices after procreation, it's called responsibility. When women make sacrifices to procreate, it's called an injustice. You [1]**unabashedly** sexist [2]**piece of shit.** Answer me you little [3]**weasel,** why do men have to pay child support? Why are they punished for keeping the human race going?

我的母親，跟我的父親一樣，了解身為父母是個責任，所以他們才會結婚。我父親的雇主沒有因為他為人類的延續繁衍了後代而加薪。男人在生殖完後做的犧牲，叫作責任。女人生殖完做的犧牲，就叫做不公。你這塊不要臉的、性別歧視的狗屎。回答我，你這隻小黃鼠狼，為什麼男人就得付小孩的撫養費？為什麼他們就該為人類繁衍後代受到懲罰？

Marcus: Whatever you say, your [4]murican pride has blinded you. I'm not arguing with you anymore, peace.

不管你怎麼説，你自持的美國人驕傲已經蒙蔽了你自己，我不想再跟你爭辯，掰。

Glossary 髒話大解

❶ unabashedly，副詞，不要臉的、沒有羞恥心的、一點都不會為做錯某件事感到不安的意思。

❷ piece of shit，名詞片語，piece 是一塊、一片東西的意思，所以 piece of shit 就是 Joe 罵 Marcus 是一塊狗屎。

❸ weasel，名詞，黃鼠狼，是用來罵鬼鬼祟祟、狡猾的人。

❹ murican，名詞，用來蔑稱美國人的用詞，是對美國這個國家內的人表示厭惡的説法，American pride 其實是美國人所自豪的事，但是被稱做 murican pride 就是諷刺美國人驕傲的説法了。

強制最低刑期

十多年前一個身上藏有大麻的男人，因強制最低刑期而被判刑 55 年，新聞記者剛剛採訪了他現在已經是高中生的兒子，聽到的回覆真的讓人感到很心酸。

Ted: Everyone's heard of this one, "drugs can ruin your life, so when I catch you, I'm going to ruin your life". Quoted from a police officer.

大家都聽說過這個，「毒品可以毀滅你的人生，所以當我抓到你的時候，我就會毀了你的人生」。來自一位警察先生的名言。

Aubrey: There were people arrested on just allegations with drugs, through [1]**frame-ups**, [2]**racial profiling** and incarceration by [3]**plea bargaining**. There were also cases of overrated sentences of people who are supposed to be treated in [4]**rehab** then to be sent to prison for smaller drug cases. Putting drug offenders on lifelong imprisonment.

有人只因為被指控跟毒品有關就被捕，經由被陷害、種族分析還有通過監禁辯訴交易。也有高估量刑的案件，有些應該進勒戒所接受治療，而不是被送進監獄的小型毒品案件，給毒品罪犯判終身監禁。

Ted: The idea of prison as a way to reform people, kind of breaks down on its own, when the punishment takes away their entire life, and all you end up with is reforming people into corpses.

以監獄為感化人的方式，差不多就會自動瓦解了，當處罰奪走了他們的整個人生後，你所剩下的就是將人感化成一堆屍體。

Glossary 髒話大解

❶ frame-ups，名詞片語，讓無辜的人受害，這裡是指被陷害進監獄。

❷ racial profiling，名詞片語，racial 是形容詞，種族的意思。profiling 就是分析，在法律上，racial profiling 的意思是利用種族這個特性，來推斷一個人有沒有可能跟非法活動有關係，比如說有個黑人家裡很窮，被查到跟某個竊盜案有關，雖然沒有證據確鑿，警察還是可以逮捕他，就因為他的身家背景，認為他一定會做壞事，充其量就是個變相的種族歧視，還是合法的。

❸ plea bargaining，名詞片語，指的是檢察官跟被告之間協議，讓被告認一個比較輕的罪名，但是作為交易，要為檢方做些其它事，像是做證之類的，有時候被告明明沒有犯罪，但是卻也沒有辦法證明自己沒罪，所以往往非常有可能會接受交易。

❹ rehab，名詞，rehabilitation 的簡稱，在這裡是指吸毒的人去的勒戒所，但是英文的 rehabilitation 是復健的意思，吸毒的人是需要復健的，摔斷腿的人也是需要復健，兩種狀況雖然差很多，但是都是同一個字，所以如果聽到有人需要去 rehab，不見得表示他是因為吸毒才去的喔。

 情境對話 *Track 116*

Ed 跟 Walter 剛剛一起看完這個週末的總統大選辯論大會，兩人開始討論彼此的感想。

Ed: When Trump started speaking, I literally [1]**facepalmed** so hard that my head hit the wall behind me. This motherfucker is leading the polls right now!

當川普開始說話的時候，我真的給他臉摀得太用力，我的頭還去撞到後面的牆。這個幹他老母的混蛋現在正在選舉人民意上領先！

Walter: Well, one thing is in his favor. He tells the truth a lot. Something MANY of our current politicians simply can't do.

嗯，有件事對他是有利的，他非常的誠實，是件很多我們目前的政客們沒辦法做到的事。

Ed: There's a fine line between telling the truth and being an asshole. Also, insulting people to their faces shouldn't award him any respect. Where do you think he gets his huge [2]**ego**? You do realize a large portion of the people he insults are fellow Americans? Also, why does our claim to fame as a country has to be that we're rude and [3]**obnoxious**? Wouldn't you like

說真話跟做為一個混蛋只有一線之隔。還有，當面侮辱別人不應該給予他任何的尊重為獎勵。你認為他那龐大的自負到底是哪裡來的？你明白一大堆他侮辱的人都是我們的美國人同胞嗎？還有，為什麼我們國家的名聲一定要

to be known for anything else? I for one would be pleased to not be known as the "dumb, [4]loudmouthed American" everyone seems to think we are because of people like Trump.

是，我們很粗魯還有很討人厭？難道你不想要以其他事情為名嗎？我個人會很高興不要被認為是個，現在大家都認為我們是的，「愚蠢、大嘴巴的美國人」，就因為有人喜歡 Trump。

Glossary 髒話大解

❶ facepalmed，動詞過去式，是一個用手摀臉的動作，通常是因為受不了某件事、羞恥、或是憤怒而做的動作。

❷ ego，名詞，這個字的用法很廣泛，在這裡是比較負面的指一個人的自負、自以為是。比較一般的用法就是指一個人的自尊，"Your criticism wounded his ego"，你的評論傷害了他的自尊。還有就是指一個人內心的自我。

❸ obnoxious，形容詞，用在非常令人厭惡、讓人極度反感的人身上。

❹ loudmouthed，形容詞，用來形容嘴巴很大、口無遮攔的人，例如 Donald Trump。

社會保障津貼

 情境對話  *Track 117*

美國的國民社會保障津貼已經瀕臨破產，對此項問題，Zach 跟 Tyler 抱持著不同的看法。

Zach: Social security is one of the most [1]**foolish** and [2]**mindless** ideas ever conceived in the history of mankind, and it's the primary reason we are 19 trillion dollars in debt.

社會保障津貼是個人類有史以來構想出最愚蠢的主意，而它就是我們會負債 19 兆美元的原因。

Tyler: Social security is to take care of those people who already gave back to society. Seriously, even the most conservative people I know say that it's an American's duty to pay for and care for the elderly and disabled.

社會保障津貼是用來照顧那些已經對社會有過回饋的人。認真講，就連那些我認識的最保守派的人都說那是做為美國人的一項義務，出錢來照顧老人家跟殘障人士。

Zach: Why the hell can't people simply save up their own money for retirement? Social Security benefits even those who gave NOTHING to society, and does not benefit those who choose to continue to benefit society by staying in the work force. Or do you believe the law can

那些人該死的為啥不能自己為退休存錢？社會保障津貼甚至使那些對社會沒有貢獻的人受惠，而對那些留在工作崗位上，不斷對社會有貢獻的人沒有益處。還是你認為法律就永

never be wrong, which would make you a ³**mind-boggling** ⁴**hypo-critic.**

遠都不會有錯，那你就是個令人難以置信的偽善者。

Glossary 髒話大解

❶ foolish，形容詞，指某人或事的表現是思慮不周的、愚昧的意思。

❷ mindless，形容詞，也是指某人或事很蠢，因為沒用腦袋或沒有腦袋，所以做出蠢事。"a mindless creature" 就是指一個沒腦袋的生物。也可以用做漫不經心，"mindless of all dangers" 對所有的危險都漫不經心，所以不見得是用來罵人。

❸ mind-boggling，形容詞，通常是因為負面的事情，而讓人感到不敢置信的意思。

❹ hypo-critic，名詞，指那些自以為是的、愛批評人的人，其實自己好不到哪裡去。就是那些嚴以律人、寬以待己的人。

Chapter 118

現代人生活真辛苦

現代的人賺錢養家不容易，在過去，一個人的薪水就夠養一大家子的人，為此 Ryan 忍不住地抱怨⋯

Ryan: The fact of the matter is that with my salary alone I couldn't pay for a house. Double that, say, by giving my wife an equivalent wage, and suddenly we can indeed buy a house. Back in my father's day, one bread earner could pay for a house by his lonesome and pay for all family expenses.

事情的真相就是我一個人的薪水根本付不起一間房子。把它加倍，就說如果我太太也賺一樣的薪水的話，突然之間我們就確實可以買房子了。在我父親那個年代，一個賺錢養家的人就可以負擔起一間房子，還付得起全家人的開銷。

Parker: [1]**For God's sake**, that is not true. The lifestyle of the average American in the 1950s, when the life expectancy was 65, no one had air conditioning or cellphones, 21% of income was spent on food, and television was a luxury, and there was half as much living space per person, could EASILY be afforded on one wage. There is NO PROOF that one wage went further in 1950 than it does today.

看在上帝的份上，那不是真的。1950 年代一般美國人的生活方式，當平均壽命是 65 歲的時候，沒有人有冷氣機或是手機，21%的收入是用來買食物，而電視是奢侈品，還有每個人的生活空間比現在少一半，一份薪水很容易就可以負擔得起了。並

People are simply ^{2}**spoiled** and expect more today, you ^{3}**numbnuts**.

沒有事實證明一份薪水在 1950 年代能比現今負擔的更多。現在人們只是被寵壞了，所以才會期待更多，你這蠢蛋。

Glossary 髒話大解

❶ for God's sake，感嘆詞片語，字面上是說看在上帝的份上，其實就是「你馬幫幫忙」的意思，通常是在很受不了對方的情況下加上的，讓人知道你真的很受不了他。

❷ spoiled，動詞過去式，在這裡是指現在人被寵壞了。這個字也可以用來表示食物或是物品腐敗了，"milk spoils if not refrigerated"，牛奶不冰的話會壞掉。還有就是指物品的質量消弱或受損害，"bad weather spoiled their vacation" 壞天氣毀了他們的假期。

❸ numbnuts，名詞，其實是兩個字合起來的，numb + nuts，numb 是麻痺的意思，nuts 是指男人的蛋蛋，合起來就是麻痺的蛋蛋，被用來罵笨到沒藥救的人。

外包（一）

 情境對話  *Track 119*

美國的大企業近年來為了節省開銷，開始將生產線外包，但是最近記者報導到，時常發現這些企業在海外非法雇用童工的問題。

Mark: Who exploits those people? Socialists? No, go visit Wall Street and you'll see the [1]**culprits** getting along very well amongst the [2]**dollar lickers** like you.

誰在剝削這些人？社會主義者嗎？不，去拜訪一下華爾街，你就會看到罪魁禍首跟像你這樣的貪財鬼相處得很愉快。

Matt: Exploitation? Grow the fuck up. You mean offering the most [3]**desperate** people in the world a chance to double their wages, instead of taking your moral high ground by denying them their factory jobs so they can be relegated to the inferior alternative, sustenance farming or starvation. But yes, the true exploitation of these people was done by socialists. India self-identifies as a socialist democracy and China self-identifies as Communist. Both countries have seen their standards of living rise dramatically since they cut back on their socialism and opened their doors to foreign corporations. Do you think the

剝削？你他媽的成熟點。你是說提供給世界上最絕望的人們一個可以給他們的薪水加倍的機會，而不是以你的高道德標準剝奪他們的工廠工作，使他們得以降級到更劣質的選擇，只夠餬口的農耕或是餓肚子。但是沒錯，真正在剝削這些人的是社會主義者。印度自己認定自己是民主社會主義者，而中國自己認定是共產主義者。兩個國家自從降低他們的社會主義，對外國公

Indians and Chinese working in Nike factories are just stupid, and that they take those jobs not because their alternative is worse?

司敞開大門後，都看到了他們的生活水準大大地提升。你認為那些在 Nike 工廠上班的印度人跟中國人都只是笨蛋，而他們做那些工作不是因為他們其他的選擇更糟嗎？

Glossary 髒話大解

❶ culprits，名詞，指應該要對某項罪惡或不當的行為負責的罪魁禍首。在法律上，指的是不肯認罪、在等候審判中的人。

❷ dollar licker，名詞片語，dollar 指的是錢，licker 就是舔東西的人，字面上乍看之下是舔錢的人，意思就是貪財鬼，太愛錢了，愛到要舔它們。

❸ desperate，形容詞，有迫切需要的、絕望的、危急的，其實可以用來形容一個人在很多種迫切狀況下的感受。"I desperately need a job." 我迫切需要一份工作。"desperate for sex" 極欲需要性愛。或是在狗急跳牆的情況下，"a desperate killer"，就是在魯莽情況下，因為絕望而殺人。

Mark 跟 Matt 在這件事上的意見相左，兩人互不相讓，繼續激烈地辯論著到底誰對誰錯。

Mark: [1]**Jesus H. Christ**, I throw you a bone and immediately all you do is go back to beating your chests like a monkey. My mistake is for trying to reason with liberals like they were rational, mature creatures. You're willfully blind, all you do is to hear promises and start slobbering, like [2]**animals**.

老天爺，我丟給你一根骨頭，而你馬上就回去像隻猴子一樣捶胸。試圖跟自由主義者講道理好像他們是理性的、成熟的生物是我的錯。你們是故意無視，你們就只會聽那些承諾，然後開始毫無節制的流口水，就像畜生一樣。

Matt: Yes, [3]**wogdumb**, it's the multinational corporations who give these children jobs, and socialist governments ensure they take these jobs to avoid starvation. And your morally superior solution is to force them into the starvation path by taking away the factory job option? Idiot. American capitalism could exist without socialism, but socialism could not exist without American capitalism.

是啊，白爛，是那些跨國大企業給這些小孩工作的，然後社會主義政府則是確保他們會做這些工作來避免挨餓。而你充滿道德優越感的解決方案就是用奪走這些工廠工作的選擇，強迫他們走上挨餓之路？白癡。美國的資本主義不用社會主義就可以存活，但是社會主義卻不能沒有美國人的資本主義。

Glossary 髒話大解

❶ Jesus H. Christ，耶穌基督的名字，外國人普遍都有 middle name，也都會用頭一個字母做縮寫，這邊是 Mark 給他加上去的。Jesus Holy Christ，當然 Holy 不是真的是耶穌的 middle name，算是有創意的吶喊方式吧。

❷ animals，名詞，這個字平常作為動物是很無害的一個字，但是在這裡是罵人是畜牲的意思，滿沒禮貌的。

❸ wogdumb，名詞，翻做白爛，指的是那些笨，還自己搞不清楚狀況的白目，讓身邊的人很受不了。wog 其實是帶有濃厚種族歧視的字，指非白人的人種，所以基本上只要不是大英帝國出來的都被罵到了，但是 wogdumb 這個字是不帶種族歧視意味的。

  *Track 121*

幾個高中小女生正在熱烈討論學年舞會的事。Paris 是去年舞會的皇后，所以 Stephanie 跟 Gigi 正在跟她討教。

Stephanie: So Paris, what are your tips for this year's prom?

那個 Paris，你今年學年舞會有沒有什麼撇步可以提供？

Paris: Well, first off, don't spend too much on a dress. Anything more than $1,500 is so [1]**ratchet**.

嗯，首先呢，別花太多錢在禮服上。任何多於 $1500 的都很顧人怨。

Gigi: $1,500?! I think that's what my mom makes in a week!

$1500？！我想那是我媽一星期的薪水欸！

Paris: Tip number two, practice your picture pose. Avoid [2]**duckfaces**. So ratchet.

第二個撇步，練習你的拍照姿勢。避免鴨子臉。超級顧人怨。

Stephanie: So ratchet. Okay, let's move on to our next topic: Promposals.

非常顧人怨。Okay，讓我們接下去下一個話題：舞會邀請。

Gigi: What's that?

那是什麼？

Stephanie: It's a really cool elaborate way for a boy to ask you to the prom.

那是個很酷、很鋪張的男生邀請你去學年舞會的方式。

Paris: Yea, like if he makes a big poster of Legos and it spells out "Lego to Prom". Do you get it, Gigi? Do you understand?

對呀，像是如果他做了一張樂高玩具大海報，拼出「一起去舞會」。你懂嗎，Gigi？你懂不懂？

Gigi: Yes, I do you ³basic bitch!

是的，我懂，你這個無聊的婊子！

Stephanie: Gigi, chill.

Gigi，冷靜點。

Glossary 髒話大解

❶ rachet，這裡翻譯為顧人怨，就是很討人厭的意思，可以做為名詞或形容詞，指的是那些以為他們的存在是上天給世人的恩典的自大狂，只有聽說過用在女孩子身上，像在這裡一直用 rachet 這個字的 Paris 自己就是標準的 rachet。

❷ duckface，名詞，鴨子臉，其實就是嘟嘴臉，是個現在年輕小女生中很常見的愚蠢現象，照個相嘟嘴嘟個屁！是不知道怎麼笑嗎？

❸ basic bitch，名詞，basic 是基本的意思，bitch 是婊子，basic bitch 指的是那些在穿著打扮跟言行上都是跟其他女生一樣，但是又自以為引領潮流的女生。

墮胎

  Track 122

Cindy 剛剛得到消息聽說 Amy 墮胎了，立馬跑去跟 Ana 還有 Morty 分享八卦。

Cindy: Did you hear that Amy just had an abortion?

你們有聽說 Amy 剛剛去墮胎嗎？

Ana: No! Omg! I hope she's doing fine.

沒有！喔我的老天！我希望她沒事才好。

Morty: What a [1]**hoe.**

真是個爛貨。

Cindy: Morty! You should be ashamed of yourself! Who are you to insult and judge people?

Morty！你應該要為你自己感到羞愧！你以為自己是誰，可以這樣羞辱跟評斷他人？

Morty: Seriously? She's a murderer! Why are you defending her?

你認真的？她是個殺人兇手！你為什麼要維護她？

Ana: Yah Morty, I think she made a wise choice, since she is most likely not ready or capable of having a child right now.

是啊，Morty，我認為她做了一個很明智的選擇，因為她現在八成是還沒準備好或有能力養一個小孩。

Morty: Are you two fucking kidding me right now? She murdered a child! She is a fucking selfish ²tramp. I hope she will never have another baby.

你們兩個他媽的在跟我開玩笑嗎？她謀殺了一個孩子！她是個她媽的自私賤貨。我希望她永遠都不會再有其他小孩。

Cindy: Alright Morty, you don't know her circumstances; therefore you have no right to judge her. So instead of being an ³asswipe, you should be offering your support, or just shut the fuck up.

好了 Morty，你不知道她的狀況，因此你沒有權利評斷她。所以與其做一個混蛋，你應該要提供你的支持，要不就他媽的給我閉嘴。

Glossary 髒話大解

❶ hoe，名詞，一般的用法是指鋤頭，但是用來罵人的時候是罵女人是像妓女一樣的爛貨。

❷ tramp，名詞，用在男人身上是指流落街頭的流浪漢，用在女人身上則是稱呼她是妓女的意思。

❸ asswipe，名詞，ass 是屁股或屁眼，wipe 就是指用來擦東西的紙巾，所以 asswipe 字面上就是擦屁股的紙巾，也就是罵人是混蛋的意思。

Chapter

123

漂白過的好萊塢

 情境對話  *Track 123*

奧斯卡金像獎剛剛發表完提名，很多人對於名單有很多的疑問，今年提名名單內清一色是白人，因此有許多人對此感到不滿。

Aaron: Hollywood [1]**Whitewashing**, how is this still a thing? It's fucking 2016! They're saying that Hollywood just don't provide enough good roles for black actors. I'd say even when there are good roles for non-white actors, they still get played by white people.

好萊塢粉刷，現在還有這種事？都已經是他媽的 2016 了！他們在說好萊塢只是沒有供應足夠的好角色給黑人演員。要我說，就算有非白人演員的好角色，它們還是由白人來演出。

Hunter: It's all about the [2]**green** man, white lead actors sell. Just look at Tom Cruise in the Last Samurai. When I saw that I was like "He's the last samurai? Fuck you!"

這都是跟錢有關的老兄，白人主角才會賣座。看看 Tom Cruise 在最後武士。當我看到的時候我就說「他是最後的武士？操你的！」

Paul: The character Tom Cruise played, Nathan Algren, is NOT the Last Samurai, that would be the character Katsumoto, who is played by Ken Watanabe who is not only Asian, but Japanese. Get your

Tom Cruise 演的角色，Nathan Algren，不是那個最後的武士，那應該是 Katsumoto 這個角色，是由 Ken Watanabe 來

258

facts straight you [3]**dumbasses**! So the white guy from America is actually played by a white guy from America, and the Japanese Asian dude by an actual Asian dude from Japan! Who would have [4]**thunk it**!

演的，他不僅是亞洲人，還是日本人。把事實搞清楚你們這些蠢貨！所以來自美國的男人確實是由來自美國的男人來演，而日本亞洲老兄也確實是由一個日本來的亞洲老兄來演的！誰會想得到啊！

Glossary 髒話大解

❶ whitewashing，名詞，一般用法是指粉刷，在這裡是指因為 2016 年度的好萊塢得獎提名清一色是白人，所以說是被「粉刷」過的名單。這個字還有兩個很下流的用法，一個是指很賣力的口交，把舌頭當油漆刷子來用一樣在用，另一個也是在性愛的時候，有母奶的女人把母奶擠進對方的屁眼裡這個動作也叫 whitewashing。

❷ green，名詞，美金鈔票都是綠色的，所以在美國，錢也可以叫做 green。

❸ dumbass，名詞，罵人是蠢貨的意思。

❹ thunk it 其實是 think of it，thunk 是 think 的過去簡單式與過去分詞，thunk 的用法較不標準，think 較正確的過去式與過去分詞是 thought。thunk it 文法是錯誤的，但是這裡是 Paul 想要強調語氣故意這麼說的。

 **情境對話** *Track 124*

美國參議院酷刑報告顯示美國的罪犯審訊程序恐怖得令人不敢置信。

Dave: I just thought that our government should think about changing the way they conduct interrogation. America should not be a country that tortures people, because it is brutal, medieval and beneath us. There was a Nazi that was in charge of getting information out of people, instead of torturing people, he walked with them through the woods, no handcuffs, or anything, just the two of them. He would ask the prisoner casual questions, and get the prisoner comfortable. The prisoners would end up spilling way more secrets than they would have if they were tortured.

Tim: That is ridiculous [1]**hogwash**. [2]**No offense**.

Dave: Nope, it's true, you can look it up.

我認為我們的政府應該要考慮改變他們審訊的方式。美國不應該是一個會拷打人的國家,因為那是慘無人道、仿中世紀還有比我們低等的。曾經有個負責從別人身上取得訊息的納粹黨員,並非用虐待的方式,他跟那些人在樹林裡散步,沒有手銬或任何東西,就他們兩個。他會問囚犯一些輕鬆的問題,讓囚犯放輕鬆。最終囚犯都會吐出比起被拷打要來得更多的秘密。

那真是荒謬的狗屁。沒惡意。

不是喔,那是真的,你可以查查看。

Tim: If I had a Nazi taking me out for a stroll in the woods, I'd be scared [3]shitless. I'd most probably spill out everything before even asked.

如果有個納粹黨員帶著我到樹林散步，我會嚇到挫屎。我八成大概會在被問之前就吐出所有的事。

Glossary 髒話大解

❶ hogwash，名詞，跟 bullshit 是一樣的意思，但是比較沒那麼髒，算是比較有禮貌的説狗屁的方式。

❷ no offense，名詞片語，沒有惡意、沒有要冒犯你的意思，這句話其實很討人厭，每次聽到有人説這句話，要不就是他已經説了，或是準備要説會冒犯到你的話，但是好像説了這個你就不能生氣似的，別人都説沒惡意了，你還生氣就是你沒風度了，但是明明就是對方嘴賤在先，所以跟髒話比起來，筆者最討厭的還是這句話。

❸ shitless，形容詞，被嚇到屎都挫了一地的意思，怕到屎都流光光了。

網路性騷擾（一）

 情境對話  *Track 125*

網路的發達，成為了一項非常容易對他人造成騷擾的工具。Jamie 看著自己的 Twitter 網頁，有感而發的說道…

Jamie: So sick and tired of these [1]**Internet trolls** always trying to get reaction out of people by leaving stupid comments.

真受不了這些網路山怪老是試圖用很白癡的留言想讓人做出反應。

Nora: That's nothing compared to the direct threat that can make people fear for their safety.

那根本不算什麼，跟那些讓人很害怕他們自己安危的直接威脅比起來。

Alan: Oh you women always like to get so dramatic and overreact on measly little things.

喔你們女人總是喜歡很戲劇化地對一些很微小的事情過度反應。

Nora: Well congratulations on your white [2]**shaft**. Do you know that women in general receive a lot more horrible messages online than men? My sister got a threat from some [3]**dirtbag** saying he's going to stick an egg in her [4]**pudenda** and punch it.

那真是恭喜你有根白老二，你知道女人普遍在網路上收到的恐怖私訊比男人還要多很多嗎？我的妹妹從某個混帳那收到一則恐嚇說，他要拿顆蛋塞進她的陰部裡然後揍它。

Jamie: That's poignant.

那真是讓人感到憂慮。

Glossary 髒話大解

❶ Internet troll，名詞，網路山怪，指那些老喜歡在別人的網站上找人吵架的人，故意用很不禮貌的口氣，挑釁的態度，通常都是很無聊的辯論，所以最好的應對方式就是無視，然後檢舉對方，陷進去你就輸了。

❷ shaft，名詞，本身是指桿狀物，所以因為形狀上相似，可以被用來指稱男人的陰莖。

❸ dirtbag，名詞，字面上是裝土的袋子，也就是罵人是混帳的意思。

❹ pudenda，名詞，指女性的外陰部，拉丁文裡的 pudenda 這個字是 "the shameful (parts)"，很丟人的部位的意思，維多利亞時代開始有人用這個字來委婉地稱呼女性的陰部。

網路性騷擾（二）

Jamie、Nora 跟 Alan 剛剛聊到網路上的騷擾可輕可重，嚴重的時候甚至可能鬧出人命。

Ana: Women aren't just threatened and harassed online. The Internet has come up with a whole new way to wreck our lives.

女人不只是在網路上被恐嚇跟騷擾，網路已經出現了毀掉我們人生的全新方法。

Alan: What's that?

那是什麼？

Ana: [1]**Revenge porn.** That's when naked pictures of people are posted online without their consent. It actually happened to my neighbor who's a high school teacher. She let her [2]**ex** take some private photos while they were going out. But after they broke up, he put the photos online and sent the link to the school she teaches at.

色情報復。那是當人們的裸照在沒有經過他們同意的就貼上網。那真的發生在我一個做高中老師的鄰居身上。他們在交往的時候她讓她的前任照過一些私密照。但是他們分手後，他把照片傳上網，然後把連結送到她就任的學校。

Alan: What a [3]**scumbag!**

好個人渣！

Ana: She attempted to commit suicide

她在那之後曾經嘗試自

after that, her family and friends have been incredibly supportive and helped her get through it.

Jamie: A girl on Tumblr was nearly driven to suicide because she drew a picture that some people considered racist. People are stupid, and we need to educate them, especially the children, to be better on how to use the internet responsibly.

殺，家人朋友們非同一般地支持幫助她渡過那段煎熬。

一個在 Tumblr 上的女孩子差點被逼到去自殺，因為有人認為她畫的一張圖有種族歧視的意味。社會大眾是很愚蠢的，我們需要教育他們，特別是孩子們，如何比較負責任的網路使用方式。

Glossary 髒話大解

❶ revenge porn，名詞，色情報復，就像對話內容裡面說的，未經他人允許，擅自把對方的裸照或是歡愛影片上網公開。revenge 是報復的意思，porn 是色情片或色情書刊的意思，pornography 的簡稱。

❷ ex，名詞，前任的意思，ex-girlfriend、ex-boyfriend、ex-wife、ex-husband 的簡稱，如果聊天聽到人說 "my ex..."，就表示他們在說前任的事。

❸ scumbag，名詞，scum 是渣子、廢物的意思，scumbag 就是裝廢物的袋子，也就是罵人是混蛋、人渣的意思。

Chapter 127

專利詐騙（一）

  *Track 127*

專利制度近來越來越容易被濫用，有不肖人士用隨便申請專利的方式對真正發明某用技術的人進行提告然後從中獲利。

Austin: Just received a letter from a company called Uniloc, they said they're filing suit against me for patent infringement.

剛剛收到一封從一家叫做 Uniloc 的公司寄來的信，他們說要對我提告專利侵權。

Kyle: What? Where did that come from?

什麼？哪來的事？

Austin: They said they own the idea of computer program checking essential server for authorization.

他們說他們擁有授權電腦程序檢查必要伺服器的智慧財產。

Kyle: Ha! One of those again, [1]**patent trolls**. These [2]**underdogs** don't even really invent or sell anything. They simply buy patents and sue the [3]**living shit** out of people. In fact, you don't even need to make something to be targeted. You just need to use something. I've heard an employment placement company for disabled people, was threatened to pay $1000 for each employee they have for

哈！又是那些個東西，專利山怪。這些敗類根本沒有在發明或是銷售任何東西。他們就光只是買專利然後把人活生生告到挫屎。事實上，你根本不用製造任何東西就會被設定為目標，你只需要使用某樣東西。我聽說過一家專門服附殘障人士的就業安

the use of their copy machine with the scan-to-email function because they own the patent for that process.

置公司，被恐嚇要為每個使用他們影印機掃瞄到 e-mail 這個功能的員工各付$1000，因為他們擁有那個功能的專利。

Austin: Wow... these people are trying to take advantage of a company helping disabled people? That's fucked up!

哇…這些人試圖利用一家幫助殘障人士的公司？那真是他媽的糟糕！

Glossary 髒話大解

❶ patent troll，名詞，專利山怪，指那些買專利用來騙錢的人。像之前提到的 Internet troll 一樣，troll 這個字本身是山怪的意思，一種幻想生物，但是因為在故事裡 troll 是很不討喜的，所以被用來稱呼很煩人的人。

❷ underdogs，名詞，用來罵敗類、沒出息的人。這個字的由來就是從打架打輸的狗，就是 under + dog，被壓制在下的狗，而反之贏了的那一方就是 topdog，贏家的意思。

❸ living shit，名詞，指一個人還活著的時候體內的屎，通常是加強語氣時說的，像是 "I'm gonna beat the living shit out of you" 我準備把你打到挫屎。

Austin 剛剛從 Kyle 那邊學到原來有專利山怪這種人的存在，為此感到不可思議之於同時也感到疑惑。

Austin: Now that I think of this further, why the flying fuck can you patent a process?

我仔細想過後，你他媽的為什麼會可以申請程序專利？

Kyle: Because software concepts are so vague and easy to imply on things, ever heard of the Fine Bros?

因為軟體的概念都非常的模糊而且很容易就能影射在東西上，聽説過 Fine Bros？

Austin: No, I've been [1]**living in a cave** for sometime.

不，我住在山洞裡有一段時間了。

Kyle: The Fine Bros are two brothers who had videos of old people reacting to stuff kids like and had videos of kids reacting to stuff old people like. They got greedy and decided to copyright the term REACT, which would have shut down thousands of people's YouTube accounts or would force people to give them money anytime they make a video of a person reacting to

那個 Fine Bros 是兩個兄弟，製作了一些老人家對小孩喜歡的東西的反應，還有小孩對老人家喜歡的東西的反應的影片。他們起了貪念，決定要申請反應這個詞的版權，如此將會造成成千上萬的人的 Youtube 帳號被關閉，或

something else.

是強迫人們每次製作有人對某件事做反應的影片時要付他們錢。

Austin: [2]**Pricks.**

渾球。

Kyle: So everybody decided that we can't let these [3]**yids** trademark a concept like that, and they went [4]**ape** at the Fine Bros.

所以大家決定我們不能讓這些猶太鬼把一個概念做為商標，所以大家都群起攻擊 Fine Bros。

Glossary 髒話大解

❶ living in a cave，living 是動詞進行式，cave 是指山洞，住在山洞裡，意思是跟社會脫節，沒在關心時事，不是 Austin 真的住在山洞裡。

❷ prick，名詞，用來稱呼毫無存活價值的渾球，另外也可以用來稱呼男人的陰莖，用法跟 dick 一樣。

❸ yids，名詞，指意第緒人(Yiddish)的後裔，也就是猶太人，算是有種族歧視意味的詞，所以別看到猶太人朝著人家叫 yid，很沒禮貌。

❹ ape，形容詞，指人極度生氣的狀況下，像猩猩一樣暴力抓狂，場面失控。

Chapter 129

藥物濫用

 情境對話  **Track 129**

處方藥物氾濫在市面上，只要打開電視，就可以看到它們的廣告，很顯然地，大型製藥廠花在行銷上的錢比花在研發上的錢還要多。

Karen: Drug companies are always finding ways to push sales; some even push doctors to prescribe pills for non FDA approved uses.

製藥公司總是想盡辦法推銷他們的產品，有些甚至去強迫醫生開不被食品藥物管理局認可的處方。

Rachel: A doctor once tried to prescribe me Depicote for chronic headaches. My brother takes that for his bipolar disorder, it's an anti-psychotic drug. Needless to say, I didn't take it and found a different doctor.

有次有個醫生試圖開給我 Depicote 做為慢性頭痛的藥。我的兄弟因為躁鬱症吃那個藥，那是抗精神病的藥物。不用說，我沒有吃那藥，還找了個不同的醫生。

Karen: See, you can't just give people potentially dangerous drugs and see what happens. You are a Fortune 500 company, not a white guy with [1]**dreadlocks** at [2]**Burning Man**.

你看，你不能隨便把危險性很高的藥物開給人，然後看看會發生什麼事。你是世界財富 500 強的公司，不是一個在火人祭頂著一頭髒辮的白人老兄。

Rachel: A friend of mine who's a drug

我有個朋友是個藥物銷售

rep once told me his favorite selling line of Wellbutrin, "hey doc, remember the happy, [3]**horny**, skinny drug?"

員，他曾經告訴過我他最喜歡的 Wellbutrin 銷售台詞是，「嘿醫生，記得那個開心、淫蕩、苗條藥嗎」？」

Karen: I thought the only happy, horny, skinny drug is [4]**crystal meth**, hahaha...

我以為唯一的開心、淫蕩、苗條藥是冰毒，哈哈哈…

Glossary 髒話大解

❶ dreadlocks，名詞，是指一種髮型，在長期不洗頭的狀況下，頭髮會黏在一起，可以很輕鬆地把它搓成粗粗的條狀，其實滿噁心的，在歐美國家算是流行，很多大明星都頂過這種頭。

❷ Burning Man，名詞，火人祭，是美國內華達州一年一度舉辦的盛祭，燃燒人這個名字來自盛會的最後一天，會焚燒巨大的人形木雕像。其實就是一群以藝術為名的人，開狂歡派對、飲酒、吸毒、亂交的地方，因為舉辦的地點很偏僻，基本上沒有警察會去管，所以大家都知道那是一年一度想亂來的人可以去的地方。

❸ horny，形容詞，淫蕩的、指某人在發騷的意思。

❹ crystal meth，名詞，安非他命的結晶品，俗稱冰毒。

Chapter 130 到底該不該投票？（一）

  **情境對話** **Track 130**

總統競選過程越來越激，這次的候選人都不是很理想，所以到底該投給誰呢？

Greg: So uh, vote for Bernie OK. Cause ya know, the rest are just some [1]untrustworthy [2]dunce. Especially Jeb and Hilary.

所以啊，投給 Bernie 知道嘛。因為你知道的，剩下的都只是些靠不住的蠢貨。特別是 Jeb 跟 Hilary。

Ron: Oh no, I'm politically neutral.

喔不，我是政治中立的。

Greg: You don't wanna take action? Politically neutral, HAH! That's more [3]malarkey than a certified pre-owned car. You're fucking lazy and that car is fucking used! But seriously everyone else is either insane or [4]corrupt. Just fucking vote for him anyway. Unless you have a masterplan for fixing our problems within the next 6 years.

你不想採取行動？政治中立，哈！那簡直比認證過的二手車還要像胡說八道。你他媽的是懶，而那車是他媽的被用過的！但是認真講，其他的要不就是有神經病，要不就是貪汙。反正就他媽的投給他就對了。除非你有甚麼可以在接下來 6 年內解決我們問題的完美計畫。

Ron: There are 318.9 million people in

美國總共有 318.9 百萬

the US. I doubt my vote will change anything. Statistically, I'm not even a drop in the bucket. Unless Bernie has a plan to make National Churro Day a thing, then I'm staying away from any and all booths!

人。我懷疑我的票會改變什麼。統計上來說，我甚至不是水桶裡的一滴水。除非 Bernie 計畫要設一個西班牙油條國慶日，那我就會遠離所有其他的投票亭。

Glossary 髒話大解

❶ untrustworthy，形容詞，表示一個人很不值得被信任，用來形容後面的字 Dunce，罵的是除了 Bernie 之外的總統候選人。

❷ dunce，名詞，這個字的由來是從 16 世紀的時候，一開始是人文主義派用 "dunses" 或 "dunsmen"，來嘲笑蘇格蘭哲學家 John Duns Scotus 的追隨者，後來演變成罵學生悟性不高，到現在變成罵人是蠢貨、癡呆、無知。

❸ malarkey，名詞，指被設計用來掩飾、誤導或留下深刻印象的言語，也就是廢話、胡說八道之類的，用法類似 bullshit。

❹ corrupt，形容詞，這裡是用來形容政治人物的腐敗、貪汙、墮落。

 情境對話  *Track 131*

Greg 對於 *Ron* 對選總統這種國家大事的漠不關心感到很火大，決定好好跟他溝通溝通。

Ron: Voting in a system where [1]**gerrymandering** is possible yet believing that your vote will carry out to your advantage is just [2]**nescient**.

在傑利蠑螈很有可能發生的系統之下投票，還相信你自己的選票會對你有利真的是無知。

Greg: To some extent, yes, but gerrymandering can only mitigate votes it can't eliminate them entirely.

從某種程度上講沒錯，但是徇私只能減輕票的效益，並不能完全把他們消除掉。

Ron: You also say that we need a master plan to get rid of corruption or need to vote and that not making one or the other makes me lazy. That's [3]**asinine**. I believe in the advancement of civilization through technological and moral progression, and getting rid of corruption doesn't affect it in the slightest. I ask for a churro because churros are at least reliable for longer than politicians, even if that means half a day.

你也説了我們需要一個完美的計畫來擺脫貪污腐敗或是需要投票，而不做其中一項的話就是我懶。那真是愚蠢。我相信以通過技術和道德的進步發展而出的文明，除掉貪污腐敗並不會對它有多大的影響。我會要求要西班牙油條是因為西班牙油條比起政客們可靠性的時效要多些，就算它只是半天。

Glossary 髒話大解

❶ gerrymandering，動詞進行式，這個字可以做為名詞或動詞，由來是 1812 年給美國麻州的議員代表 Elbridge Gerry 的名字跟 salamander 合起來的字，因為當時他的所在黨為了贏得票選自動重新劃分選區，也就是公然作弊，當時重新畫出來的選區因為在地圖上看起來像蠑螈，就被記者寫成 gerrymander，那之後如果出現選區劃分不公，就被稱做 gerrymander。

❷ nescient，形容詞，從拉丁文 "nescientem" 來的字，不知道的意思，後來被用來罵人沒常識、無知。

❸ asinine，形容詞，也是從拉丁文來的字，"asininus" 意思就是像屁股一樣，後來演變成罵人是愚蠢的、無知的、荒唐的。

Chapter 132

別惹電玩咖

 情境對話  *Track 132*

女權主義作家 Anita Sarkeesian 因為對電玩中的女性角色設計太過性感，遊戲內容太過暴力，認為有損女性形象，發表了一系列的抨擊言論，因此引發電玩界的公憤。

Gary: I think Sarkeesian is a fedora tipping SJW retard. Everything I've heard from her reeks of what they call "rush to judgment." Basically, everything that she publishes is a first draft that should be checked again against actual research and enlivened with some actual attempts at being interesting.

Wallace: Who's this Sarkeesian person? And what is SJW?

Gary: I'll try to catch you up to speed really fast. Anita Sarkeesian is a [1]**feminist** who says all men are [2]**rapists** and video games that do nothing but portray women as [3]**sex dolls** for male pleasure. SJW stands for social justice warrior and basically they're the kind of people who

我認為 Sarkeesian 是個斜戴軟呢帽的 SJW 智障。所有我聽她說過的話都冒出所謂的「匆忙做出判斷」的惡臭。基本上，她所有出版的東西都是第一草稿，需要和實際研究作比較，還需要學著嘗試讓它更有趣。

Sarkeesian 這個人是誰？還有什麼是 SJW？

我會儘快解釋，讓你跟上。Anita Sarkeesian 是個女權主義者，她說男人都是強姦犯，還有電動玩具除了將女人們描摹成性玩偶提供男人樂趣之外，什麼用都沒有。SJW 是

think they're sticking up for minorities. So if I said a person was stupid and that person was black they'd jump on me for being a racist. They are basically the Internet political correctness [4]**nazis**.

社會正義戰士的簡稱，基本上他們就是那種自以為在為少數民族出頭的人。所以如果我説有個人很笨，然後那個人是黑人，他們就會因為我的種族歧視立刻跳出來修理我。他們基本上就是網路觀點正確性的納粹警察。

Glossary 髒話大解

❶ feminist，名詞，女權主義者，倡導婦女應當擁有跟男人同等社會、政治、法律、經濟權力等等，通常言詞都比較犀利，常常讓人覺得吃不消，雖説要求的是「平等」的地位，但是常常有太超過的行為出現，變成好像在打壓男人似的。

❷ rapist，名詞，強姦犯，在沒有經過受害人同意之下非法強迫性交。

❸ sex dolls，名詞，性玩偶，通常是塑膠做的充氣性愛娃娃，供給男性自慰時能有更多的樂趣，這裡雖然是指二次元的電玩角色，但是對 Anita Sarkeesian 來説功能都是一樣的，所以稱作 sex doll。

❹ nazi，名詞，大寫的時候是指德國納粹黨員，但是小寫的時候是用來罵那些喜歡強迫規範別人的人。

難搞的女人

Lindsay 看著雜誌突發奇想的問 Tara 跟 Kathy…

Lindsay: So if you have to pick one of us to be in a relationship with, who would you pick?

所以如果你們要選我們其中一個交往的話，你們會選誰？

Tara: Ahh... I'm not answering that, nope.

啊…我不想回答，不。

Kathy: Tara!

我選 Tara！

Lindsay and Tara: (both yelled) What?!

（同時喊）什麼？！

Lindsay: You're choosing her over me?

你選她不選我？

Kathy: Yah, because she's sort of a [1]**pushover**, very easy to handle, and you're ahh... a bit [2]**high maintenance**.

對呀，因為她差不多是個濫好人，很容易掌控，而你呢…有點難搞。

Tara: Hey! I'm not a pushover!

嘿！我才不是濫好人！

Lindsay: High maintenance? What are you talking about? Tara, tell her I'm not.

難搞？你在說什麼？Tara，告訴她我不是。

Tara: Umm... You kind of are.

嗯…你有點是欸。

Lindsay: Oh I can't not believe you. And you! (pointing to Kathy) You are [3]**flaky**!

喔你真讓我不敢相信。還有你！（指向 Kathy）你很不可靠！

Kathy: Well... maybe I am.

嗯…或許我是吧。

Glossary 髒話大解

❶ pushover，名詞，是指一個人是濫好人，不知道怎麼說不，很容易被說服跟誘惑，女人被人這樣稱呼不是好事，因為人家會認為你很好上。

❷ high maintenance，形容詞，maintenance 是保養、維護的意思，所以被人說需要高度保養，也就是說你很難搞的意思，動不動就大驚小怪，現在人常說的有公主病的女孩子就是 high maintenance。

❸ flaky，形容詞，被用 flaky 來形容的人就表示他很不可靠，朝三暮四，可能早跟你約好了吃飯，結果當天卻爽約，可以稱這些人叫 flake。

Chapter 134

怎麼把妹？

 情境對話 ✛  *Track 134*

Jack 跟 *Ned* 兩個單身漢正在討論把妹到底需要什麼樣的技巧？到底要如何搭訕？

Jack: You just have to learn how to talk to women. I know how to do that because I do careful observations.

你只是需要學著如何跟女人說話。我知道怎麼做是因為我很小心仔細地觀察。

Ned: Really? You never told me that before.

是喔？從來沒聽你提過。

Jack: That's because I'm not an arrogant [1]**jackass.** The problem most men have is that they don't know how to talk to women.

那是因為我不是個自大的驢子。大部分男人的問題是他們不知道如何跟女人說話。

Ned: You know what my problem is? I'm not interesting. What am I supposed to say? That I'm a prize-winning chess master? (Does impression of a woman) Oh please [2]**do me,** chess master!!

你知道我的問題是什麼嗎？我沒興趣。我應該說什麼？說我是個西洋棋高手嗎？（裝女人的說話方式）喔拜託快來上我吧，棋子大師！！

Jack: Listen, talking to women is about

聽著，跟女人說話是要問

asking questions, that's it! Because women don't ³**give a shit** about what you have to say, all they want to do is talk about themselves. Remember, just ask questions. Also, be somewhat ⁴**cocky**, women love that.

問題的，就這樣！因為女人才不關心你想要說什麼，她們想要的只是述說關於她們自己的事。記住，問問題就對了。還有，稍微臭屁一點，女人很愛那種的。

Ned: Okay, I think I can do that.

好吧，我想我可以做的到。

Glossary 髒話大解

❶ jackass，名詞，指公的驢子，也可以用來罵人是愚蠢的混蛋。

❷ do me，動詞片語，就是跟人家說「來上我吧！」的意思。同樣的用法，人稱不同也是可以的，do + 人稱，就是上某人的意思，do him、do her、do your sister。

❸ give a shit，動詞片語，當你對某件事不感興趣，到了連拉坨屎給他們都懶得做，就可以感覺得出來有多不感興趣了。

❹ cocky，形容詞，通常是用在男人身上，因為只有他們有 cock，也就是那一根東西，用 cocky 來形容人表示那個人太看得起自己，太過自以為是，有自信是好事，但是太多就是自大了。

川普真的很討人厭

 情境對話  *Track 135*

Nick 跟 Don 剛剛看過總統大選的最新報告，結果讓人感到驚駭無比，川普目前在共和黨內遙遙領先，很有可能成為共和黨的代表。

Nick: The US presidential election has officially became what I call, the [1]**clown town** [2]**fuck-the-world** [3]**shitshow** 2016.

Don: I hear you, with Donald Trump winning 7 States on Super Tuesday and two more last night, the fear has become even more real now.

Nick: Gosh I hate that name, knowing that everytime his name is said out loud, he has a shattering [4]**orgasm**.

Don: Hahaha... He's like America's back mole. It may have seemed harmless a year ago, but now it has gotten frightenly bigger. It is no longer wise to ignore it.

美國的總統大選已經正式成為我說的，2016 瘋狂酒醉去他媽的世界爛秀。

我知道你在說什麼，Donald Trump 已經在總統初選秀贏得了七個州，昨晚又贏了兩個，這恐懼真是越來越真實了。

老天我恨那個名字，我知道每次他的名字被大聲說出來，他就會有驚天動地的性高潮。

哈哈哈⋯他就像是美國背後長的痣，一年前看似無害，但是現在它變得越來越大，無視它不再是聰明的舉動了。

Nick: He is somewhat objectively funny though. I remember once he posted a twitter to say happy 911 to haters and losers. I can see why his supporters would like him.

其實客觀的看來他還算好笑的，我記得有次他在 Twitter 上面貼說：911 快樂，給所有的酸民跟魯蛇們。我可以了解為什麼他的擁護者會喜歡他。

Glossary 髒話大解

❶ clown town，名詞，字面上看是小丑鎮，這個地方呢，不是誰都去得了的，想去的人首先得喝酒喝到斷片，然後毫無知覺地到達這個地方，通常要幾天的宿醉過去之後才會發覺到自己做了什麼。簡單講就是醉到不知道自己在哪裡做了什麼，就表示你去了 clown town。

❷ fuck-the-world，名詞片語，指一個人的心理狀態已經緊繃到斷裂，終於爆發出來的情況，這人什麼都不管了，全世界的人都死光也不關他的事。

❸ shitshow，名詞，描述一個事件或是情況失去控制到荒謬的程度，完全就是混亂到無法收拾的地步，像現在 Trump 領先的狀況簡直就是狗屎秀！

❹ orgasm，名詞，性高潮的意思，在這裡是用來嘲笑 Trump 每次聽到自己名字的表情。

Leader 043

學校沒有教的「髒」英文

作　　者	欒復倪 Fu-Ni Luan
發 行 人	周瑞德
執行總監	齊心瑀
企劃編輯	陳欣慧
執行編輯	魏于婷
校　　對	編輯部
封面構成	高鍾琪

內頁構成	菩薩蠻數位文化有限公司
印　　製	大亞彩色印刷製版股份有限公司
初　　版	2016 年 5 月
定　　價	新台幣 360 元
出　　版	力得文化
電　　話	(02) 2351-2007
傳　　真	(02) 2351-0887
地　　址	100 台北市中正區福州街 1 號 10 樓之 2
E - m a i l	best.books.service@gmail.com
網　　址	www.bestbookstw.com

港澳地區總經銷	泛華發行代理有限公司
地　　址	香港新界將軍澳工業邨駿昌街 7 號 2 樓
電　　話	(852) 2798-2323
傳　　真	(852) 2796-5471

國家圖書館出版品預行編目資料

學校沒有教的「髒」英文 / 欒復倪著. -- 初版. --
臺北市 : 力得文化, 2016.05
　面 ；　　公分. -- (Leader ; 43)
ISBN 978-986-92856-2-9(平裝附光碟片)

1.英語 2.讀本

805.18　　　　　105005945

力得文化
Leader Culture

Lead your way. Be your own leader!

力得文化
Leader Culture

Lead your way. Be your own leader!